Wolf's Law - Che

Analeen is terri beasts murdered her mother n from her family by ruthless saves Analeen's life when it escapes the carnage, only to be capt a wild man.

Law wants little to do with humans and refuses to take a human female as his mate. But when he brings the beautiful Analeen into his care, he can't stay away. It isn't long before both succumb to their desires. Passion burns deep, but it's only a matter of time until Analeen learns what Law truly is.

Scarlet Sweet - Anya Bast

Loosely related to Blood of the Rose.

As the Scarlet of the Tuatha Dé Danaan, the fate of her people lies in Cerian's hands. To win against their foes, she must become what none of the sidhe have ever been—a Vampir.

The dark and powerful man sent to transform her is compelling and seductive. He is a dangerous aphrodisiac she must resist. She has stood alone for too long to allow anyone to breach her defenses.

But one taste of Cerian makes Rhys ravenous for more, and when he hungers he doesn't relent.

Writers Unblocked - Diana Hunter

What happens when two writers of the hottest, steamiest, sexiest romance novels marry each other, yet hide their inner desires from each other? Jack and Jessica Blackburn know. Their spicy novels are on the best seller lists, but their everyday life runs more to the mundane. Until a simple computer mistake reveals their true natures and changes the course of their lives.

Looking Forward - Mary Wine

Earth in the 23rd century is crowded and unable to feed her ever-growing population. Homesteading once again beckons to the struggling masses —only this time, the adventure will take humankind to the deep reaches of space. Leah eagerly embraces the struggle even when she finds herself facing a Tailarmarian warrior and his demands that she become his mate. Beyond time and customs there still waits the spark of attraction that can bridge the hearts of two strangers. Some call it love, Leah discovers it is destiny.

Raptor's Prey - Delilah Devlin

Part of the Desire series

After a month-long sleep filled with dreams of a dark-skinned lover in a castle beneath the sand, Captain Andromeda O'Keefe awakens in her suspension chamber to discover her dangerous cargo has escaped. Worse, naked and at his mercy, she learns her sexy, forbidden dreams weren't hers alone.

Khalim Padja of the Raptor Clan has a date with a prison cell. Using his dream-share gift, he invades the wary captain's dreams to seduce her. But time is running short to win her heart and his freedom.

Voyeurs: Overexposed - Sherri L. King

First in the Voyeurs series, which is linked to the Horde Wars series.

The war between the Shikars and the Daemons must be kept secret from all human knowledge. Alek, a human with photographic proof of the Horde's existence, must be dealt with quickly, before his pictures leak out.

Agate, a Shikar spy whose fascination with human custom knows no bounds, is the perfect liaison to send to divest Alek of his pictures and his dangerous memories. If only she can keep her libido in check. After all, Agate has never been one to shy away from her sensual side and Alek makes her hotter than any sex toy she's ever dared to invent.

It's too bad he won't be allowed to remember her come the morning…

ELLORA'S CAVE
ROMANTICA PUBLISHING

ELLORA'S CAVEMEN: TALES FROM THE TEMPLE III
An Ellora's Cave Publication, September 2004

Ellora's Cave Publishing, Inc.
1337 Commerce Drive, #13
Stow, OH 44224

ISBN 1-4199-5118-1

ISBN MS Reader (LIT) ISBN # 1-4199-0050-1
Other available formats (no ISBNs are assigned):
Adobe (PDF), Rocketbook (RB), Mobipocket (PRC) & HTML

ELLORA'S CAVEMEN: TALES FROM THE TEMPLE III edited by The Legendary "Queen of Steam" *Jaid Black.*
Cover design by *Darrell King*. Photography by *Dennis Roliff*.

ELLORA'S CAVEMEN: TALES FROM THE TEMPLE III

Wolf's Law

By Cheyenne McCray

Scarlet Sweet

By Anya Bast

Writers Unblocked

By Diana Hunter

Looking Forward

By Mary Wine

Raptor's Prey

By Delilah Devlin

Voyeurs: Overexposed

By Sherri L. King

WOLF'S LAW

Cheyenne McCray

Chapter One

Law scented the woman long before he heard the clank of chains. The smell of her terror and her anger overshadowed her pleasing woman scent.

Two men laughed and shouted, their cruel voices shattering the peaceful quiet of D'euan Forest.

The wolf slipped between trees, his paws silent upon pine needles and matted leaves. His keen senses absorbed all that surrounded him. The rich perfume of moist earth, spring flowers and cool evening air filled his nostrils, along with other familiar forest smells… A rabbit trembling beneath a bush, just feet away; a fox skirting the edge of Law's territory; a herd of deer just over the rise. Leaves whispered in the light breeze and wind caressed his muzzle as he loped through dappled sunlight.

He assimilated everything while never removing his attention from the woman. Her distressed thoughts echoed in his mind as he neared her. Her fury, and again her fear.

I'll kill the bastards, she was thinking, and Law would have smiled at her strength and courage if her situation hadn't been so dire.

His own fury mounted, raging through him like white-hot fire, and he bared his fangs. For he heard the thoughts of the men just as clearly as the woman's. They intended to rape her as soon as they made camp for the night.

Analeen stumbled and dropped to her knees on the hard-packed earth of a wheel rut. Chains binding her wrists clanked as they hit dirt and the rope around her neck grew taut.

"Get up, bitch." Dyrke brought his horse to a stop just as she thought he intended to drag her behind him and strangle her to death.

Her breathing came in hot angry gasps. Tears of fury built up behind her dirt-encrusted eyes, but she refused to cry. Dust covered her aching body and fire burned at her wrists where chains had rubbed them raw. Her bare feet were cut and bloodied from sharp rocks from the one-day journey from her village.

"If the wench won' get up, drag 'er," Jove ordered as he rounded back on his own horse. Analeen raised her head and her gaze met his cruel, cruel pale blue eyes. "Even if the wench is hav dead by the time we make camp, we'll still have our fun wit' 'er."

Analeen would rather die than let these bastards touch her. But she had to live. No matter what they did to her, she would escape and return to her family. Her younger sisters needed her, and she couldn't leave them in this world alone.

"She won' bring much of a price if she gets any uglier." Dyrke yanked the rope when Analeen eased to her feet. Her foot caught on the hem of her dress and she almost fell again. "Get up, whore."

She wanted to rage against the bastards, wanted to claw their eyes out and cut off their pricks. Already she was so exhausted, so weak, she knew she wouldn't be able to fight them both off. One, maybe, but two… Her chances were not good. Not good at all.

And it was almost nightfall.

Dyrke yanked the rope, and Analeen began plodding behind his horse again. Gods, how her muscles ached. She had never been so bone-weary in her life.

And never in her worst nightmares had she ever imagined being kidnapped from her family to be sold as a pleasure slave. She was not pretty at all. Her life had been relatively dull, and she lived in a tiny village, in a small modest home, taking care of her younger sisters. Her father performed odd jobs in the village while she watched the four girls—that was, when he wasn't drunk or gambling at the tavern's *litho* tables.

A fierce growl rose up from beside the road.

Analeen's heart jumped to her throat.

"What the devil?" Jove wheeled his horse around. He ripped a dagger from his belt.

"Wolf!" Dyrke shouted just as a huge black object rushed past Analeen and straight at Jove.

Analeen's terror was immediate and absolute. *Oh, gods, not a wolf!*

As the wolf attacked the men, she fought against the rope around her neck with everything she had. Dyrke had knotted it too tightly and the loop was too small to fit over her head. She yanked against Dyrke's hold on the rope as hard as she could.

While Analeen fought the rope, Jove's mare gave a high-pitched scream. The wolf snarled and clamped his incisors deep in the horse's flank. The mare reared and screamed again.

At the same time, Jove threw his dagger at the wolf. With a lithe movement, the beast released his grip on the horse and dodged the blade. Analeen saw the wolf's furious gray eyes, the rage in them so intense it iced her spine.

Jove's horse bolted into the forest, blood flowing down her flank. The man on her back almost lost his seating. He yanked on the reins and shouted for the horse to stop. The mare thundered through the trees and Analeen could only hear the dying pounding of her hooves.

Dyrke's gelding had never stopped whinnying with fear and trying to dance away from the wolf. The horse dragged Analeen. She tumbled forward, dress tangling around her legs. Her face slammed into hard-packed dirt. Stars sparked behind her eyes. She clawed at the rope, trying to breathe.

The man shouted, "Bloody wolf!"

Analeen scrambled to her knees in time to see the man cock his arm back, ready to fling his own dagger at the huge black menace.

The wolf lunged, its fangs flashing white against its black face. Instead of clamping his incisors onto the horse or the man, he snagged Analeen's rope in his mouth. With one strong snap of his powerful jaws, he bit the rope cleanly in two. This time she stumbled backward. She landed hard on her hip and pain seared her body.

Dyrke's features held a mixture of fury and fear as he flung his dagger. Analeen barely saw the blade flip through the air before she scrambled to her feet and fled into the forest. She still couldn't yank the rope over head, so she caught up the end and clenched it in her fist as she ran.

Blood pounded in her ears as her bare feet pounded against forest floor. Rocks and sticks poked into her soles and bushes snagged her torn dress, ripping it from one breast and further into shreds. Behind she heard Dyrke's cries, the horse's screams, and the wolf's snarls.

She didn't want to die like her mother had. Her throat so mangled and torn that their father wouldn't let any of the daughters see her before her body was burned.

Everything behind Analeen went quiet. No sounds came from the direction of the road, and her terror mounted.

Analeen came to an abrupt stop. She heard only wind murmuring through branches above her. Not a bird, not a squirrel. And nothing, nothing at all from the fray she had left behind.

A wolf's howl shredded the silence and another cold wash of fear rushed over her.

She swallowed, hard. Her body trembled. What should she do?

A tree. I could climb a tree. Wolves couldn't climb trees, could they?

The tree in front of her, the branches rose too high; the one next to it was too spindly to hold her weight. Feeling more and more desperate, she whirled—and slammed into something hard.

A man.

She stumbled back. Big hands grabbed her by her shoulders as she started to fall.

The man caught her to him. Her body flush against solid muscle. Huge hands gripping her arms. Tall, so tall, with long, wild, black hair.

And silvery-gray eyes as fierce as the wolf's.

Renewed terror and fury gave Analeen the strength to fight, to forget her wounds and her exhaustion. She shoved her hands against the man's bare chest and struggled against his hold, but his grip didn't lessen.

"No!" She screamed and clawed at his bare chest, fighting like a forestcat. She tried to bite his arm, kicked at his bare legs and tried to twist out of his grip.

And then she realized the man was entirely naked.

Shocked, Analeen went completely still. Her gaze fixed on his cock, a part of her registering its impressive size. And damn it all, her nipples tightened at the sight.

But the larger part of her grew rigid with fear. She became very aware of her breast hanging through her torn dress and the shreds that barely held the gown to her shoulders.

Her gaze shot to his.

"Are you finished attempting to claw my eyes out, kitten?" The man's deep voice penetrated the haze of terror that suffused her very being. His voice held a hint of irritation that matched the reflection in his eyes.

Analeen swallowed. Her entire body trembled and exhaustion crept back into her bones. Weariness overcame her so fast her head spun and her body went limp. The punishment she had been through at the hands of Dyrke and Jove, the terror of the wolf and her flight, and now a frightening naked man capturing her—it was all too much.

Darkness wove itself through her consciousness until everything went black.

Law frowned as he caught the woman tighter to him. Rage still burned within him at what the men had done to this small creature, and he desired only to kill both of the bastards. He would have hunted them to the ends of Dair if he hadn't been concerned about the woman running through the dangerous forest alone.

Analeen, he had read in her thoughts. *Her name is Analeen.*

His frown turned into a scowl. What did he care what the woman's name was? He had no interest in human women. He would simply return the wench to her village and be done with her.

Yet a deep, primal part of his being did not want to let go. Her scent of woman's musk and wildflowers mingled with the smells of blood from her wounds, and dirt clinging to her skin and clothing. Her eyes were closed but he remembered their blue-green depths, and her spirit combined with fear in her gaze. He could not help but admire the way she had fought him, the way she never gave up even though she had been physically abused and terrified beyond reason of the wolf.

Of him.

Law held the woman against him with one powerful arm, and stroked a clump of matted hair from her face. He couldn't stop himself. Even covered with dirt, dried blood crusting her wounds, her brown hair wild and filthy, and her clothing in shreds, she was quite simply the loveliest being he had ever seen.

His fingers left her hair and he trailed them down the slope of her delicate nose to her slightly parted full lips, and over her chin. Before he realized what he was doing, his fingers neared her beautiful bare breast, traveled up its slope and then rested on the hardening nipple.

A growl rose up in his throat and his cock went rigid against Analeen's belly. Unbidden visions filled his mind.

Of caressing every inch of her bare flesh. Of sucking her jensai red nipples, licking a path down her body, and tasting the heat of her juices between her thighs. Gods how tight she would be, her quim sheathing him as he fucked her hard and so very deep.

With a cry that neared a howl of frustration, Law jerked his hand away from her nipple as if Analeen's body had scalded him. His need for her, his desire for this woman, was so intense that his body began to shake.

No. This woman was human. He would not take a human for a mate.

Chapter Two

Analeen moaned in Law's arms and he sensed dark dreams chasing one another in her mind. He could not leave her, would not leave her. He could do nothing but scoop her up in his powerful grasp and carry her through his forest to his den.

Cool air brushed his naked skin and his cock remained at full attention. He could not tear his thoughts away from the image of taking this woman over and over.

When he reached the den he chose to reside in during spring and summer months, he strode in through its opening, down a long passageway, and deep into a crystal cavern. What was left of the day's sunlight poured in through an opening at the top of the cavern. The minimal light reflected through crystals, causing rainbows to glitter and dance upon the floor.

He lived alone, having left his uncle's pack long ago. Once his family had been murdered, he had not wanted bonds of any kind.

Law carefully set Analeen upon a pile of tanned hides and used a rolled-up doeskin on which to rest her head. He found a knife in his supplies and sliced the rope from around her neck.

She slept. Her body needed to recover from the trauma she had been through. He covered her with a soft doeskin blanket, checked on her frequently, and gave her sips of water even as she dreamed. He wiped dirt from her eyes, her face, and her neck with a soft wet cloth. When he finished, he cleansed the wounds on her arms and feet. And still she slept.

He felt fiercely protective of this woman and could barely stand to let her out of his sight, even to hunt for his own meals.

For two days she slept fitfully, tossing her head. Her eyelids fluttered and her cheeks burned hot with fever. He forced pulverized bits of willow bark through her lips along with sips of water. Finally her fever broke and she rested.

On the third day, he decided she had slept long enough. He carried her outside the cavern and down to the pool.

Analeen woke to the gentle brush of a moist cloth against her cheek. For a moment she relaxed into the caress, feeling safe and loved by her mother's soft touch. She heard the soft slosh of water against shoreline, the call of the nordai and the kiss of wind against her cheeks and over one breast.

Her eyelids flew up and her lips parted to scream, but a large hand clamped over her mouth. She went entirely still as her gaze locked with the fierce gray eyes of the man who had captured her in the forest. He knelt beside her, his powerful body as naked as before. He was so large he blocked everything from view. All she could see was this huge man who held her prisoner.

"Scream and I will have to turn you over my knee, kitten." Amusement flared in those eyes, but they immediately darkened with what looked like desire. He gave a shake of his head and tossed his hair back with the movement, as if shaking away that desire. "I will release you, but if you make a noise, I will gag that sweet mouth of yours."

Analeen bit her lip beneath his palm and gave a slow nod. She could tell this was not a man to trifle with. She would escape him, yes, but she would have to wait until the right time.

He moved his hand from her mouth and resumed washing her face with careful strokes. She flinched when the rag trailed over a wound on her chin, and he frowned. "Bastards," he growled. He continued wiping the cool cloth over her face and neck until he seemed satisfied.

"You took care of me," she murmured as memories came pouring back to her. She had been ill with fever and he had wet her face with cool cloths and had fed her bitter tasting powder that must have been willow bark.

He shrugged. "You were ill. Three days you slept."

Her eyes widened with surprise. "Three days?" She tried to push past him, to sit up. "I must get back to my sisters. They need me."

The man grasped her hand as he rose to his feet, pulling her up with him. For a moment the world spun and she sagged against his muscled form. His chest was hot against her one bare breast and her cheeks flushed with their own heat.

"Are you all right, Analeen?" he asked softly against her hair.

She jerked her head up and bumped his nose. "How do you know my name?"

He simply looked at her as if memorizing her features.

Analeen swallowed. "Who are you?"

"I am called Law." He cupped the side of her face and rubbed his thumb along her cheekbone. "You, my lady, have stumbled into my territory. What comes here leaves or stays by my word alone."

"Excuse me?" Analeen's frown was immediate. "You can't keep me here."

His eyes darkened and she took a step back. "You will stay until I allow you to leave."

She glared at Law and tried to jerk away from him, but she almost fell, she was so weak. He caught her and held her in his firm grip.

Before she could respond, he caught her chin in his hand. "Come. You need a bath."

Analeen was in no shape to fight the man. He supported her with one arm and led her toward a pool just feet from where she had been lying. A springy carpet of moss felt soft against her injured bare feet as she gazed in wonder about her. All thought of what he had just said slipped away from her mind as she took in the beauty of the sanctuary, more beautiful than the Mairi Sea.

Trees grew thick around the pool, countless leaves hanging in soft lacy curtains, drifts of the greenest green, spilling down to the water's surface. Flowers sprouted in haphazard clumps of red, pink, and purple, and the pool shimmered a deep crystal blue-green.

"The same color as your eyes," Law murmured, and she glanced up at him in amazement.

"It's unbelievable." It was more than that, but that was all she could think of to say as he led her into the water.

Again she was surprised. It wasn't freezing cold, but simply a gentle coolness that energized her body and cleared her mind the deeper they walked into it. Her aches and injuries nearly vanished with just the caress of water.

Law led her to a rock alcove near the shore, far enough into the water that it rose to just beneath her breasts. Her shredded dress billowed around her legs, and her one breast that wasn't bared begged to be set free.

"You are a lovely creature, Analeen." Law took her by the shoulders and forced her to turn her back to him. She felt him untie the back lacing to her dress. "A sore temptation for any man."

She frowned. *Why would he say such things?* She knew she wasn't pretty, just a breath above ugly, as she had been told countless times by her father.

Law whipped her around to face him so fast she cried out. She would have lost her footing if he hadn't been holding her shoulders so tightly. The scowl on his face caused her heart to thud.

"You are a beautiful woman, Analeen." His voice was a low roar. "By the moon, I will teach you to see your own beauty before I let you go."

All she could do was stare at him in surprise. He seemed so serious. And it was like he had just read her thoughts as clearly as if she'd spoken them aloud.

Law's gut churned as he lifted Analeen's hair from where it caught in the neckline of her dress. The abuse she had gone through extended far beyond what the bastards Dyrke and Jove had done to her. He desired nothing more than to track the men, and then to hunt down her father, and make them all pay for the damage they had done to this woman. His fangs nearly exploded in his mouth and he felt the tightening of his skin that came before change. It took all his power to fight back the wild beast threatening to overcome him.

Analeen audibly caught her breath as he lowered her dress slowly over her shoulders, down her arms and beneath the water to her waist, where he let it fall to her feet at the bottom of the pool. Both her breasts were bared now and he nearly moaned aloud.

Almost without thought, he brought his hand out of the water and trailed his wet knuckles down the curve of her slender neck, over her collarbone, and to the tantalizing swell of one breast.

She stilled and he sensed her fear and her anger at being touched without her permission, yet her arousal, too. He forced himself to stop and reached behind a hidden shelf on the rock alcove and brought out a jar of soap that smelled of mint. While she watched, he dipped his fingers into the white substance and scooped out enough to wash her body.

Slowly he soaped her shoulders and arms, down to her fingers. Analeen trembled beneath his touch. Her thoughts were so easy to read. She wanted to slap him, wanted to run, wanted to stay, wanted him to stop, never wanted him to stop.

After he soaped her arms, he washed her back, and then her belly. When all that was left untouched were her breasts, he took her hands and put soap in her palms.

His voice came out in a hoarse whisper as he said, "Wash your breasts."

Analeen's cheeks flushed and she hesitated. "You have no right telling me what to do."

"Now," he demanded in a voice so menacing that Analeen brought up her hands and began massaging her breasts.

Law's cock jerked at the sight.

"Your nipples." He could barely keep from touching her.

She bit her lower lip with her small white teeth and tugged at her taut pink buds.

"Rinse off," he ordered, his tone curt as he struggled to maintain control and not ravish this woman where she stood.

She paused only a moment, then dived beneath the surface of the pool and came back immediately. She swung her long hair out of her face. Her hair glistened and beads of water rolled down her fair skin.

He put more soap into his palm. "Turn," he demanded. "I am going to wash your hair." She stared at him for one long moment, her eyes narrowed, then slowly faced away from him.

Analeen was a good foot shorter than he was, just the right height. He worked the shampoo into her hair, and he felt her tremble with desire at his touch.

Gradually Analeen relaxed as he massaged her scalp, despite her intentions to stay stiff and unyielding. She leaned back against him, feeling like her muscles could no longer hold her upright. Law's skin felt hot and sensual next to hers, and his cock grew harder yet against her backside. All in all, it was an exquisite set of sensations.

Despite the fact this man was a stranger, Analeen felt herself becoming more aroused by the moment. She had always been curious about sex, but always assumed such pleasures would be denied her, except for random, sweaty encounters in the dark—clumsy and hurried, such as she had known. She wasn't a beauty like her sisters, and she had no wealth to attract a suitor.

Yet here she was, in an exquisite pool, with an exquisite specimen of maleness paying her tender attention. Her quim ached and her nipples were hard as Mairi Sea Pearls.

Analeen sighed. "That feels so incredibly good." She was this man's captive, but somehow she didn't feel threatened. She wanted him with a desire that shocked her.

In truth, she had never actually felt that he would harm her in any way, a fact that puzzled her. Just by the look in his incredibly fierce gray eyes, she knew he was wild and deliciously wicked.

"Rinse time," he said, the second before at least a gallon of water sloshed over her head.

Analeen sputtered and started to yell at him when he doused her yet again. She whirled to face Law, who held a wooden bucket, and glared up at him. But for the first time since she had met him, he was smiling.

"You were getting far too comfortable against me, kitten." His mouth curved into an arrogant grin. "It is obvious you want me."

"Oooh!" Analeen slapped her hand onto the pool's surface, sending a spray of water right at the cocky bastard's face.

Surprise crossed his features and he slung his long hair out of his face just as she splashed him again. He narrowed his eyes, his gaze fixed on her like a predator about to take down his prey.

With a cry, Analeen turned and tried to hurry through the water toward the shore. Her feet tangled in her forgotten dress and she dropped into the water.

The next thing she knew, Law's arms were around her waist. He brought her up out of the water, and she gasped for air. He was laughing, his voice deep and throbbing, and she had to return his grin.

His gaze caught hers and she went completely still. Those beautiful silver-gray eyes clouded with desire and she shivered with the intense need she saw there. Her nipples ached even more, and her quim flooded with her juices.

He slid his hand into her hair, cupped the back of her head, and drew her body flush against his. His cock was a hot and hard rod between them, and her breasts were pressed against his powerful chest.

"Law." A waterfall of sensation tumbled through Analeen's belly. "I—"

He let her thoughts flow around him like the gentle warmth of the pool. She was as aroused as he was, but she didn't know him.

Fierce need gripped his body and he ached to thrust his cock into her heat and fuck her until they both cried out with completion. All Law knew was that he wanted this woman more than he had ever wanted any woman in all his years.

And he couldn't have her. She was human.

Chapter Three

"I would never hurt you, kitten." He pressed his lips to the soft skin of her forehead and she shuddered with what he knew was desire. Her womanly scent was rich and inviting. It sang to him like a mate's howl when the full moon rose high and proud in the night sky. "I would never take you without your consent."

What was he saying? He would not be taking her at all.

His hand still cupping her head, he chased droplets of water sliding down the slope of her nose with his tongue. He tasted the salt of her skin, a trace of mint from the shampoo, and the sweetness of the pool's water.

Analeen's chest rose and fell against his, her heart pounding loud enough for his sensitive ears to hear. It throbbed throughout his being, pulsing like his cock pulsed against her belly.

"Law..." This time his name came out as a whisper of desire, no fear or anger in her tone. She placed her hands against his chest and looked up at him with those beautiful blue-green eyes.

A low growl rose up within him. By the moon, how he wanted this woman. He moved his lips over hers and gently nipped at her lower lip. She gasped and he slipped his tongue into her mouth, forever imprinting her taste in his memory. Tentatively her tongue mated with his, but as he kissed her, she became more confident, more demanding. She made small mewling sounds, like a kitten.

His kiss became harder, more fierce. He demanded all of her and she gave him that and more. He clenched his fist in her hair, and with his free hand he stroked the curve of her shoulder, down the indentation at her waist and over the flare of her hip to cup her ass and force her impossibly tighter to his erection.

She moaned and rubbed her slender body against his cock. He broke the kiss, his breathing heavy and all the heat in his body pooling in his groin. Analeen whimpered and tried to bring her lips back to his.

"You take my very breath from my body." His voice grew huskier with his desire. "I think you have bewitched me."

Her face flushed, and her eyes were heavy-lidded. "I don't know what you're doing to me, Law. I feel as if my heart has known you a lifetime, yet I don't know you. I know nothing about you. I should be angry with you, but somehow you have taken that anger away."

"It is enough that you are a woman and I am a man." Law scooped her up in his arms and she did not even cry out in surprise. She simply clung to his neck, a small creature at ease with him, giving him a measure of trust. What would happen to that trust when she found out what he was? The very thing she feared more than anything?

Rational thought fled his mind as he laid her upon a bed of soft moss. The way she looked up at him nearly sent him over the edge. He slid between her thighs, his cock pressed against her pussy, and her cheeks flushed a pretty shade of pink. She wrapped her arms around his neck and pressed her mound against him.

He could not wait to slide into her, could not wait to fuck her long and hard.

No. If he did it could start the transformation process and she would become the thing she most feared. Such a betrayal would be unthinkable!

But he had to taste her, had to give her pleasure.

Law kissed Analeen again, and her belly fluttered from the slow, languorous kiss that took her breath away. Too soon he slipped his tongue out of her mouth and moved his lips over her chin and down the curve of her neck. His long wet hair trailed over her skin as he moved, a gentle caress that caused her to shiver.

Analeen didn't know what she was doing. She should be angry, should try to flee. But all she knew was that she didn't want him to stop. She had never felt such incredible sensations in her life and she ached for this man's touch.

He moved his lips to one of her nipples. "So beautiful," he murmured before he latched onto the nub and sucked.

She cried out from the sensation, so loud that nordai startled in the trees above and took wing. Without even realizing what she was doing, she arched up, pressing her breast harder against his mouth.

Law groaned and moved to her other nipple and she cried out again. Her hands found his hair and she buried her fingers in the wet strands. When he released her nipple and moved his mouth between her breasts, she whimpered, not wanting him to stop the incredible feelings.

"Do you enjoy my mouth upon you?" He trailed his tongue down her belly, nearing the soft curls of her mound.

She could barely find the breath to speak. "Yes." Her tone was low and hoarse with desire. She forced herself to raise her voice and said, "Don't stop."

The man's laugh was soft but so carnal it made her blood boil.

And then she couldn't think any longer. Not at all. His tongue was tracing lazy circles through the soft brown curls of her mound, his hands gripping the insides of her thighs. Her legs trembled and she couldn't believe what he was doing. He wasn't going to put his mouth—

His tongue swiped her folds and she cried out her surprise and her passion. Oh, my gods, did that feel incredible. His hands gripped her thighs tighter as he sucked and licked her quim. She clenched her fingers in his wet hair and moaned and thrashed. What was happening to her? She felt the most incredible sensations rising within her, sensations that stole all breath from her chest, and all thought from her mind.

He thrust his finger inside her quim and she screamed. Fire seared her body, expanding outward from her belly to her breasts to the roots of her hair, and down her legs, all the way to her toes. Her body bucked and jerked and brilliant colors flashed behind her eyes.

She couldn't believe what had just happened to her body. She had heard the local tavern wenches speak of pleasures with a man, but the one experience she'd had with the son of a farmer had been less than pleasurable. He'd forced her to suck his cock, and she hadn't enjoyed it at all.

Law continued sucking and licking her, and thrusting his finger inside her quim until the sensations became too much to bear. She begged him to stop. She couldn't take any more of the sweet, sweet torture.

He seemed reluctant to halt, but did and eased up her body. His cock was against her belly, his arms braced to either side of her shoulders, and his silvery-gray eyes stared down at her with so much desire in them it was almost frightening. Her breathing came hard and her body was covered with sweat. She could smell her own juices mingling with the scent of the moss at her back and the lacy trees drifting down to the pool.

"Your taste—incredible." Law lowered his head and brought his lips a breath above hers. "I want you to sample your own nectar." He pressed his mouth to hers and slipped his tongue through her lips. She tasted her unique flavor and more quivers went through her belly to know this was what he had sampled when he had brought her such exquisite feelings.

"It was unbelievable. I still feel bursts of pleasure shivering my body." She glanced down to where his cock was hard against her belly. After the experience he had given her, she wanted to repay him in kind. His cock looked far more delicious than the farmer's son's. "Tell me how you would like me to pleasure you."

Fire burned in Law's gut as he eased to his feet. His long black hair lay loose and drying about his shoulders and wind caressed his nakedness. Analeen's skin pebbled with gooseflesh from the cool breeze and her nipples stood out taut and hard.

"On your knees," he commanded, his voice coming out rough with desire. "Wrap your hand around my cock."

She shivered and obeyed, slipping her small fingers down his length and her big blue-green eyes focused on his erection. This time he did groan aloud. "Put my cock into your mouth."

Analeen licked her lips and then slid them down his length, taking him deeper than he thought possible.

By the moon, she felt so hot and wet around his erection, and all he could think about was driving into her quim and fucking her until she screamed her release.

"Move your hand and mouth up and down my cock." He was hoarse with his need and could barely speak.

Analeen looked up at him as she sucked his cock. He had never felt anything so incredible in all his many years, as the feel of her mouth on him.

He grasped her head and thrust his hips against her face in time with her movements. His climax built within him until he knew he was near the peak and there would be no going back.

"Analeen," he groaned as he watched his cock move in and out of her mouth. "My seed will fill your mouth if you do not stop."

She sucked harder. Like the lava of Mount Taka, his come burst from his body and down Analeen's throat. She didn't stop. She took his fluid, swallowing it as he burned and his mind soared. The orgasm that slammed into his body was so powerful it very nearly drove him to his knees.

Chapter Four

When he could take no more, Law pulled his cock out of Analeen's mouth, then knelt so that they were both on their knees facing one another. He slipped his hand into her folds and she gasped and clung to his arms. He slid two fingers deep into her channel and her eyes nearly rolled back in her head.

Holding back the fierce need to take her, he brought his hand from her folds. He wrapped his fingers around his semi-erect cock that quickly grew to its full size again. He pushed it against the soft curls of her mound and slipped it into the lips of her quim, brushing it against her clit.

Analeen pushed closer to him. "I want you inside of me."

With a groan Law closed his eyes. He wanted this woman so badly it made his body scream with need. But it was more than that. It was her innocence, the strength of her spirit he had witnessed in her thoughts, and the caring he had seen for the ones she loved.

He felt her fingers wrap around his cock and his eyes opened.

"*No.*" The word came out harsher than he intended and she jerked her hand away, a hurt expression upon her face.

"I understand." She tilted her chin up, her eyes glassy as if they ached with unshed tears. "As my father always says, I am a breath above ugly. I am surely not pleasing enough for a bonding with you."

Fury seared his very being at the treatment this lovely woman had received at the hands of her father. He jerked her to a stand and she recoiled from the anger she surely saw in his expression. "I told you that you *will* see yourself as the beautiful woman you are. You will no longer listen to the voices of weak men who belittle others to make themselves feel more powerful."

She just stared up at him with her eyes wide and disbelief in her expression.

"On your hands and knees," he demanded. "And look into the pool."

Analeen felt the desire to knock this big man on his ass, but she knew she was no match for him. When he braced his arms on her shoulders and pushed down, she complied and settled on her hands and knees at the water's edge and stared into its blue-green depths.

"Look at your reflection and tell me what you see." His voice was softer now, but still held a note of anger in it.

She blinked and then saw her reflection wavering in the pool. "I see myself, and you."

"Tell me what you look like."

Analeen swallowed. "My hair is straggly, my eyes are too big, my nose too small and my lips too large. My face is thin and pinched."

A growl rose up beside her and she jerked her attention to Law. He had sounded so much like a wolf that fear nearly exploded her heart.

"Let me tell you what I see." He gently pushed on her cheek so that she was looking in the water again. He slipped his fingers into her folds from behind, and began stroking her clit as he spoke. "I see beautiful blue-green eyes filled with innocence." His finger circled her swollen nub as he continued, "I see an adorable nose that gently slopes down to full lips made to be kissed." His fingers moved faster and faster, and Analeen saw her lips part and her lids lower. "Your face is oval-shaped, the perfect size for all your lovely features."

Analeen felt on the verge of explosion. Her thighs trembled and her breasts bounced as she thrust back against his hand.

"And your hair." He took a strand of now dried hair that hung around her face. "Gentle waves of honey-brown that frame your face perfectly."

He increased the pace of his fingers and she thought she would die from the pleasure. "You have the loveliest quim and luscious nipples made to suck."

Law pinched her clit and she cried out, her voice echoing around the pool. Her body jerked and her mind filled with light and color as the orgasm rippled through her like a rock tossed in that beautiful pool

When she finally came down from the place he had sent her to, Law ordered her to look at her reflection again. Analeen studied her features in the water, her heart beating fast from what he had done to her. She still saw the plain woman she had always been.

Law growled again and rose to his feet. He held out his hand and reached down for her. She took it and let him pull her to a stand.

"As I told you before, you will not leave my forest until you discover your own beauty."

Anger rose up in her, and the heat filling her was not just from her orgasm. "You can't make me stay!"

"I can and I will." When she tried to respond he cupped the back of her head and put his hand over her mouth. "I will know if you lie to me, so do not think to tell me until you truly believe it."

Two weeks passed. Every day Law taught Analeen the many ways they could pleasure one another—every way except for the bonding. He let her see through his eyes how beautiful she was, and he saw her confidence grow in herself and in him.

He came to cherish every moment with her, every minute they spent together. He could no longer imagine life without her, and that fierce need to protect her had grown to the desire to keep her as his own. He would take her for a mate, but not until she knew what he was, and what she would become. One bite, one time pumping her with his seed, and she would become a werewolf, too, on the next full moon.

Law only hoped she would not hate him for it. All he knew was that he couldn't let her go.

Over the two weeks, he had shared much about his own life with Analeen. He owned a tanner's shop in a nearby village and had a home there where he stayed in the winter months. During the summer, he lived in the cavern while he hunted in his forest and collected pelts to tan and sell come wintertime.

He didn't tell her exactly how he hunted the animals, and how he ate their flesh raw, ripping it from their bones while it was still hot with their blood.

In turn, Analeen shared with him about her family, even how her mother had died and how much she missed her. He witnessed fear in her trembling voice and in her eyes when she told him about the wolf.

She talked about her four younger sisters and sensed her pride in each of them. And he sensed how much she missed them. Several times she had tried to escape. When he foiled her attempts, she begged him to let her go. Her sisters needed her. But he forced her to remember that the next oldest girl was eighteen, just a year younger than Analeen, and more than capable of caring for her three younger sisters.

No, he demanded that she would have to wait until he was certain she truly had discovered her own beauty. She tried to make him believe she had, several times, but he knew she was only saying it so he would let her go. That alone set his heart to aching. Day after day, he had hoped she would have no desire to leave him, but even though he read her thoughts and knew she found great pleasure in being with him, he did not sense she loved him.

As he now loved her.

Analeen lay back on the soft pelts in the cavern and stared up at the crystal ceiling. It sparkled and glittered, casting thousands of rainbows across the cavern floor. She raised one hand and a rainbow striped her skin. She studied it, seeing the beautiful red, orange, yellow, green, blue, indigo, and violet against her flesh.

Yet she didn't completely see it. In her mind she pictured herself with her captor, rolling across the pelts, kissing and licking and biting one another. Bringing each other to climax after incredible climax with their hands and their mouths.

Yet Law refused to bond with her.

Over and over he had told her she truly didn't know him, didn't know what he was. When she knew, he had told her, she could make the choice then.

She was certain who he was. A fierce, protective, and loyal man. A man who taught her how to care about herself as much as she cared about others. And a man who taught her she was beautiful inside and out.

Finally, clear as day, she could honestly see it, as if the mask others had placed upon her had fallen away to reveal the woman she truly was.

With a sigh she rose up from the pelts and her feet pattered across the smooth rock floor of the cavern. She was now completely comfortable with her nakedness, not having worn clothing since the day she had arrived.

Every day, Law had blocked the entrance with a large boulder, keeping her prisoner.

She didn't imagine that most prisoners were made love to the way Law made love to her.

At first, she had been angry, and had searched and searched the cavern for some way out. But over time, she gradually came to accept her temporary imprisonment. Law had promised to release her when she truly appreciated herself.

Under Law's constant attention, by the way he cared for her, she felt like a newly opened jensai bloom. The rare flowers always started out as plain black buds that were nothing special to look at. But when they bloomed, they were the most incredibly beautiful and precious flower one could ever hope to see.

That was how Law made her feel. Beautiful. Rare. Precious.

Even though she knew the entrance would be blocked, Analeen slipped from the coolness of the cavern, into the long passageway that led to the outside and to Law's pool. They had spent countless hours there, laughing and playing in the water, bathing, and exploring one another's bodies. Cool air brushed her naked skin and her nipples tightened as always as she imagined it was Law caressing her body. She could never tire of being with him.

She had fallen in love with Law.

Analeen paused in the passageway, her scalp prickling with the realization, and she held her hand to her pounding heart. "Oh, my gods," she whispered. A sense of giddiness came over her and her heart felt near to bursting.

Just as quickly it faded. Likely Law didn't feel the same.

But what if he did?

She slipped into the passageway that seemed brighter than normal. It was about time for Law to return from hunting, and even though she couldn't get out, she could wait for him.

Analeen rounded the corner and saw the cave entrance was open. Slowly she walked toward it. Maybe Law was already back? Or could he have forgotten to move the boulder before it?

The thought raced through her mind that now she had the opportunity to escape, to return to her family.

But just as quickly that thought fled. She didn't want to leave Law, the man she loved. Even if he didn't love her, she would take what time she had with him, and then she would go home.

She hurried out the cave entrance and onto the soft grass that led down to the pool, a smile on her face.

Shock ripped her being.

Blocking the path was an enormous black wolf.

Chapter Five

Sheer terror nearly drove Analeen to her knees. But she couldn't move. Couldn't run. Could do nothing but remain trapped in the silvery-gray gaze of the black wolf.

The wolf that had gone after Jove and Dyrke and had chased the bastards away.

His head was raised, studying her. Beside him was the pelt of a deer and Analeen hoped the wolf was full. Of course, even that wasn't a guarantee he wouldn't tear out her throat anyway.

She slowly took a step back.

The wolf stepped forward.

Analeen went still again. And then felt blood drain from her face as the wolf began to change before her very eyes.

The beast rose up on his hind legs that transformed into a powerful man's legs. Fur melded into skin, fangs into straight white teeth. The only thing that didn't change was his silvery-gray eyes.

Law's eyes.

Her head grew light and the world seemed to topple sideways. She started to fall but in the next moment she found herself in Law's arms.

She went wild. "No!" she screamed as she fought and clawed him. This time she had more strength than she had the first time she had tried to escape Law. She fought with everything she had, put every bit of rage left in her from when her mother had been murdered by that wolf. All Law did was hold her, press her tight against his bare chest. He didn't try to stop her from hurting him, but he didn't let her go. He just held her.

When she had worn herself out, Analeen went limp in his embrace and cried. Law scooped her up in his arms and carried her into the cavern.

"You lied to me," she shouted through her tears. "You're not who I thought you were."

"I never lied to you, kitten." His voice was firm, but his eyes soft and understanding. "I told you that I would not bond with you until you knew who I am. What I am."

Analeen swallowed as he carried her into the sparkling crystal cave. He spoke the truth. He hadn't come out and told her, but he hadn't lied to her either. And when he had attacked Jove and Dyrke, he *had* saved her. He hadn't attacked her—he had snapped his jaws through her rope.

When he reached the pile of pelts that they slept on, he lowered her onto the soft fur, then settled next to her. His long dark hair was wild about his face and passion burned in his silvery-gray eyes. His glorious body was naked as always, only scratched and bleeding where she had taken her fear out on him. His cock stood out thick and long. He wanted her, even now.

And she couldn't deny the fact that she wanted him. She still loved him.

She clenched her hands into fists. "Why didn't you tell me?"

Law sighed and ran one finger down the bridge of her nose to the tip. "I am sorry I did not tell you, kitten. But I did not want you to fear me. I know how afraid you are of wolves."

Analeen bit her lower lip. "But a werewolf? Why do you have to be a wolf?"

His features were serious as he said, "Does that mean you cannot love me any longer?"

Her eyes widened and her cheeks burned. How did he know? She had only figured it out moments ago.

"I have another confession to make." Law traced her lower lip with the pad of his finger. "One of the many talents of a werewolf is the ability to sense feelings and to read minds."

She frowned. "You've been reading my thoughts? I don't think I like that at all. As a matter of fact, it makes me want to punch you."

Law shrugged one shoulder. "It is a part of me, as breathing is a part of you."

For a long moment Analeen studied him and then her heart betrayed her. No matter that he was a werewolf with talents beyond her imagination, she still wanted him. She still loved him.

With a smile, Law lowered his mouth to hers. "I love you, too, kitten."

Heat of a different kind rushed through her as he took possession of her mouth. A long, slow, deep kiss that showed her his love for her. His hands roamed her body and his lips tasted her everywhere, from her nipples, down her flat belly and to the soft hair of her mound. He licked and sucked her clit, but just when he took her to the brink, he stopped and rose up between her thighs and placed the head of his cock at the entrance to her core.

Analeen stopped breathing.

"I want to bond with you. I want to make you mine, forever."

Without hesitation, she nodded. "I want you more than anything."

"I have yet another confession." He pressed the head of his cock in just an inch and she gasped at the feeling. She could tell he was holding himself back from plunging into her. "When I penetrate you it will start the process of transformation."

"Transformation?" Her heart thudded against her rib cage. "You don't mean that I'll become a werewolf, too?"

Law nodded. "And you will have the long life that a werewolf leads, as will our children." He pushed in a fraction more and clenched his jaw. "Say yes, Analeen. Tell me you will be my lifemate. I cannot live without you."

As clear as the crystal of the cavern, her heart answered, *Yes*.

"Say it out loud, my love." He pressed into her a fraction more. His arms trembled and sweat broke out on his forehead. "Tell me you love me and you want to be mine—completely mine."

"Yes, Law," she whispered, and then louder, "*Yes*."

Law drove into her, plunging deep inside her. Analeen cried out at the girth and length of him driving into her, and then moaned as it turned into complete and total pleasure.

By the moon, Analeen felt so good around him as he fucked her. He thrust in and out of her tight sheath, enjoying the sensation of her channel gripping his cock. He couldn't take his gaze from her as he plunged in and out. Her blue-green eyes gazed up at him, and he could read the love in those depths, as well as in her thoughts. She was holding nothing back from him, and she had accepted him for what and who he was.

And she had agreed to become his lifemate. To be with him, always.

Their sweat mingled and droplets slid from his forehead and onto her hair. Her face was tilted back, her heavy-lidded blue-green eyes focused on him. She was definitely the most beautiful creature he had ever known.

His climax grew and grew within him like a thunderstorm of the most powerful proportions. But he held back, drawing out Analeen's pleasure as she cried out, moaned, and writhed beneath him.

Analeen had never felt so full, so happy, so complete. In her heart, she knew it didn't matter that Law was a werewolf. He was a good man, a caring man. And he was now a part of her…her life, her love.

It felt so incredibly good as he fucked her. He had called it that before, fucking, and she liked the word. It was erotic and made her more excited.

"But now I am making love to you," he murmured as he bent to nuzzle her ear. "It is not simply fucking now."

"Will I be able to read your mind, too?" She grasped his buttocks and thrust up, urging him to fuck her harder.

"Yes, kitten." He kissed her with a long fierce kiss, thrusting his tongue inside her mouth at the same time he thrust his cock into her quim. Harder and harder and harder yet. She felt her orgasm building, the sensations spiraling and spiraling out of control until she screamed her release. Colors burst in her mind, like the rainbows of the crystal cavern. Her mind sailed out of her body, existing in another world for that fraction of time.

In the distance she heard Law shout her name and then his teeth sank into her shoulder at the same time she felt his cock pulse inside her. She cried out again from the pain of the bite, but then the sensation melded into pleasure.

Law collapsed on his side, and brought her into the circle of his arms, his cock still in her core. Their breathing was loud and the smell of their sex heavy in the air.

Analeen brought her hand up and caressed Law's stubbled cheek. "I love you, my wolf-man."

He smiled and held her closer. "I love you, kitten."

Epilogue

Law slipped through the dark village on silent paws, and came to the home where Analeen had lived. He had heard the men's voices long before he reached the village, and had convinced his wife to walk behind him. Her dress made soft swishing sounds as she followed.

When Law reached the shadows outside the home, his eyes focused on a huge, slovenly dressed man who bellowed, "Get on out of here," to the two men before him. Law recognized the bastards Dyrke and Jove.

Jove clenched his fists. "The bitch ran off and we cain't find her nowheres. I'm a bettin' she's in there, locked up with the rest of your whore daughters."

The large man was surely Analeen's father.

He hitched up his breeches over his fat gut. "I sold the bitch to you fair 'n square. If she got away it's your business, not mine."

Law's hackles rose and he heard Analeen gasp behind him.

"You sold me?" Before he could stop her, she marched out of the shadows to stand in front of the huge man, ignoring Dyrke and Jove. "My own father sold me?"

"Grab the bitch!" Jove shouted.

Rage flooded Law, clouding his vision red. He bolted out of the darkness and clamped his jaws around one of Jove's wrists. The man screamed as bones crunched, flesh tore. The wolf bit clean through his wrist, severing his hand completely.

"My hand!" Jove screamed again as blood spurt across the ground. "The godsdamn wolf bit off my hand!"

But Law's attention had turned to Dyrke who had his dagger out.

"Law!" Analeen screamed as the dagger flipped through the air and straight at the wolf.

He easily dodged the dagger and charged the bastard. He knocked Dyrke to the ground, flat on his back. The one who had called Analeen ugly.

The man screeched and tried to fight the wolf off. With a snap of his powerful jaws, Law ripped out a chunk of the man's cheek and spit it out, then tore off the end of the bastard's nose.

Dyrke scrambled to his feet and ran. He kept screaming, holding his hand to his face, blood pouring everywhere.

Law sensed movement and Jove's dark thoughts as he cradled his mutilated hand to his chest. The wolf whirled to dodge another attack with a dagger. Analeen had a chunk of firewood in her hands and was behind Jove. Before the bastard could charge Law with the knife, she swung the log at the back of Jove's head. He dropped like a rock.

Analeen's breath came in harsh, angry gasps. She knew Law was okay, and turned her attention to her father, who had been staring transfixed at the carnage.

Law's hackles rose and a fierce growl rose up from his throat.

"Get that wolf away." Her father backed up toward the door of the cottage. "You know what one of those bastards did to your mother."

The change had already started within Analeen and she caught a fraction of her father's thoughts.

"You're the bastard." Still wielding the hunk of wood, Analeen slowly walked up to her father. "Mother didn't die from a wolf's bite. You sold her, just like you sold me."

Her father's face blanched. "Like I told you, she's dead."

"Yeah." Analeen fought back the tears. "She was murdered when she tried to get back to us."

She wiped one hand across her eyes and then said, "You are going to leave my sisters and never, ever come back."

The man she used to think of as her father took a step toward her. "Listen you little bitch. I'll do with them what I please."

Law growled, his fangs glimmering in the moonlight, his hackles rising and a menacing rumble rising up from him. He slowly stalked her father, who stumbled back in his haste to get away and fell.

"I mean it." Analeen took a step toward him. "You don't take anything from the house. You never see my sisters, or me, ever again. If you don't leave now, I'll let Law tear into you like he did those two."

When her father hesitated, Law rushed him. The man scrambled to his feet and ran as fast as he could, his fat jiggling over his belt. He stumbled and fell a couple of times, but soon he was completely out of sight.

Analeen knelt beside her wolf and hugged him tight.

She could see in his mind how they would guard and help her sisters—and how if her father dared to return, he would learn the true ways of the wolves—how the pack protects its own.

And this wolf was hers. Hers alone. He always would be.

About the author:

Cheyenne McCray is a thirty-something wild thing at heart, with a passion for sensual romance and a happily-ever-after...but always with a twist. A University of Arizona alumnus, Chey has been writing ever since she can remember, back to her kindergarten days when she penned her first poem. She always knew that one day she would write novels, and with her love of fantasy and romance, combined with her passionate nature, erotic romance is a perfect genre for her. In addition to her adult work, Chey is also published in young adult literary fiction under another name. Chey enjoys spending time with her husband and three sons, traveling, working out at the health club, playing racquetball, and of course writing, writing, writing.

Cheyenne welcomes mail from readers. You can write to her c/o Ellora's Cave Publishing at 1337 Commerce Drive, Suite 13, Stow, OH 44224.

Also by Cheyenne McCray:

Erotic Invitation
Blackstar: Future Knight
Seraphine Chronicles 1: Forbidden
Seraphine Chronicles 2: Bewitched
Seraphine Chronicles 3: Spellbound
Seraphine Chronicles 4: Untamed
Things That Go Bump In the Night 3 - anthology
Vampire Dreams - with Annie Windsor
Wild 1: Wildfire
Wild 2: Wildcat
Wild 3: Wildcard
Wild 4: Wild Borders
Wonderland 1: King of Hearts
Wonderland 2: King of Spades
Wonderland 3: King of Diamonds
Wonderland 4: King of Clubs

SCARLET SWEET

Anya Bast

Chapter One

"He's a drunk," Cerian said under her breath. "The only hope for our people is *that,* down there." She gestured toward the dark-haired, broad-shouldered man sitting in the tavern below them. "A star-cursed, drunken, outlander Vampir." She swung her head to gaze at Lympia with disbelief shining in her eyes.

"You don't know for certain he's drunk," said Lympia. She batted her blue eyes there were fringed with light pink lashes.

A loud crash jerked Cerian's focus back to Rhys ap Griffyn. He'd toppled the table over in front of him, sending his tankard rolling across the wooden floor and sloshing the potent spirit it formerly contained all over his neighbor—a very large Ystani warrior. Now the cursed Vampir roared at everyone around him, yelling in some foreign language at the top of his very powerful lungs.

Cerian gripped the edge of the window set into the tavern's slanted roof and stared down in disbelief. They'd crawled up here so they wouldn't have to enter the packed tavern to get a clear preview of the man sent to save their people. She squeezed her eyes shut on the spectacle below. The knot in her stomach grew tighter by the moment.

"Well, at least he's a *good-looking,* star-cursed, drunken, outlander Vampir," offered Lympia with a weak smile.

Low, angry voices had Cerian staring below again. The Ystani warrior had taken issue with the spirit now soaking her mottled leather tunic. She rose to her full seven feet of finely honed muscle and hissed at the Vampir, baring dark red teeth. Cerian could almost smell the warrior's fetid breath. Rhys ap Griffyn was getting a whole face full.

Rain began to fall and Cerian shifted uncomfortably on the straw-thatched roof. Cold drops plopped onto her head and back, soaked her hair and clothing.

Could this get any worse?

Several other warriors stood from a small table in the corner and pushed through the crowded tavern toward the Vampir. For the most part, they looked primate evolved, like a human or a Tuatha Dé Danaan, but Cerian knew better. Their abnormally well-developed musculature and the three indentations in their jutting chins gave them away.

As they crossed the floor, they unsheathed their short blades. They did it discreetly, as though they planned a quick, unobtrusive, and deadly attack. Cerian realized then that things *could* get worse.

Much worse.

"Sarthes," breathed Lympia.

"Sweet goddess," Cerian cursed. "How could they know?" She glanced nervously at Lympia. "Do you think they know? Maybe they're here by chance," she finished hopefully.

Lympia pursed her lips and frowned. "Whatever the reason, the Vampir is vulnerable in his condition."

Cerian watched as the Vampir whirled. His broadsword was strapped crosswise from shoulder to hip against his back. He drew it, as though sensing the danger approaching from behind. With the firelight from the tavern's hearth glinting off the blade's edge, he didn't look vulnerable. Then he tottered unsteadily to one side.

Cerian sighed and glanced at Lympia, who nodded. They flipped themselves over the edge of the windowsill and dropped down silently into the throng, drawing several half-interested looks from the jaded clientele.

The acrid smoke from the cook fire and the sweat and oily skin of the tavern's occupants caught and held in her nostrils and throat. Grimacing, Cerian ignored it and opened her mind, sensing the pulsing waves of thought energy around her. Weaving, prodding, and molding that energy, she made a way through for herself and Lympia. Short swords drawn, they stalked past the hulking bodies of the tribal aliens around them, prompting them to step aside.

When they reached the Vampir, he'd engaged the three Sarthes already. The tavern's inhabitants backed away, all except for the Ystani who stood in the shadows, likely waiting for her chance to take a bite of the Vampir.

Rhys ap Griffyn stood with both large hands wrapped around the grip of his broadsword. The three Sarthes circled him warily, their short swords in hand. They also had disruptors, Cerian was sure, even though they'd been outlawed on Gaman since the Thirty Year War had come to a tenuous end. They wouldn't work on the Vampir, though. His brain didn't follow the patterns the weapons were designed to fracture.

She had an outlawed disruptor of her own strapped to her waist, though she wouldn't use it unless it was very necessary. The last thing she needed was the Union to come down on her people for her misuse of weaponry.

Cerian frowned. Despite his totter to the side and his loud show earlier, the Vampir didn't look drunk. His dark brown gaze was steady and alert. The solid muscles of his body were tensed and ready for action. His gaze didn't waver. His steps didn't falter now.

Whether he was drunk or not, Cerian needed to put an end to this before it became a full-blown battle. The Vampir couldn't handle three Sarthian warriors and an affronted Ystani all by himself.

She stepped forward, catching the eye of the Sarthes, and held up a hand. "*Karslan y butif Scarlet ti Tuatha Dé Danaan gar les. Gar! Butif!*"

The Sarthes stilled for a moment, considering her. Then the blond Sarthe fired back an answer in his guttural language. They wouldn't hurt her, the intended consort of their leader, but the Vampir had to die before he completed what he'd been sent here to do.

Something inside Cerian withered. Ta'bat, leader of the Sarthes, knew what she intended. Somehow he knew, and wanted to stop it.

One of the Sarthes stepped toward the Vampir with a battle cry and all the fury of the Underworlds broke loose. Metal met metal. Blades soared through the air like dangerous birds.

Cerian and Lympia charged into the fray, forming a back-to-back circle with the Vampir. Rhys ap Griffyn quickly understood they were there to help him, though he growled at Cerian once, the low, hair-raising sound coming from between his shapely lips. His message was clear. He knew they were there to help, but didn't necessarily welcome it.

One of the Sarthes met Cerian's blade and the thrum of the contact echoed down her arm and into her shoulder.

The Sarthes were doomed from the beginning. After all, they couldn't hurt her. Ta'bat would likely subject them to a fate worse than death for that. They had to take her slashes and cuts, though it wasn't she, in the end, who felled them.

The Vampir fought like a man possessed. In a shower of ringing clashes of blade and brawn he hardly let either Lympia or herself get a poke in sideways. He cast a territorial glance in her direction as he made short work of the last one. Then he smiled triumphantly, standing over the three. Cerian watched his nostrils flare, probably at the scent of the fresh blood all around them.

Cerian rolled her eyes. "Not bad for a drunk."

"I wasn't drun—" He whirled to the side, his sword at the ready, as the Ystani warrior rose behind him, red teeth bared.

Cerian was faster. She grabbed a hurling pick from her pocket and threw it, catching the Ystani in the neck. The warrior looked stricken, grasped her throat, and fell with a loud thump to the floor of the tavern.

The tavern's inhabitants had retreated to the bar and the edges of the room. Not unfamiliar with such brawls, they simply looked on with average interest, though the three Sarthes and the Ystani lay bleeding on the floor by their feet.

"Come on," said Cerian. "Where there are three Sarthes, there are bound to be twenty. They want you dead, Rhys ap Griffyn." She shuddered. "And what the Sarthes want, they usually get. Let's move."

He ignored her and pulled his bloody shirt away from where it clung to his skin, swore low in some language she didn't understand and yanked it and his scabbard over his head.

Cerian tried not to look at his wide shoulders, hard chest and rippling abdominal muscles. Tried not to trace the thin line of dark hair that trailed down his stomach and below the line of his leather trews.

Lympia was right. He was a good-looking, star-cursed, drunken, outlander Vampir. His musculature was sculpted and strong—the body of a warrior. His hair was short and dark, and he had a face that would make any woman's heart beat faster.

She shook it off. Not hers, though. She had no time for such indulgences.

Lympia stood beside her. Her body was taut as a bowstring from the fight. "Let's get going," she echoed.

As if he had all the time in the world, he pushed a hand through his hair. The action showed the curves of perfect biceps. "Why do you think to order me? Who are you?" he asked.

Cerian's gaze snapped to his. She motioned the Ystani. "Looks like I'm your savior."

"You're the one I was supposed to meet. Cerian, leader of the lost faction of Tuatha Dé Danaan. The *Scarlet*." It was more statement than question.

She nodded curtly. "We're not lost. You found us, more or less." She gestured at her friend. "This is Lympia. She's a Zaenian, but an adopted member of the Danaan."

Lympia bowed slightly, her black, ringleted hair falling over one slim shoulder.

Cerian headed toward the door. "Can we please leave now?"

They exited the tavern. The rain still came down hard. Cerian led the way toward the rover. She threw an angry glance over her shoulder at Rhys. "Were you the only Vampir the Council of the Embraced would send? Do we rank so low on the scale that they'd send a lush—"

He moved so fast it astounded her. With his free hand, he grabbed her by the upper arm firmly, yet he did not hurt her at all. "I told you once already, I wasn't drunk. I've been followed since I landed, but I didn't know by whom. I bluffed, that's all, trying to get them to attack me while I was ready for them and they believed me vulnerable. Better then than while I slept at night." He flashed white teeth in a smile that was far more feral than friendly. "Understand? I was drawing them out."

The man looked like a predator, long, sleek and dark. Like a huge cat slipped out of midnight to ambush her. He didn't look anything like she thought he'd looked. Hadn't expected the man to make places low in her body go tight and sensitive with sexual awareness. Although, after she'd received word that the Council of the Embraced would send someone, she hadn't thought much at all. She'd simply been relieved she'd have a way to stave off the Sarthes.

She fought the urge to twist from his grip like a child. "Yes, fine. I understand."

He released her and walked to the rover. "Alcohol doesn't affect the Embraced, only large quantities of blood inebriate the Vampir."

"I didn't know that."

He flicked her a darkened glance. "Better start learning."

Unease flickered through her. She masked it and stepped into the beat-up silver rover with Rhys and Lympia behind her.

* * * * *

Rhys sat down in the right seat and watched Cerian sink into the left and push a series of buttons that lit when she touched them. The ancient, dented vehicle revved to life. Raindrops hit the huge windshield in a relentless rat-a-tat-tat. She flicked the wipers on.

She was beautiful, even more beautiful when that sour look was wiped clean of her face in the heat of battle. Thanks to some odd coupling in the line of her ancestors, she was a unique marked Tuatha Dé Danaan. Marked meant she was predestined to be Embraced—fated to become Vampir. Soon she would be a Vampir sidhe—the first of her kind.

He'd been sent to Embrace her.

The Embraced fell into two categories. The Vampir were those who were born at birth with a caul, *marking* them to one day be located by their *pere de sang* or *mere de sang* and be Embraced. Or they were unmarked humans who were Embraced and were strong enough to pass through the ordeal and attain fully Embraced status.

Those not strong enough to pass all the way through the transformation made up the second category—the Demi. The Demi fed from lust and sex, not blood.

He shifted his gaze to Cerian. She was smaller than he thought she'd be, small and curved in the nicest ways possible. Though it was clear enough the woman could fight. Leather cupped her shapely ass and tight, worn fabric stretched across her full breasts. The strap of the scabbard fastened across her back, like his, and was pulled between her breasts, offering him an exceptional view.

Her hair was a riot of different hues of brown, light as Ursi sugar, dark as deep turned earth and every shade in between. It fell past her waist in a series of tiny braids. He'd noticed earlier how the secured ends brushed her ass when she moved.

She flicked a glance at him and jutted her jaw slightly as she guided the vehicle into the forest. "What are looking at?"

He smiled slowly. "You."

She gave him a sidelong look and flushed. He knew he wasn't the only one feeling the flare of sexual awareness between them.

Cerian stiffened visibly. "Well, stop it. Look at Lympia," she snapped.

He turned his head and watched the Zaenian woman. She dropped her exotically colored lashes and then looked up with heat in her beautiful light eyes. It was a blatant invitation. Her chocolate-colored skin gleamed soft and supple in the dim light within the rover. He watched the rise and fall of her full breasts.

She was a rare breed, too, on this war-ravaged planet. Gaman was a dumping ground for various races across the universe. They all vied for a piece of this place and fought tooth and nail to get it. Only strict laws, backed up by the threat of unforgiving violence by the Union of Gaman, maintained any peace at all. The Union, the governing body set up by the strongest of the tribes in order to end the Thirty Year War, ruled with an iron fist and showed no mercy to those who flouted their decrees.

"I haven't seen a Zaenian in a long time, Lympia." commented Rhys.

Her pale blue eyes clouded like a storm on a summer's day and filled with as much volatility. "I am one of the last of my kind," she answered. "The Thirty Year War decimated us."

"What tribe waged war on you?"

Lympia focused her gaze past the windshield of the rover and into the darkness-swathed forest. "All of them." Her gaze flicked back to his. "But I have a special interest in seeing the Sarthes fail in their conquest of the Danaan."

Still in sitting position, he bowed from his waist in deference to her and her people. "That is why I am here," he answered.

He turned back to Cerian. "Why does Ta'bat want you so badly?"

Cerian glanced at him. "Crystals, very rare ones. My people mine them under the mountains where we live. We've had several tribes try and take them from us, but the Union has ruled that none can do it by force. However, the Sarthian ruler, Ta'bat, can take me as his consort. That's the only way they'll ever get their hands on what we mine."

"Why didn't those Sarthes just try and take you back there? Why doesn't Ta'bat press you into it?"

She shook her head and her braids made a susurrus of sound as they brushed. "Can't. The Union won't let them force me physically, but they will let them cut off our food supply to compel my hand." She turned to him with desperation in her eyes. "My people are starving, Rhys."

It was the first time she'd said his name in a nonformal way and it took him aback for a moment. "Why is my Embracing you going to save your people?"

She smiled. "You *must* know the answer to that. The Sarthes hate the Embraced. Ta'bat's people will never allow their leader take one as consort. There'd be a bloody civil war. If I'm Embraced he'll be forced to leave us alone, at least until he figures something else out. It will depend on how badly he wants our crystal, in the end."

The lights flickered on and off in the rover as they crashed through the forest. The whole vehicle sounded as if it would fall apart at any moment, creaking and banging and shivering beneath them. Although he didn't need the bright headlights of the rover to see them, the high beams revealed many large, felled trees. Their upturned roots rotted in a tangle against the riven ground of the old forest. Victims of the long and bloody Thirty Year War, he surmised.

They cleared the trees and Rhys saw a mountain in their path. They seemed to be on a direct collision course with it.

"*Caerli vey ia se,*" Cerian muttered beside him.

A boulder on the road in front of the rover rolled away and the vehicle entered a cave. She mumbled more foreign words and the boulder slid back in place behind them.

They bumped and jounced down and down into what felt like the heart of Gaman itself, and finally entered a huge room with rough-hewn stone walls and a high ceiling. Beautiful crystal dripped from all sides of the cavern. The floor was made of a smooth, opaque crystal. There had been splendor here once, Rhys could tell. It was obvious in the worn wooden tables and chairs scattered through the main residence of the Tuatha Dé Danaan that the wars had taken their toll. Danaan, all dressed in thread-worn clothing, milled the large cavern-room.

They climbed out of the rover and Cerian turned sad eyes on him. "This place used to be teeming with laughter and music." Her gaze hardened. "I'd have it that way again. On our own terms. Not by the leave of the Sarthes."

For just a fleeting moment, Rhys loved her. Loved that hard resolve in her eyes and the passion she had for her people. This was a good leader. She had his respect.

He watched her take her pack from the rover's baggage hold and walk away.

And by the all gods above and beyond, how he wanted her. Images of her fine body moving over his like silk, her skin sheened with the perspiration of their coupling, flooded his mind. How would her cries sound as he thrust into her, holding her wrists captive over her head? Would her hair spread in an earthy riot of color across the pillow?

He stifled a groan. He wanted her long, strong legs wrapped around his waist as he shafted her toward climax. His body thrummed with the awareness of her, attuned to her every breath and movement.

* * * * *

"Go ahead, find yourself quarters. We've got enough vacant ones since two-thirds of our people are dead.

Choose one." Cerian slung her pack over her shoulder and headed toward her own room. "Guess you won't need a ration of herbed flat bread and gruel, will you?"

"No," Rhys answered. "A willing donor is all I need."

"I'll let you feed from me, and you can share my quarters anytime." Cerian heard Lympia purr.

She chuckled at her friend's boldness. "Go ahead," called Cerian over her shoulder as she walked away. "Share Lympia's quarters." The sex-starved Danaan females would be all over the Vampir. Funny how that thought made her stomach clench just the slightest bit.

He was at her side the moment she stepped into the shadowed corridor leading to her room. He pressed her up against the wall, his hooded gaze roving almost territorially over her body. A sexual growl trickled from between his lips. "I'd rather share yours, Cerian."

Her name on his lips was like a seductive spell that wove itself around her breasts and her sex. She took a careful breath. This was a dangerous man. Very dangerous indeed.

Cerian had been alone for too long, had wanted and needed a consort for too many years. She didn't have the ability to sleep with this man and not hope for...*more*. At one time, she could've done it without a backward glance, but not now.

That left him with the capability to ravage her body with pleasures and her heart with an elusive, illusory promise of companionship, support...things she wanted so very badly. Then he would leave her with nothing but an increase of the bitterness in her heart after the centuries of the war her people had already endured.

She wanted him badly, but the cost was too high. She needed to stay strong, her emotions unfettered. There would be no way she could take this man to her bed and maintain the cold aloofness she needed to survive and be a leader to her people.

She swallowed hard, masking as best she could the hammering of her heart, the heaviness of her breasts and the slickness coating her sex at the thought of him strong and lean between the sheets of her bed.

"Get off me, Rhys," she commanded evenly. "Your attentions are unwanted."

He slid a finger over the plump of her breast, up to trace her collarbone and let it come to a rest on her chin. He tipped her face to his. When he spoke, she could see the sharp points of his fangs flashing within his mouth. "Oh, I disagree, though you're a good liar."

There was an accent to his words, spoken in a thick, aroused voice. Welsh, she supposed. She knew enough about the Vampir to know he was old...very old. The Council had sent a little information on him before he'd arrived. He'd been Embraced in Wales sometime around 1100 A.D. Earth reckoning. Cerian was centuries old, but the Vampir was far older. Cerian wondered if he'd always exuded this confident sexuality, or if he'd honed it over all that time.

"I will have you, *cariad*." His voice was like velvet against her skin. "Once I've decided to seduce, *I seduce*." The dark threat hung in the air between them, pregnant with erotic possibility.

And arrogant presumption.

It was that last that really annoyed her. She brought her knee up and he twisted out of her way at the last possible moment.

She drew a shaky breath and turned on her heel. "If you'll excuse me, I have a date with a hot shower." She threw a pointed look at him. "*Alone.*"

Cerian walked down the corridor to her room. The glow of three lanterns lighted the large chamber. One of the women must've flamed them in anticipation of her arrival. The crystals they mined emitted a natural radiance, which was why they were so coveted. In the bedchambers constant light was not a desirable thing, so regular oil lanterns scattered the rooms.

Flame threw flickering light over the rough-hewn walls and rug-covered floor. It was a simple chamber, furnished with a large bed, a table, some chairs and a wardrobe. A door off to the left of the room in the back led to her private bathroom. That's where she was headed. She couldn't wait to wash the Sarthian blood from her skin.

She threw her pack down on her bed, stripped her rain and blood-soaked clothes off, and headed into the bathroom. She stepped into the shower, turning the knob that let the water from the hot spring deep in the mountain travel down the conduit and pour out of the showerhead. They might be lacking in food, but not water. The mountain was filled with it, both in cool, secret lakes and hot springs.

The warm water sluiced down her body, drawing all the tension out of her muscles. She braced a hand against the rough rock and rotated her head and shoulders under the massaging stream, groaning. The only thing that could make this shower feel any better would be… She broke the thought off. It had been way too long if she was thinking about the Vampir.

But it *had* been a long time.

Once there had been Tuatha Dé Danaan males, but the Thirty Year War had taken all but very old and the very young, plus a goodly portion of their females. The last time Cerian had known a man's hard body moving against her had been nearly five years ago. Could she be faulted for imagining Rhys in the shower with her now? She was a young, healthy woman, not made of stone.

Shivering, she gave in to the fantasy. The heat from his muscular chest would bleed through the skin at her back to her very heart as he pressed her up against the shower's wall. The firm planes of his stomach and the hard pressure of his thighs would brace her as he spread her legs and drew a strong, sure hand up her inner thigh to hold his palm against her aroused sex.

She cupped her breasts at the thought, running her thumbs back and forth over the sensitized tips. Then she slipped a hand down to her clit and rubbed it until it plumped full and responsive before she sank a finger within her pussy.

She'd part her legs for him and he'd slide his long, thick cock into her, stretching her muscles exquisitely. Then he'd thrust...and thrust and thrust. Giving her no quarter, no time to draw a breath, no time to even *think*. His dark hair would brush her shoulder as he kissed along her throat, nipping as he went. He'd fist his hand in her hair as he drove into her from behind, drawing her head to the side so he could bite the place where her shoulder and neck met.

The combination of his cock plundering her sex and his mouth drawing on her throat would push her straight into a mind-bending climax. She'd cry out and claw at the walls as the muscles of her pussy contracted around his pistoning shaft. He wouldn't stop until she'd been well and thoroughly fucked.

Cerian plunged her fingers in and out of her pussy, and shuddered as her climax hit her. Waves of sensation washed over her, and the muscles of her vagina convulsed around her fingers. She leaned back against the wall and caught her breath.

Dear Goddess Danu, she was in trouble.

Chapter Two

The next morning, Rhys sat at a long table and considered the people around him.

About four thousand years ago, a part of the Tuatha Dé Danaan left Earth and traveled out here to this fractious planet. They'd been the ones who hadn't wanted to conceal their natures when the Milesians had come to Ireland and defeated their people. The Milesians had demanded the conquered Danaan either go into hiding or leave.

These people were their descendants, and were far different from the Danaan who'd remained on Earth. The Earth-dwelling sidhe were a gentle yet commanding race. They loved music and dancing. Their psychic abilities were extraordinary and they could do powerful magic, beautiful spells that could take your breath away.

These Tuatha Dé Danaan were tired, beaten by this cruel planet. It was almost as if war had ground their magic with its boot heel.

Or maybe they were simply hungry.

Rhys watched as a server placed a heel of flat bread and a few spoonfuls of thin gruel on each passing Danaan's plate.

Lympia had explained that they were not a farming people, instead choosing to barter for their food stores. Ta'bat had intimidated all those they traded with, cutting off the ability of the Danaan to trade their crystal for food, until Cerian conceded to him.

Rhys fisted a hand. He really hoped he'd meet Ta'bat one day.

Of course, after Lympia had explained in full the plight of these Tuatha Dé Danaan, she'd invited him into her bed. He'd declined without slighting her. Lympia was beautiful and would make any man more than happy for the offer—with the exception of himself. His sights were set elsewhere. He looked toward the corridor where he knew Cerian's room was located.

After a time, she came from the opposite direction, covered in a thin layer of glimmering white crystal dust.

She strode toward him, her gaze sweeping over the rations line. Her beautiful face was set in grim lines.

"Is everything all right?" Rhys asked.

She glanced at him. "No, not really. We found the person who leaked the information about your arrival to the Sarthes. We had to chase her into the crystal mines to finally capture her."

He stood. "Why didn't you call me to help?"

She flashed him a look of irritation. "You're here to Embrace me, not play guardian of the domain."

"What will you do with her?"

Cerian shrugged a slim shoulder. "I don't know yet. I've ordered her locked in her room. She can't be allowed to help the Sarthes any more than she already has, but—" She pursed her lips together and looked away.

Rhys didn't press her. Something more was wrong than the obvious. "You need to eat," he said, motioning at the line. "I will Embrace you tonight. You need to be strong for that."

She shook her head and walked toward the corridor. "I'm fine. I'll be fine."

Gods, the woman was infuriating. He watched her stride into the shadowed corridor and then went after her so he could berate her in private.

When he finally reached her, he took her by her upper arm and spun her around to face him. "You need to take the Embrace seriously, Cerian. I know you want the food to go to your people, but at the same time, there are risks to even a marked person during the transition to Vampir. You must be strong enough to endure the process."

Her green eyes flashed with sudden anger. Better that than sorrow. "I *will* eat, Rhys. I just don't want to right now."

He released her.

"Sometimes..." She dropped her head and her dark brown lashes fanned out over her skin. Crystal dust glimmered on them and on the smooth curve of her cheek. He wanted to brush it away.

"Sometimes what?"

She swallowed and looked back up at him. The naked vulnerability in her eyes socked him low in the gut. "Sometimes I think I should just give in to Ta'bat. My people would have food and protection—"

"At what cost, Cerian? They'd rape you of your crystal and take freedom from your people."

She smiled sadly and shook her head. Her braids moved around her body with the motion and brushed his arm. "How long do you think we can hold out, Rhys? Most of my people are dead from the wars, nearly all the men."

Anguish tightened her voice. "We're weak and highly susceptible to the domination of another Gaman tribe. It will happen eventually. The Sarthes are hardly the worst. We could bear them—"

He wound a finger around one of her braids and pulled her forward gently. He tasted her lips and she stiffened. He closed his eyes and savored her, rubbing his lips over hers slowly. "No more talk of giving in to the Sarthes," he murmured.

She lifted her gaze to his. Unmistakable sexual heat flared there. Finding that look of desire mirroring his own lust for her tensed his muscles and hardened his cock. What he wouldn't give to have her sweet flesh envelop him.

* * * * *

Cerian warred with herself as Rhys lowered his mouth to hers once more, stealing all her words and her breath along with them. She knew this wasn't a good idea, but a part of her wished for the release she knew he'd bring her and, perhaps more importantly, the blessed reprieve from all rational thought that a long, hard fuck could provide.

His lips slid over hers like silk, then the tip of his tongue feathered over them, entreating her to open to him. Pure desire shot down her spine straight to her sex. She parted her lips and he explored her mouth with his tongue. It was not a taking, but a sweet, hot savoring.

He withdrew and moved his lips over her cheek, flicking out from time to time with the tip of his tongue, until he'd trailed down her chin and throat. "You taste like crystal," he murmured. He brushed his lips across the bare skin between her collarbone and shoulder. The hard sweep of his fangs followed.

She stiffened. "Don't."

She'd heard the bite of a fully Embraced Vampir was an exquisite bliss. Even the half-Vampir, the Demi, were said to bestow sexual ecstasy on their victims. If he bit her, she would part her thighs willingly for him right this very minute. Sweet Danu, she might part them for him anyway.

He froze and lifted his head. His eyes glowed with a predatory light and his fangs were extended. "You know, I'm going to have to bite you tonight. I'm also going to have to touch you. In fact, you'll *want* me to touch you…intimately."

"What?"

He smiled. "You don't understand what will happen, do you? Granted, I can't say for sure what it will be like. I've never Embraced a sidhe. *No one* has ever Embraced a sidhe. You're the first marked of your kind. An aberration. But I can tell you that with a human, it's very sexual."

"Sexual?"

"Oh, yes. Males usually Embrace females and vice versa, unless another arrangement is preferred, simply because most of the time the two end up," he leaned in so close she could smell his intoxicating breath, "fucking." He gave her a sly smile and a hooded gaze.

She blinked. An Embraced's breath was always heady. Their bodies did something with the blood they consumed, turned it into pure life force. She'd heard their breath was a lure, predator to prey. Making it easier for an Embraced to lull and take blood from a donor. As a sidhe, that part didn't work on her.

Her desire was all natural.

She took a step back and he took a step forward, closing the distance between them again. Cerian tried to twist away, but her muscles just wouldn't cooperate. Her resolve slipped yet another notch.

He held his hand so that it hovered over her heart, yet did not touch her. She felt his power, his heat, bleeding through her clothing and into her skin, as though he actually caressed her.

Her eyelids fluttered closed briefly. "What are you doing?" Her voice sounded so heavy, so aroused to her own ears.

"Shhh… Let me, Cerian. For once, don't fight."

He ran his hand over her breast, still an inch away. She felt his touch on her, as though he cupped the weight of her breast in his hand, rubbing back and forth over the aroused tip. Every inch of sensual awareness she possessed flared to glorious life.

She sucked in a breath. What would it be like if he really touched her? Skin to skin, breath mingling with breath…sex interconnecting with sex.

"Do you want that?" he murmured close to her ear. "I do, Cerian. Very much."

Danu! She'd been so relaxed, she'd slipped and broadcast that last thought.

A flush crept up her cheeks as her heart rate sped up and her nipples hardened. She shut her mind to him and didn't answer.

He brought his hand down over her abdomen to her sex.

He wove a seductive spell around her without so much as touching her. She felt his warm fingers on her slick folds, delving into her pussy and brushing her clit. Goddess, she *did* want his hands on her. His real hands, skin to skin.

She moaned. How much was she expected to take? Her resolve crumbled completely.

"Please," she whispered.

"What, Cerian?" His voice came harsh now, an aroused accented roll off his tongue. "Tell me what you want."

Images of the fantasy she'd had of him the night before in the shower rolled over her. She didn't block them, rather sending them full-force to Rhys. *He pressed her face-first against the wall of the shower, his hands playing over her breasts, caressing and plumping as he pressed the head of his cock into her pussy and drove into her from behind. He braced his hands on her hips and shafted her slow at first, then faster and harder until she clawed at the wall in front of her. He licked the skin of her throat and then bit as the first throes of her climax gripped her…*

He growled, low, deep and dangerously.

"Please touch me," she said, barely loud enough to hear.

She didn't have to ask twice. He took her by the small of her back and pressed her to him. His mouth came down on hers as his hand made its way down the waistband of her trews and into her underwear to cup her aching sex. His finger roved hungrily over her flesh. Finally, he slid two fingers into her pussy and seated his palm over her clit.

At the same time, he kissed her. Hard. Deep. A taking, this time. One she welcomed.

Cerian nearly lost her balance. Goddess...the man could kiss. He parted her lips and tangled his tongue with hers as though starving. His hand moved on her pussy, his fingers thrusting as he worked magic over her.

He ripped his mouth away and groaned. She felt his hard cock pressing into her. "Cerian," he murmured so close to her lips that the words brushed her. "You feel like heaven."

Her climax burst over her in a near drowning wave. He covered her mouth with his, consuming all the sound she made.

"Oh. Oh, sweet Danu," she cursed softly. Her breath came heavy and a flush had settled in her cheeks. She was lost to him now. Lost to his mouth and hands. She would have him in her bed, in her shower, and every inch of floor in between.

He pulled her against him and kissed the top of her head in a gesture that was so full of caring—so wonderfully *domestic*—that she nearly wept. Maybe she could afford herself the illusion. Just for a little while. Just for a few short hours.

"Come to my chamber," she murmured.

His response was cut off by the sound of screaming from the main cavern. The shouts were mixed with masculine commands fired off in Sarthian.

"Cerian!" Ta'bat's roar echoed through the caves and into the corridor they stood in. "Give me the Vampir!"

Cerian froze, her mind stuttering over the fact that Ta'bat was actually *in* her mountain. Then she grabbed Rhys' hand and pulled him down the corridor with a hard yank. She'd never dreamed the Sarthes could infiltrate their caves. They'd gotten through all their magical safeguards. How?

More traitors, perhaps. More Danaan like the one they'd found this morning who believed she should give in to Ta'bat.

"Wait." Rhys stopped.

She whirled and faced him, her eyes wild. "We have to hurry. The Sarthian warriors will be all over these corridors very soon. No time to chat."

"They're out there with the Danaan."

She shook her head. "They can't do any direct physical violence to them by order of the Union. They won't harm a hair on their heads. They want *you*, Rhys. And while you may be able to fight three of them at once, you won't be able to fight five hundred. Plus," she looked pointedly at his scabbard-less side, "you don't have a weapon. And there are no Union laws against direct physical violence against you, an outlander."

"I need to Embrace you *now*, Cerian."

She paused. Yes. It was the only way. They needed to go forward with that which Ta'bat meant to prevent. "Come with me."

They ran down the corridor and she led him through a series of fissures in the rock-face. If Ta'bat thought he had her, he was badly mistaken. Renewed determination flowed through her. This mountain was *hers*, and she knew it like she knew her own body. Ta'bat would take neither as his own.

She led him through the mine passageways. Sometimes they were so narrow she feared Rhys' height and breadth wouldn't allow him to pass. Sometimes they were so wide they had to dodge boulders in their path. All around them, the crystal embedded in the walls glimmered, giving light.

The room she sought opened up before them. In the bottom of the mines, this mountain chamber would take Ta'bat and his men a long time to find. If they were lucky, Rhys could Embrace her and then flee. He could evade the Sarthes and get out of the mountain undetected.

"This is where you want me to Embrace you, Cerian?" he asked behind her.

She turned. "Yes. Is it all right?"

His gaze roved the chamber. "Perfect."

She looked around. She supposed it was very beautiful to a person who didn't see the crystals every day. In light green, pink, silver and red, the translucent, faceted crystals dripped from the ceilings and jutted from the walls, emitting a low incandescent shimmering. A small pool of water, warmed by nearby underground hot springs, stood to their left. The area was mostly cleared of rock and boulder. A thick Gaman cave moss grew on the ground here.

"We'll be safe here. For a while, anyway," she said.

He dropped his gaze to hers and held it. The look he gave her was so full of heat that it quickened her pussy, flooding it with moisture. His dark eyes were filled with everything he planned to do her. He let a low, territorial and sexual growl slide past his lips as he walked toward her. Every nerve ending in her body jumped to life.

Suddenly, it didn't matter that Ta'bat was searching the mountain. It didn't matter that she had traitors within the Danaan. All that mattered was what lay between herself and Rhys. It was time to see it through.

"Are you ready for me?" he murmured darkly as he strode toward her.

Chapter Three

She held up a hand to stay him. "Explain what's going to happen to me, Rhys. I know some, but not all."

"First, I'm going to trigger your mark, Cerian. That's when things will start to get strange, if you react anything like a human. Then I'm going to drink your blood, let it mix with mine. When you drink my blood, it will be a biochemical cocktail straight from my veins to yours. That cocktail is going to cause internal changes. DNA-level changes."

"But we don't know what will happen because my DNA is already so different from a human's." She recognized the note of unease that had entered her tone.

She'd known since she'd been small that she was marked, but she'd never planned to be Embraced. Now being Embraced was the only way to stave off Ta'bat. It was something she simply *had* to do. A transformation she had no choice but to undergo. But she'd never truly considered the process, since she'd never thought that part of her would ever see the light of day.

He smoothed a tendril of hair behind her ear. "Don't worry. You're meant to be Embraced. All will be well. Do you trust me?"

She shrugged. "You've given me no cause to distrust you."

"You're about to become what you were born to be."

He put his hands on her shoulders and looked into her eyes. White light seemed to flash through the depths of his gaze and mirror in her own mind's eye—a spark within him that awakened a spark within her. For a moment the brilliance blinded her. Then knowledge of a breadth she hadn't known in her centuries of living flowed into her. She gasped, turning away from Rhys as the onslaught began.

Cerian dropped to her knees and closed her eyes, trying to control the mental assault and failing. The sensation was overwhelming, beautiful and terrifying all at once. Information flooded her mind. What the Vampir were, why they existed, the entire history of the Embraced bombarded her.

The Vampir had evolved from humans during the same time humans had evolved from primates. A desperate need for a defense against an ancient race calling themselves the Dominion had triggered their development. It was a lot of knowledge to have about a race that existed light-years from Gaman on a backwater planet like Earth.

After several shocking moments, the hurricane in her brain slowed and came to a stop. Cerian opened her eyes to a new world. Everything looked sharp and perfect. She sucked in a breath. The sidhe already had exceptional vision, but this surpassed unbelievable. If she concentrated, she could see every single facet in every single crystal glimmering above them. She could hear Rhys breathing behind her, every rise and fall of his chest. She could feel every tiny thread of soft moss pressing into her knees where she knelt on it.

She stood and turned to him. "Rhys," she whispered with wide eyes. "Finish it."

He walked to her and smoothed his hand over her cheek, then further down to trail over her jaw, neck and shoulder. He drew his fingers sensually over her collarbone and breast, all the way down to press the small of her back, leaving a trail of fire where he touched. He pulled her to him as though to kiss her.

He brushed his lips lightly across hers but didn't linger. Instead, he traced them over her jawbone and her cheek. He put his other hand to her nape, and massaged the muscles there for a moment before twining his fingers through her hair. Slowly, gently, he tilted her head back, exposing the line of her throat. All the while, he nuzzled her, making small noises of reassurance. His tongue flicked out and tasted her earlobe. Then he laid a line of kisses down her neck.

Cerian's heart rate and breathing picked up. Her body began to tighten and prime itself for him. He nipped at the skin where her shoulder and throat met and she felt her pussy drench.

She whimpered. "This is torture. Please, bite me."

His tongue licked at her pulse, and a tremor ran up her spine. She twined her arms around him to support her suddenly shaky legs. Sharp fangs brushed her skin once, twice, and then bit. She stiffened and gasped at the sweet jagged pain. Then warm pleasure spread out, enveloping her.

Liquid desire filled her from the toes up. Her nipples tightened and she shivered every time he moved and brushed his hard chest against them. The suction at her throat increased and the pleasure became almost unbearable. It seemed to tighten some unseen line straight from his mouth to her pussy, making her sex swell for him, ready for his attentions.

Her knees faltered and she would've collapsed if his arms hadn't supported her. He lowered her easily to the moss-covered ground, still with his mouth at her throat.

Her fingers tightened on his shirt until she was sure her knuckles were white. Her thighs parted for him almost of their own volition, and he slid snugly between them. His cock was hard and pressed into her sensitized flesh. Under her breath, she cursed the clothing that separated them.

They stayed twined that way for several long moments. Cerian reveled in the long, hard pulls he took from her throat.

Finally Rhys released her, licking over the small wound he'd made, and raised his head. His eyes were dark now, filled with lust. His penetrating gaze held hers as he brought his own wrist to his mouth and bit. Dark blood welled from the wound he'd made. He lowered it to her mouth. "Drink," he murmured.

She hesitated, then flicked her tongue out and tasted what welled from the gash on his wrist. The essence of his life force coated her tongue. It tasted nothing like she'd expected. Its flavor was that of an aged wine, though somewhat different—spicier and sweeter all at the same time. It was the intermingled flavor of the life force of every person he'd fed from in his very long life.

Cerian licked his skin and closed her eyes. It was nearly irresistible. She latched her hands around his wrist, followed by her mouth, licking and sucking.

Rhys groaned low in his throat. She felt his body stiffen and his cock twitch against her. She toed off her boots. *Want* fell short of the scope her desire right now. She *needed* him inside her.

She almost broadcast her thoughts at him, but he understood. Still keeping his wrist at her mouth, a tricky thing, he shifted to the side, reached between them and undid the buttons of her trews. Every whisper of fabric through buttonhole was like a promise. He pulled them down until she could kick them the rest of the way off. Braced on his side, he worked on his own clothing, nudging his own trews down low enough to free his cock.

Finally they were both bared from the waist down. He set his cock to her pussy, teasing her clit with the head and making her whimper around his wrist, before working it inch by glorious inch within her. Now connected by vein and sex, he began to thrust into her slowly.

Danu, he filled her so completely, stretched her muscles so perfectly. She let go of his wrist and arched her back. "Yes. Oh, sweet goddess, yes," she breathed.

The Embrace had made her body exceptionally sensitive. She felt more alive than she ever had before. She knew somehow that this was only the beginning stage of the change she would undergo.

He shifted to cover her body with his, bracing one hand on the ground beside her head. The other, he trailed slowly from her cheek, over her upthrust breast, around to cup one buttock. First he drove into her slow and easy, then faster. Cerian gripped his shoulders, feeling the bunch of his muscles beneath her fingers.

He pulled her shirt up, his mouth latching onto one taut, aroused nipple. He alternated between nipping and pulling and taking it deep into the warm recesses of his mouth. He twisted his hips so the head of his cock rubbed the pleasure point deep within her. Relentlessly he stimulated it, until she was panting and scraping at his shoulders and back with her nails.

Her climax shattered through her, bursting over her body like none she'd ever had in the past. She stifled a scream as her vaginal muscles contracted around his cock. He lifted up and pressed two fingers to her clit, rotating and manipulating in just the right way. On the heels of her first orgasm, a second one rocketed through her. It bowed her spine and made her call Rhys' name.

He answered with his own climax. She felt his cock jump within her and his body shudder. He buried his face in her hair and groaned. They stilled, both panting.

Rhys shifted to the side and held her against him. She snuggled into the warm, protective curve of his body. She knew the second phase of her transition to Vampir had begun. She could feel it within her bloodstream. She felt hot and cold at the same time and, worse, she was beginning to feel weak.

She fought to keep her eyes open. She couldn't afford vulnerability right now. Retaining consciousness was paramount.

"Don't struggle. You'll black out soon. There's no way to prevent it," Rhys murmured, smoothing her braids away from her perspiration-dampened forehead.

She swallowed against a suddenly dry throat. "No. I can't—"

"Don't fight it, *cariad*. It's a part of the process. Better you're unconscious for the next part of the change."

Her eyelids drooped and her vision dimmed. It was too strong. The darkness beckoned too seductively for her to resist. "You've got to get out here, Rhys," she whispered. "Get out before they find you. I'm sorry I can't help."

The darkness swallowed her whole.

*****

Rhys laid a lingering kiss on Cerian's lips before standing. To ward off the dampness of the cavern chamber, he dressed her, and then stood looking down at her. Her face, for the first time since he'd met her, was peaceful. Her chest rose and fell with the depth of her slumber. Before she'd lost consciousness, he'd given her small mental compulsion for good, healing dreams. She needed them. Shadows graced the woman's eyes at all times. He found himself curiously and inexplicably driven to chase them away.

Permanently.

Rhys had spent centuries roaming Earth and centuries more roaming the universe on behalf of the Council. Sent back and forth at their whim on official missions was his life, his career.

He was bone weary of it.

In his long life he'd met a lot of people—a lot of women. None of them had as much grace, dignity and quiet strength as the woman lying on the ground before him. He felt the urge to protect her. She'd probably want to slap that urge right out him, but he had it all the same.

He gave his head a sharp shake. There was no way he was going anywhere. Not when Cerian was so vulnerable. When she awakened from the Embrace, she'd likely be weak. Who knew what Ta'bat would do when he discovered she, and the crystal, were now off-limits to him? Maybe he'd be so enraged he'd forget all about the Union's rules. She wouldn't be prepared to fight him, then, as a fledging Vampir.

Rhys didn't bother dressing. Instead, he shifted to his animal form. On large, silent paws, he traveled back through the fissures in the rock, back toward Ta'bat and his men.

In the concrete empires of late twenty-second century Earth, the animal form of cougar was not very practical. They just didn't blend in very well. Especially since people tended to scream and run in fear when they saw one. But here, in these caves, *this* was cougar heaven. He could maneuver here far better in his animal form.

Rhys made his way silently into the main part of the caverns and then sought high ground. He leaped onto a high, jutting crystal and traveled that way, silently traversing from one crystal to the next.

Below him, Ta'bat's men searched chamber by chamber. Besides the occasional look of hatred or fear, the Danaan seemed unharmed. The Sarthes had commanded them to their rooms, it appeared, with only a few chosen as gophers for the Sarthian warriors. Rhys watched a Sarthe slap a pretty Danaan on the ass as she passed by with a water pail. She took the abuse calmly, only turning to spear the man with a look of withering scorn.

Rhys continued on through the myriad and many corridors of the mountain, searching for his one objective—Ta'bat. Take the leader and you demoralized the warriors. You created chaos in the ranks. He could only hope there was no strong second-in-command. With a little luck, there'd be a scramble for power if Ta'bat were killed.

Finally Rhys heard harsh commands barked in Sarthian. The voice was the same he'd heard call to Cerian earlier. He followed the sounds into a huge chamber he'd never seen before. The man Rhys assumed was Ta'bat stood in the center along with three warriors. He was a middle-aged man, the Sarthian leader, with black hair and a muscular build.

Rhys studied the chamber. Great gods, it was a ballroom, he realized. The floor was of smooth rose marble veined by silver crystal; tapestries depicting the history of the Tuatha Dé Danaan hung from the shimmering walls. This was a place where the Danaan had once danced and celebrated. By the looks of it, it hadn't been used in a very long time.

Ta'bat finished delivering his orders to three warriors in front of him. One of them fired an angry retort back at their leader. Ta'bat barked back, louder and angrier.

Dissension in the ranks?

The warriors turned and left the chamber. Rhys eyed their swords as they walked under the elegantly arched doorway. He needed a weapon badly if he wanted to take Ta'bat. The only one around seemed to be in Ta'bat's scabbard.

Not ideal.

However, if he wanted to approach Ta'bat while he was alone, this was an opportunity Rhys knew he couldn't pass up. At least the element of surprise was on his side.

Ta'bat turned and paced the room, the heels of his boots clicking on the floor. Rhys leapt down a few crystals, then waited for him to turn and pace back his way.

Ta'bat saw him and went very still, his black eyes going wide. Rhys supposed they didn't have cougars on Gaman.

Rhys growled low, then pounced.

Chapter Four

Cerian roused, becoming aware of the absolute soundlessness. The intensity and breadth of the silence was near deafening. The depths of Gaman were like that, a silence so heavy it could crush you if you listened too long.

She pushed herself up and blinked several times, her vision clearing. Glancing around the chamber, she saw that Rhys was gone. Wistful happiness filled her. Hopefully he'd get out alive. She forced the wistfulness back. After all, she'd known he wasn't hers to keep.

She struggled to her feet, testing out her new body. Her head hurt and she felt weak…but…. "Oh," she breathed, her eyes widening. "Oh, dear goddess Danu."

Her magic before had been only a spark compared to what she felt now. She flexed her metaphysical muscles and felt the swell and contraction of the very air surrounding her.

She held her palm out and created a spark in the center of it. Patiently, she coaxed the spark brighter and bigger until it was heatless fireball in her hand. She bounced it up and down, and laughed. She'd been working to accomplish that illusion for the last fifty years.

So an Embraced sidhe meant enhanced magic.

Cerian let the ball float in the air before her, guiding her way. It was time to find Ta'bat and show him her new fangs.

She traveled back into the main cavern, extinguishing her fireball before breaching the opening of the last fissure. The place was swarming with Sarthes. Calmly she looked on until they recognized her.

A warrior stalked over to her and grabbed her roughly. He narrowed his eyes, turned his head to the side and spat. "You vibrate like a vampir," he growled.

She smiled sweetly. "You're too late, I guess."

He dragged her forward. "Ta'bat will still want to see you. Maybe you'll meet with an unfortunate accident, one to which the Union can't take exception." He laughed. "You have a successor, I'm sure." He jerked her hard. "Maybe she won't be so difficult."

Rage flowed through Cerian. She started to conjure up an illusion of incredible strength for herself and then stopped. She needed to keep her secrets.

The warrior led her to the ballroom. Then stilled and released her.

Cerian followed his gaze. A huge cougar crouched over Ta'bat, his very large mouth around the Sarthian leader's throat.

The only way she knew it was a cougar was because of the Records of the Ancients. The Danaan had catalogued many things about the planet they'd traveled from. To the Sarthe, the animal probably looked like a monster.

To her, it looked like Rhys.

The warrior drew his sword and stalked toward the cougar. Cerian drew her strength illusion. Mischiefing the warrior's mind to believe her invincibly strong was beyond simple. She took a running leap at him, tackling him and wrenching the sword from his hand.

Goddess, it was heavy, made for a muscular Sarthe. She hefted it and brandished it as high as she could. "Stay back," she warned. "Don't move. Don't yell. If you do, the beast will take his throat."

The warrior smiled slowly, then yelled at the top of his lungs.

A heartbeat and a half later had warriors pouring into the chamber, surrounding them.

Cerian knew she had to act quickly. Concentrating inward with all her will, she reached inside herself and touched the place where her magic lay coiled like a powerful snake. She found the waves of matter binding the ballroom. Locating the right waves to pluck and manipulate, she cast an elaborate illusion at the Sarthes. A blinding light filled the room and a piercing screech that deafened only the warriors followed it.

Metal clattered on marble as all the warriors clapped their hands over their ears and collapsed to their knees, dropping their blades beside them. The light and sound faded and the warriors stared at her in awe.

Lympia appeared in the doorway, her eyes wide.

Cerian held her friend's gaze for a long moment, though all she wanted was to close her eyes. The expenditure of magic had cost her and she was still weak from the Embrace. She felt drained enough to collapse. Instead, she let the Sarthian sword clatter to the floor, drew a deep breath, and kindled the spark in her palm, flaming it up.

"I'm sick of the killing," Cerian said loudly. "Get out of my mountain," she commanded in a low voice. She allowed the fireball to swell and drew her arm back as if to throw it. The warriors stumbled to their feet, turned tail and ran.

Lympia compressed herself to the wall so as not to be trampled.

Cerian twisted to face Ta'bat, who still lay pinned on the floor. Rhys backed away and shifted.

Ta'bat rubbed his bruised and bleeding throat. It looked like she'd arrived just as Rhys had been about to bite and tear. Ta'bat sneered at them both. "Place reeks of Vampir," he rasped. He stood, brushing off his clothes and glaring at Rhys.

Cerian extinguished the fireball and sauntered toward him as coolly and confidently as she could manage. "Ta'bat, this is over between us. You will cease to block our trade immediately."

Ta'bat took a menacing step toward her, his hand on his short sword. "*I* say when it's over, Cerian."

Rhys moved so fast he was a blur. He caught Ta'bat's throat in one powerful hand and lifted him until Ta'bat's feet hovered over the floor.

"Actually, *you* don't," said Rhys. "Cerian is Embraced now and untouchable to you. This crystal mine is a small concern in the scope of things, anyway, wouldn't you say, Ta'bat? It's clear your position within the ranks of your people doesn't go unchallenged. Some might rejoice if you met an untimely end."

Rhys grabbed Ta'bat's short sword from his belt and dropped him. Unbalanced, the Sarthe stumbled back, catching himself before falling inelegantly to the floor. The truth of Rhys' statement manifested as fear in Ta'bat's shiny black eyes.

"Go take care of your people, Ta'bat," said Cerian. "And I'll take care of mine. Maybe we can find a way to live alongside each other in peace."

Ta'bat said nothing in reply. He eyed the short sword Rhys brandished and then glanced at Cerian sideways before giving her a wide berth as he left.

Cerian held her breath until Ta'bat left, then huffed it out in a sudden rush. She'd been holding onto her strength by a tensile thread. Now it snapped. She felt herself crumple.

"Cerian!" Lympia cried from the doorway.

She heard the clatter of the short sword on the floor and felt Rhys' arms close around her as consciousness left her once more.

* * * * *

She awoke feeling protected, cuddled into a warm blanket and even warmer arms. "Mmmm," she decided and snuggled further into Rhys' embrace.

He shifted against her and kissed her lips. Her eyes came open and she kissed back. She smiled. "You're still here."

He nodded. "Had to see what an Embraced sidhe looked like." He cocked an eyebrow. "They're pretty magical, aren't they?"

Her smiled widened. "*Yes.*" She stretched and realized her hair was damp. "Did you give me a bath?"

He parted the blanket that swathed her and she made another realization—she was naked. He kissed her collarbone and then worked his way down, dragging his soft lips against her skin as he went. "Yes." He looked up, shooting her a sexy grin. "You were covered in crystal dust and moss."

"Oh," she breathed. She wished she'd been conscious for the bathing. "Is everyone all right, Rhys?"

He nodded. "Everyone is fine. Lympia was very worried about you, but I assured her I'd take care of you and you'd be fine."

Someone to take care of *her*. What a notion.

He paused to pay attention to both her breasts, enveloping each hardened peak in his mouth, sucking on each one until an ache began between her thighs and she moaned.

With a groan of his own, he glided down her body. "I have to taste you," he murmured against her solar plexus.

She sighed in anticipation. She wanted to taste him, too. How good his hard length would be to take into her mouth. Images flashed through her mind. She'd explore his cock's smooth plum-shaped head and the heavy veins roping its steel-velvet length with her tongue. His muscular body would tense as she brought him down her throat, suckling him until he climaxed and she swallowed his come.

He groaned low as he reached her belly button and gently bit her. "You're broadcasting your thoughts again."

She smiled and relaxed into the mattress as he kissed through the hair of her mound. "The Sarthes are gone," she breathed in sudden overwhelming wonderment. She'd driven them away with her own magic. "Ta'bat is defeated."

He growled softly. "No more thinking about other men." He parted her thighs and laid a kiss at the point where her upper thigh met her sex. He nipped her skin lightly.

She shuddered in pleasure. What other men?

The first touch of his tongue against her pussy erased all thought completely. He licked along her folds, darting his tongue into her. Cerian moaned and arched her back, stabbing her nipples into the air.

When he settled his hot mouth and tongue over her clit to pull and suck, she almost went through the roof. Rhys slipped a finger into her and thrust, driving her closer and closer to climax, and finally pushed her over the edge.

A wave of pleasure rolled over her and she cried out. He lengthened her orgasm with his skillful fingers and tongue until she clawed at the blankets and keened.

Rhys shifted and came down over her. He kissed her throat as he positioned himself between her thighs. "Even an Embraced magical sidhe must feed," he rasped.

She started to ask what he meant, but he chose that moment to drive into her with one powerful thrust. The pleasure of his cock filling her stole her words.

He began to shaft her slowly. The feel of his nude body moving against hers was exquisite. The brush of his fangs against her throat had her arching her neck in welcome.

"I feed, you feed," Rhys said. He lowered his mouth to her skin and bit.

Pleasure suffused her body, pushing her close to a second climax. The scent of her blood filled the air and she gasped as an unfamiliar hunger tightened low in her stomach. She recognized it as *sacyr*—the force that drove the Embraced to feed.

Her fangs lengthened and she touched them with her tongue carefully. The need to bite him suddenly overwhelming, she kissed his throat, set her fangs to his skin and sank in.

She'd never known what bliss was until this moment. Joined at sex and vein, they were one being.

Cerian felt the pleasure Rhys experienced as he drove into her wet heat. How her muscles tightened around his length like a perfectly fitted silk glove. How much he reveled in the soft brush of her breasts against his hard chest and the satin slide of her skin against his. She knew he could also feel her sensations.

Cerian felt his climax coming as sure as she felt her own. Intense and overwhelming, it crashed over them at the same time. She relinquished her hold on his throat and panted, unable to make any other noise as her pussy pulsed around his cock. It seemed to go on and on, racking their bodies with waves of pleasure.

When it was over, she lay, breathing heavily in the warm aftermath. Rhys shifted to the side and she mourned the loss of him from her body.

"Oh, gods," he groaned.

She laughed.

He pulled her to him and kissed her temple. "I want to do it again," he murmured into her ear. "And again and again," he finished with a little growl.

She turned and pushed him back into the pillows. "I still haven't gotten a good look at your body." *And I might never have another chance*, she finished silently.

She straddled him, her braids kissing over his skin as she shifted. He relaxed, sliding his hands behind his head. His biceps showed nicely in that position, and something low within her flared to life again. *Danu*, he made her insatiable.

She drew her hand over his muscled chest, noting several scars. She traced one and glanced up, asking the question with her eyes.

"From before I was Embraced," he answered.

Cerian wanted to know the story behind each one, but likely she never would. She shifted on him, following the length of one down his hip, and inadvertently rubbing her bare pussy over his cock. She felt it harden against her.

"Watch it, woman," he warned.

She grinned, feeling playful. Goddess, she hadn't felt that way in a long time. A small smile flirting with her mouth, she rocked her hips deliberately, thrusting her breasts out a little to tease him.

Cerian found herself on her stomach in record time. She gave a short scream of surprise that ended in a laugh.

He dropped a lingering kiss onto the back of one knee and another to the base of her spine, his tongue stealing out to taste her skin, before he straddled her. His now-hard cock pressed between her upper thighs. He landed a playful thwack on her buttocks and she started, letting out a gasp. Pleasure jolted through her pussy at the contact.

Brushing her braids to the side, he rubbed her shoulders and back until she nearly purred. "I could get used to this," she murmured.

Rhys pulled her hips up until she was on all fours. He covered her body with his, pressing his mouth to her ear. "So could I." His voice rumbled through his chest and vibrated into her. "How do you feel, Cerian? Are you sore?"

"I feel better than I have in a long time."

He slipped a finger into her pussy and she moaned. "So you feel good enough for this?"

"Yes," she breathed. Her body was already prepared to take him again. He set the head of his cock to her pussy and she thrust her hips up in welcome.

Rhys took her slowly this time, shafting her in long, easy strokes until she climaxed and she took him with her into ecstasy. In all her long life she'd never met a man who could draw so much pleasure from her body, she thought as he lowered her to the bed.

She turned her head and watched him close his eyes. Soon, his breath transitioned to the deep rhythm of sleep.

Tomorrow, she'd have to say goodbye.

Cerian didn't sleep until many hours later.

Chapter Five

Rhys awoke slowly, reaching around the bed for Cerian and coming up empty. Sounds of rustling fabric had him opening his eyes. Cerian stood dressed and staring down at him.

"Oh, those are way too many clothes, *cariad*," he said in a sleep-roughened voice. "Come over here and let me take some off."

She smiled weakly. "I have a lot to do today, Rhys. We got rid of the Sarthes, but there are still Tuatha Dé Danaan who lack faith in my leadership. I have trade to set back up again, if it's possible. Food to locate, if it's not."

He flipped the blankets away, stood, and walked to her, suddenly wondering if she returned the feelings that had sparked for him somewhere between the brawl in the tavern and this moment.

Cerian looked down and away. "I'll get the rover charged up, take you back—"

He cupped her chin and forced her gaze to his. "Do you want me to go?"

"What I want isn't important," she muttered. "You have a life elsewhere. I have one here. I have lots of work to do, restoring my people's confidence in my rule. They've obviously lost it, considering we have these traitors within our midst."

"There is something about being near you that makes me deeply content, Cerian."

She glanced up at him with her lips parted, a vaguely stunned look on her beautiful face.

"And if you don't mind," he continued, "I'd like to stay and explore it a little more. And maybe I could help you a little, you know, around here. That is, if you want me to stay."

She smiled and for a fleeting moment the shadows left her eyes. "Yes, I want you to stay, Rhys."

"Okay, I'm glad that's settled. Now, about those clothes…"

About the author:

Anya Bast writes erotic fantasy and paranormal romance. Primarily, she writes happily-ever-afters with lots of steamy sex. After all, how can you have a happily-ever-after WITHOUT lots of sex?

Anya welcomes mail from readers. You can write to her c/o Ellora's Cave Publishing at 1337 Commerce Drive, Suite 13, Stow OH 44224.

Also by Anya Bast:

Blood Of The Rose

Autumn Pleasures: The Union

Spring Pleasures: The Transformation

Summer Pleasures: The Capture

Winter Pleasures: The Training

WRITERS UNBLOCKED

Diana Hunter

As the flogger fell on her spread and helpless body, Jack grinned widely. Was there anything better than having a willing, bound woman before you, ready to serve your every whim? The sight of his wife, squirming and moaning as the deerskin caressed her breasts, aroused him as nothing else did. His thick cock swelled to its full eight inches, the purple veins bulging with life.

Jessica cried out as the leather landed across her nipples, stinging the aroused little buds. Already hard from Jack's pinching and the clamps that held them tight, they ached with every blow. But she would have it no other way. The submission she gave her husband was a gift she could give no other man and her pussy glistened with her kindled passion.

Jack threw the flogger to the side and mounted his helpless wife. Grabbing a pillow from the top of the bed, he pushed it under her hips; she helped by raising her shaved mound as high as her bound limbs allowed. Her pussy was pink and slightly swollen from the few blows he had landed square on those most luscious lips. With a feral growl, he thrust into her waiting wetness.

With her husband's body taking her so forcefully, Jessica had little choice but to come. Her cries played counterpoint to his; she felt the waves of pleasure course through her, tingling all the way down her bound arms to the very tips of her fingers. Several times she thrust her body forward, pushing him deeper to extend her climax. But all too soon it ended and she relaxed in contentment.

Her breathing returning to normal, her heart rate slowing down, Jessica Blackburn pulled the pillow from between her legs and stood up. It had been a great fantasy this time and she grinned as she stowed the bolster back on the bed behind the other pillows. Her husband would never notice her scent on the long, wide pillow, not after she spritzed just a dash of store-bought perfume in its general direction.

Yes, definitely a very nice fantasy this time, she thought to herself as she straightened her hair and pulled on her jeans. Every day she came home from work and every day her husband greeted her with a peck on the lips before going back to his own work on the downstairs computer. She would come upstairs and change out of her professional, constricting clothes and into something more casual. Today it was jeans and a turtleneck sweater. Never sweats. There was absolutely nothing sexy about sweatpants. Or a sweatshirt.

She sighed as she gave herself a once over in the mirror. Not that dressing sexy meant anything. Although she married Jack two years ago, he had recently told her she really didn't need to keep buying sexy underthings…that the garments didn't matter to him. Jessica was heartbroken. She had been purchasing them all along in order to spice up their rather tedious sex life. A sex life he, apparently, did not want spiced up.

In spite of the fact that she had just come, she still felt horny. Her glance fell on the frame that surrounded their queen-sized bed. It was a four-poster, with strong iron bars connecting the four iron posts. Small finials decorated the tops of the posts and she had threaded creamy sheer voile curtains to surround the intricate ironwork of the headboard. Oh, the fantasies she had spun when they bought this marvelous piece of furniture! But when she had hinted to Jack that he spread her wide and tie her down to play with her body, he had laughed out loud at the absurdity. Jessica did not mention it again.

Put back to rights, she sauntered downstairs to find her husband. She knew right where he would be—at the computer in their downstairs study, working away at his book. She rounded the corner of the doorway and poked her head in.

The sight of Jack Blackburn's blond mop never failed to elicit a little catch in her throat. At her request, he wore his hair long, the curls spilling over and around his head to brush his shoulders. Pulled back out of the way now, still his hair curled gracefully in its ribbon tie. Didn't matter that she was married to the man; his gorgeousness never failed to thrill her. Dressed as usual in jeans and a denim shirt that accentuated the powerful muscles of his back and chest, Jess knew he was unaware of his effect on her. The strong lines of his jaw were set as he hunched over the keyboard, his ruggedly handsome face scrunched into tiny crinkles as he glared at a problematic sentence. His intense, deep-set blue eyes would melt her heart as soon as he glanced her way.

She remembered the first time she had ever seen him, at a conference for writers of romance books. He had been working the room, charming the editors and the publishers as well as several of the authors. In fact, Jessica had at first taken him to be one of the cover models who often attended these affairs to look for work. But when her companions stated that, no, that was Jack Blackburn, the author of some of the steamiest romantic books ever written, Jessica just knew she had to meet him.

And so, she had done her own set of networking, slowly getting closer to the blond-haired writer with every handshake. From here she could see his strong, broad shoulders and even while she spoke with a new contact, a part of her mind analyzed the muscles that rippled under his burgundy linen shirt. Jessica didn't know how many books the man had written; she had only read one. But that one certainly explained the crowd of women around him she was now trying nonchalantly to navigate through.

Even though she endeavored to keep him in the corner of her sight as she worked the room, the press of people hid him from her. Finished with the conversation she was holding, Jessica turned to get her bearings on him again, and discovered he was no longer in the spot he had occupied for such a long time. Frantically, her eyes searched the room… A bump from behind almost made her snarl. Turning around to give the woman a dirty look, Jessica's demeanor immediately relaxed. The woman who bumped her was now shaking the tall author's hand, fawning all over him. Was it her imagination? Or did Jack Blackburn's smile seem just a bit forced?

Positioning herself to get her chance at meeting the hunk of the room, Jessica plastered on her own smile, suddenly not sure if she wanted to destroy the illusion. Sometimes it was best to admire beauty from afar. A sudden image of Lina Lamont in *Singing in the Rain* flashed in her memory and she paused. But before she could run, the woman in front of her stepped back…and right on her toes.

And from there? Well, the events that succeeded read like one of the romance novels they both wrote—he picked her up and carried her to a quiet room off the main ballroom, no matter that her toes were only bruised and there was no lasting damage. They fell to conversing as he insisted upon an icepack for her foot and finally confessed to using her as an excuse to get away. He really wasn't the crowd-type person his alter-ego writer was.

Their courtship had been covered in the papers, but thankfully, on the back pages. While she was gaining some fame as a romance writer in her own right, Jack's spotlight cast a very large pool of attention and Jessica had come to understand the man's penchant for privacy. The media hounds faded away, however, once the wedding was over and the two settled into a normal life.

A humdrum life, some might say. Jessica fixed her smile in place and waited for her husband to notice her. It was a courtesy they both gave to one another—never interrupt a writer in mid-sentence. She spent the few moments watching his long fingers dance on the keyboard…her imagination drifted…and his fingers danced over her clit as she lay bound to the bed upstairs…

"How long have you been standing there?"

Jessica jumped at the sound of Jack's voice. With a guilty look, she pulled her hand away from the front of her jeans, clearing her throat before trying to speak. "Not long. I just wondered if you had any preferences for dinner."

Jack Blackburn eyed his wife. She was undoubtedly the most gorgeous creature he had ever laid eyes on. Two years ago, he had already read her book before recognizing her at the writer's conference. Using her sore toes as an excuse to leave the room gave him a chance to get them out of sight of the ever-present paparazzi who insisted on following him everywhere. He did not miss opportunities when they presented themselves.

He had also not missed the sudden withdrawal of her hand from her crotch.

"You know me, my sweet. Whatever you feel like fixing is fine with me."

The look she shot him would have melted iron. Without a word, she turned on her heel and stalked out of the room.

Jack listened to the sound of rattling pans. What was her problem tonight? He leaned back in his chair, the steamy scene on the computer screen momentarily forgotten.

If only Jessica could be more like the women he wrote about instead of the ones she wrote about. The women in his stories generally had strong, even tough exteriors, but inside just wanted a man to dominate them. While he couched his phrases in flowery-yet-specific terms, to those who understood the D/s lifestyle, there could be no doubt about the author who wrote such strong heroes. Heroes who intuitively knew what their lover wanted and gave it to them—even when the woman was too afraid to ask for herself.

But Jessica's heroines were always strong, independent women who knew what they wanted…and got it. The relationships she detailed were ones of perfect equality where responsibilities were shared and sex was…well…where sex was vanilla. Ordinary, plain old sex couched in terms so intense as to make her readers blush with a sudden hormonal rush.

He grinned, leaning back in his chair and contemplating his wife's qualities. Yes, the woman could write, there was no doubt about that. And she did it in her spare time. Several times he had mentioned her staying home, but she always put him off. Jack dropped the issue, thinking her career as a teacher must give her something that staying home with him wouldn't. His grin widened, putting deep creases in his cheeks. On occasion, she did take a personal day and stayed home to use him for "research". He always willingly complied.

But then his smile faded and he sat up.

She had used him for research, but he had never used her. In any sense of the word. Jessica was the love of his life. How could he ever tell her the demons that hid inside of him? The demons that peeked through his writing, but he was afraid to unleash, lest she turn from him in disgust.

For a moment he stared at the scene on the screen, the words detailing yet another of his fantasies—the heroine bound against her will, the hero winning her over with his ways, the inevitable sex scene where she gave herself to him of her own volition, his desires becoming hers.

Her bound breasts, round and firm in their bindings, excited the beast inside his soul. Capturing the young London aristocrat had been a rare stroke of good fortune in a season of despair. Captain John Blakemoore stared at the white skin of the woman bound in sea ropes before him, her breasts turning pink as he twined the rough rope around them. Her submission to his will was sweeter than the honey of the tropical bees that formed their golden syrup from the flowers that thrived on the sun.

Fear glinted in the woman's eyes—fear and desire mixed. The captain had worked hard on this conquest, harder than he'd ever worked before. He never cared about a woman's reasons; her submission to him was all that mattered. The conquest. Forcing her to admit his domination over her.

Only this time his heart had gotten involved and now he bound her tightly, tying her bound hands to the beam overhead, stretching her slender body so that she was forced to her toes.

The glint in her eyes confirmed she was a willing prisoner. Her begging on the deck in port in front of all the townspeople had been a particularly sweet moment of triumph. She was a creature of passion as he was and he ached to take her now.

Instead, the torment of her body would take precedence. He would teach her how pain and pleasure were closely mixed, and how one could easily lead to the other. His fingers reached out to squeeze a nipple between his thumb and forefinger and the small whimper from her throat made his cock hard.

Reaching into his pocket, he pulled out a small set of clamps, designed at his orders and made by a jeweler in Jamaica. Stretching her nipple taut, he clamped the metal onto her sensitive little bud, then let go and watched her squirm.

She danced in such a delightful way, tears forming in her beautiful eyes. And yet, she did not ask to have it removed. Its companion dangled from the other end of the chain and when he picked it up to attach it to her other nipple, she hesitated only a moment before thrusting her breast forward and into his hand.

With a grin, he repeated his actions, first stretching the nipple out until she gasped, and then attaching the clamp and letting her breast fall to bounce off her chest.

"More," she whispered into his ear when he leaned down to kiss the white sweep of her stretched arm. Through the sheen of tears, she pleaded her submission. "Let me give all of myself to you, John Blakemoore. Let me surrender to your will."

No. His beautiful wife would never submit. Jessica would leave him instead. With a muttered curse, Jack Blackburn shut down the program and stalked out of the room.

* * * * *

"Oh, Andi, I get so tired of trying. Why bother anymore?" With the receiver crammed between her ear and her shoulder, Jessica busied herself about the house, dusting and straightening as she went. These Saturday no-mind jobs, as she referred to housework, relaxed her and gave her a chance to think. Usually she mulled over some thorny story problem, but today, her sexual frustration was the only thing on her mind. And when Andi called, that frustration spilled out onto her best friend.

"Well, it's affecting my work… Do you know, I actually wrote a scene today that…" Her voice trailed off. No, she could not even tell her best friend her fantasies. Even as she wrote the pages this morning, her cheeks burned with shame and humiliation. How could she want to be treated this way?

"Never mind, it wasn't well-written anyway." She sighed as she dusted a photo of her husband. Jack grinned that rakish grin of his, his arm around her shoulders in a protective embrace. She remembered that moment. Jack had received a book award and the two of them attended the ceremony. As they were leaving, a fan came up to her and had been rather pushy about getting an autograph. His eyes, however, had not been on her face. Instead, he had leered at her breasts, the tops of which showed in the scarlet slinky dress Jack had purchased for her. The nakedness of her cleavage made her uncomfortable, yet Jessica wore it to please him. Only recently had she begun to recognize her giving in as an indication of her submissive tendencies and it still confused her.

Jack had put his arm around her, drawing her close, and she had seen a flash of anger in his eyes. It had surprised her; she had never seen him angry. In fact, it was the only time she had ever seen such a strong emotion from him. But the photographers were there and by the time they were in the hired limo, his demeanor was placid once more.

"No, never mind, Andi. I'm just being cranky, that's all. Seriously. I just need a good fucking, that's all." She laughed, shocked at her own use of language. "I know, too much information."

She set the picture down, free of dust, and moved on. The conversation also moved to safer topics and Jessica felt as if she had dodged a bullet. It was hard enough admitting these feelings to herself. How could she ever admit them to anyone else?

Only later, sitting at her computer once more and reading over the graphic scene she had written, did Jessica finally confront what she had spent years running away from. As an independent, woman who made a good living for herself and her husband, she was a thoroughly modern American Woman; but just under the surface lurked another woman. That was the woman who wanted to submit, who wanted to be taken care of, who wanted to live on the edge of virtual slavery. While she didn't take care of the money, Jessica felt it was important for her to provide her share. Thus, she worked as an English teacher at the local high school, even though she'd much rather stay home and write full-time like he did. So why would a woman who rarely gave in and who was in total control of herself want exactly the opposite when it came to the bedroom? It didn't make sense.

Or did it? Wasn't the giving up of control in essence, also the giving up of responsibility? She controlled every aspect of her life, from what to have for dinner to what book she would write next. She did the lion's share of the housework although Jack had his set of chores as well. Outside was his responsibility; inside was hers. An equal sharing of household management. These duties she did not want to shirk. Indeed, she enjoyed most of them.

So what was it? Why had her dreams always been haunted by men who persisted when she said no? Why had she come so hard yesterday afternoon when she imagined him flogging her? Why was she now so aroused at the scene she wrote this morning?

With an oath, Jessica closed the scene on her laptop and dumped the file into the computer's trash bin. She could never show that to anyone. Jack put her on a pedestal. He loved her deeply and he would never, ever consent to what he would see as a brutal attack on his own wife. This was just something she would have to accept. Determined to quell those desires once and for all, she pushed herself away from the screen and went to find the mop. Didn't matter that she just mopped the kitchen earlier in the day, she was sure it needed it again.

* * * * *

For several moments, Jack stared at the strange file that suddenly appeared in the folder he and Jessica shared. While they each used their own computers, the two were networked and information they both needed to access was kept in this shared folder. But the one labeled, "Jessamyn's Submission" did not sound like a document the two of them would both need. Obviously it was a story Jessica was working on, but why had she put it here?

He shrugged. She had never asked his opinion on anything she had written in the past, but they often discussed points that gave them trouble. Must be she was having difficulties with this piece. Determined to be helpful, he double-clicked and opened the document.

What was there about this pirate captain that stole her heart so? Captured on her way to meet her fiancé, why had she chosen him? His oversized white shirt hung in graceful folds from massive shoulders bronzed by years of seasons in the southern sun. In his callused hands, he caressed the leather of a many-thonged flogger in the same manner his fingers caressed her skin the first time he took her.

A taking? No. A giving. Lady Jessamyn turned her back on her London upbringing and gave herself to this captain of a pirate ship. Despite his rough demeanor, his harsh words to her, his threats; she had seen the vulnerable man underneath…the man who could also love with a passion deeper than any of those landed London fops could even imagine.

And now she was his. Completely. Stretched naked before him in his cabin, her bound hands tied to the rough beam overhead, her eyes watched him run the leather straps through his hand as he surveyed his property.

Property. It was what she was in any case. Whether the property of a fop, or the property of a pirate captain, who it was that owned her was the only part of her life she could control. And she had. Her cheeks blushed as she remembered the morning she knelt before him and asked him to keep her. He told her to beg him in front of the entire crew—and she had. Her humiliation stripped the pride from her and her arousal caused her cheeks to flush. She became the Captain's woman. And she would have it no other way.

Now the flogger fell on her stretched and bound breasts, breasts turned a deep pink from the constriction of the ropes that encircled them. Her head fell back and her eyes sparkled with the passion ignited by the sting. Barely able to touch the floor with her toes, she fought to keep herself still as his blows, some soft and gentle, some hard and stinging, landed on her tender flesh.

He shifted his position now, coming to her side and coloring the skin of her bottom. The heat rose and she knew her cream flooded the small slit that separated her legs. And when his finger suddenly plunged into that slit from behind, Jessamyn moaned and pushed herself back, wanting to feel his touch inside her body.

Jack read the passage through twice, his cock hardening at the image the words provoked. An image not so very different from the one he, himself, had written earlier. Had Jessica seen that passage? Had she peeked? And what was his sweet little wife doing writing such incredibly violent scenes? Jack read the short page again, too stunned to accept that his wife might have similar desires to his own.

Jessica's humming came to him through the open doorway and, feeling like a boy with his hand caught in the proverbial cookie jar, Jack clicked the program closed in a hurry. She might have left that in the folder for him to find…or she might not have. Staring at the now-empty screen, Jack's analytical mind turned over the problem. If Jess had taken his idea and rewritten it, she would not want him to find it. But what if she had been harboring these feelings of submission for these past two years? Could she have put that there on purpose? Jack's blood quickened at possibilities too life-changing to contemplate just yet. He needed more information.

Affecting an air of nonchalance, he sauntered out into the living room where she was busy tidying up. Saturdays were housework days, and she had changed her weekday suit for jeans and a simple oxford shirt. All business, Jessica's hair was pulled back, the red scrunchie a mismatch for her maroon button-down shirt rescued from the back of Jack's closet. The oversized shirt gaped when she leaned over the low coffee table and Jack grinned when he caught an innocent glimpse of her white breasts hanging free from any confining bra. It was a sight he could look at all day.

Jess recognized that look in his eye right away. Putting her hands low on her hips, she swayed them seductively. "Hey there, big boy…wanna have some fun?"

Jack's delighted laugh pealed through the room. How could he ever think such a little minx might give into the same dark fantasies that fueled his own soul? Yet the scene he read remained in his mind. Did he dare to hope?

His grab for her was rougher than he intended. With a small cry, she fell against him and in one of those split second decisions, he decided he would not apologize.

Instead, he seized the moment, pressing his lips against her in a hard, passionate, possessive kiss.

Jessica's head reeled. Jack had never been this forceful before. While her first instinct was to recoil, her second was to yield before the onslaught of his tongue. Confused, for a moment she hung suspended, off balance, attacked. When his hand grabbed her breast through the fabric of her shirt, she whimpered and her mouth surrendered without her consent. Through her parted lips, his tongue stabbed in to twine around hers, as if her mouth were something he owned.

She had been feeling a bit naughty all day so only her jeans covered her mound and pussy. Jess left the white cotton panties in the drawer. Jack's fingers found her nipple and squeezed; her wetness spread along the seam of her jeans. The pirate king held her in his arms.

With an oath, Jack thrust her away from him with almost the same force he had pulled her to him. What was he doing? This was his wife, for crying out loud. She was proud, independent, secure in her sexuality; not a wannabe slut like the women he detailed in his books. He staggered and turned away, unable to look her in the eye. He could not face her disgust.

Jessica's shock at losing his passion was almost as great as seeing it. She said nothing, unsure what was happening. Trying to marshal her thoughts, her chest heaved with awakened and unfulfilled passion.

"I'm sorry, Jessica. I don't want to hurt you." Jack's tight voice choked out the words.

"Hurt me? How? Because you just gave me one heck of a kiss?"

"You deserve better. You are my wife. You warrant my respect."

"Yes, I do." Her brow furrowed. What was he getting at? "But I also deserve your passion. Jack, you've never kissed me like that before."

"Jess..." She stood there, so beautiful in her earnestness. What was she saying? Did she not realize how close to the edge he was? "Jess, don't tease me. There are demons that lurk inside me, demons that want to hurt you. Tease me and I will not be able to control them."

Jessica frowned in puzzlement. "Jack, I don't know what you're talking about. Tell me." He remained silent, his breathing labored and his eyes dark. Did she dare hope? "Jack, I am your wife and I deserve to see the demons you think you have. We are married. There are not supposed to be any secrets between us." Even as she said the words, her cheeks colored as her mind considered her own hidden desires.

Jack snarled and turned away. He paced to the fireplace, the pictures she had just dusted catching his eye. Jessica had glowed that night she wore the dress he chose for her. He knew she was uncomfortable with the low-cut neckline, and it had given him a rush to know she wore it anyway just because he asked her. His anger left him. She was right. She deserved to know the truth.

His body relaxed and he turned to face her, his movements slow and sure. Jessica's breath caught in her throat as she recognized the predatory look in his eye; it was the look she always imagined finding there. Swallowing hard, she set her chin with determination...and fear. Could it be? Might her husband not be as disinterested in sex as she had come to believe?

Could he also need something more than just plain sex to interest him?

With a graceful ease, Jack towered over her, his hands resting on her soft, smooth shoulders. For a moment, he gently caressed them, his eyes never leaving hers. He saw the fear in her eyes, and something more…excitement? There was only one way to find out how far he could push her before that look turned to disgust. He let his hands trace down the length of her arms; firm hands that brooked no nonsense. Jack stood a full foot taller than she did and her head hung back, not breaking from his eyes that held her spellbound. What was he doing to her?

He needed to bend as his hands reached hers. For a moment, he entwined his fingers through hers, his thumb gently caressing the soft skin on back of her hands. "I read your scene, Jessica. Is that what you want? Tell me. Is that what you want me to do to you?" His fingers tightened around hers even as his voice hardened.

She saw the change in his eyes, the possessiveness. His hands hurt hers and she almost cried out. How had he read her story? She had put it in the trash, hadn't she? His grip tightened and she whimpered. Suddenly it didn't matter how he had found it. "Yes, Jack. Yes." The pleading in her voice was stronger than she intended, but she could not, did not want to take it back.

"Jack, hurt me. Take me and possess me like the pirate king. Please, Jack. If that's the demon that resides in you, let it out. Please let me be her."

Even if he wanted to, he could not stop the animal raging against his mind. For two years he held himself back, afraid his wife would no longer love him and now here she was, begging to be treated like the whores he created in his dreams. Grabbing her shirt in both hands, he ripped it open, the buttons scattering unheeded along the floor. He shoved the material down her arms, trapping her hands inside, exposing her breasts to his hunger.

Jessica squirmed, but her hands only became more entangled in her shirt. Jack's strong hand closed over her right breast and squeezed, slowly increasing the pressure. Deeper and deeper his fingers dug into her tender flesh until she at last cried out.

But he did not remove his hand, or even lessen his grip. Instead, he tightened his fist even further, turning his hand to twist her breast, stretching the skin to its furthest limit. Only when she cried out a second time did his hand release her.

"Is that really what you want, Jessica? Pain so intense it can only lead to pleasure?"

"Yes, Jack. Please, don't stop."

Her heart beat hard; a sudden fear blossomed in her belly. It swelled to her throat and for several moments she could not breathe. What would he think of her? What would he do to her?

Not giving her time to change her answer, Jack grabbed her hands, pulling her backward through the house. Jessica stumbled along behind, the shirt still entangling her. Several times she tripped, only to have his strong arms catch her. At the foot of the stairs, he paused long enough to throw her over his shoulder before climbing to their bedroom.

Jessica didn't know whether to laugh or scream at such treatment. In one way it seemed melodramatic and overdone. And yet, there was no amusement in his eyes when he threw her onto the bed and yanked down the zipper of her jeans. With a single move, he pulled the jeans off her legs and exposed her naked mound to his view.

He did not try to hide his grin. She had dressed as a slut for him…no bra, no panties. Only the shirt and jeans.

Jessica had never seen such a grin in his eyes before. Not one of laughter and fun, but one of predator enjoying its prey. She struggled against the shirt that still bound her arms, working herself loose. But before she got far, Jack grabbed her leg.

"You're not going anywhere, my love. You wanted to see the animal inside. Here he is."

Jack knew his habit of leaving his ties on the back of the decorative chair in the bedroom drove his wife nuts. Often she would scold him for not taking care of them then hang them herself. But two lay across the chair back at the moment and Jack grabbed them both.

With a deft tie, Jack secured her ankle to the iron bedpost. Jessica, her arms now free, pushed herself up and tried to pull her leg away, but it was caught fast. Too late to prevent him, he grabbed her other ankle, yanking it down to fasten it to the other bedpost. Her legs spread wide and in spite of her sudden fear, her juices gushed to fill her slit.

The closet was only a stride away and Jack was back with several more ties. What did he need so many for? Two more would secure her wrists, and she did not fight him as he pulled first one arm, then the other, and used the ties to spread-eagle her body on the bed.

"Is this what you want, Jess? Is this the way you want me to treat you?" Jack's voice was rough and gravelly with his own passion. Let her get a taste of the animal inside him. It would teach her not to play with fire.

She was where she dreamed of so many times before. Helpless before her husband, open to his every whim. Her voice barely a whisper as she faced her own hidden desires, she answered. "Yes, please. Let me submit to you, Jack Blackburn."

The heroine bound against her will, the hero winning her over with his ways, the inevitable sex scene where she gave herself to him of her own volition, his desires becoming hers.

His thoughts from the morning filtered back through his consciousness. Could it be true that her desires and his were the same? His voice still rough, he barked out his question. "Why didn't you tell me before?"

She could not meet his gaze. With tears in her eyes, she admitted the truth to him at last. "I didn't want you to think ill of me. You saw me as independent and strong. But I don't want to be strong all the time, Jack. I don't want to have to make so many decisions. I want to be here, used by you in whatever way you want. I want to be your slave, Jack."

The tears fell free; tears of shame mixed with relief that now her secret was told. Jack had every right to leave her over this—she wasn't the woman he thought he married.

For several moments, Jack simply stood there, partially stunned at her revelation, mostly rejoicing. "Jessica, I did not want you to see the Dominant I really am. I can be very demanding in the obedience I require. Are you saying you will submit to me in *every* way?"

She knew what he was asking, and had to be honest with him. The time for equivocation was past. "Jack, I do not know if I can submit in everything. But I do know I want to submit here. In the bedroom."

He nodded. "It's a good place to start. I can see your arousal from here."

His reminder that nothing was hidden from him about her body caused a blush to color her cheeks. She smiled through her tears and bent her back to raise her pussy to him—her gift.

"Eager little slut, aren't you?" They both knew the power of words; what effect would that one have on his wife?

Humiliation deepened the blush, but she forced herself to answer. "I am a slut, Jack. A selective one. I choose you."

In answer, Jack turned and walked out the door. Jessica writhed on the bed. Had she said something wrong? Where was he going? "Jack? Jack!"

He heard her calling and grinned. There was more to domination than just taking a woman's body. Jack wanted his wife's mind as well. She wanted to submit to him in the bedroom? Very well, he would have nothing but total submission from her while she was in that room.

Unlocking the bottom drawer on his desk, he slid open his past. Several items lay in neat order inside. He was a dominant long before he married Jessica, and these were the tools of his trade. Locking them away when he married, he thought he'd locked away the feelings as well. Apparently the lock held only so long. Reaching in, he chose one item then closed and relocked the drawer, quietly climbing the stairs once more. She wasn't yelling anymore, but he could hear her twisting about on the bed, trying to get loose. He paused in the doorway, leaning his large frame against the doorjamb to admire the view.

Jessica's lean body glistened with beads of perspiration from her struggles. Convinced he was punishing her for her admission, she had decided to get loose. But Jack's knots were well tied. Damn the man for having been a Boy Scout! Several strands of her dark hair had come loose from her ponytail and now clung to her face. Desperately she tried to use the pillow under her head to brush the wisps away, but she could not manage it without the use of her hands.

With a start, she realized Jack had reentered the room. He stood over her with his hands clasped behind his back and an amused smile on his face. "Here, love. Let me get that hair for you." He knew how she hated having hair in her face. Several times she had threatened to cut it all off, but he had protested. Now he leaned forward to smooth back the offending few strands, wiping her forehead dry with his hand as he did so.

"Feeling a bit vulnerable, are we?"

Jessica didn't know what to say. This was too new. His hand trailed along her neck to brush the top of her naked breast. He could touch her any way he wanted. She could not stop him.

His wife had ample breasts, now flattened a bit as she lay on her back. The nipples, however, betrayed her excitement. Dark and round, the little nubs were raised to the air and as Jack flicked his finger over the one closest to him, he felt it harden. His cock mirrored her nipple.

But prolonging her torment would only increase both their pleasure. Jessica's eyes widened as he brought his other hand out of hiding. The lashes of a long leather flogger hung menacingly from a strong wooden handle. She whimpered as Jack brought the thongs up to lie on her naked skin. With slow, deliberate movements, he trailed the lashes along her breasts, over her darkened areolas and across those raised and sensitive nipples.

Jessica strained to see the flogger and noticed the lashes were a darker shade at the ends than at the handle. This had been used before, Jessica realized, her breath catching in her throat. Jack was no novice! Elements of domination always entered his writings, but until this moment, Jessica had not realized they were elements based on real-life experiences. But what were those ends stained with—sweat or blood?

Jack waited for Jessica to protest his introduction of the flogger. But she did not, her eyes only following the ends of the lash as he caressed her naked flesh with the soft leather thongs. Testing her further, he slapped it gently across her breasts.

The suddenness made her gasp, but it did not hurt. It barely stung. Still her body flinched as he landed a second light blow in almost the same spot as the first. Closing her eyes, she raised her breasts to the flogger as it landed again.

"How far do you want me to go, Jessica? What are you really willing to do?"

Jessica opened her eyes and stared into the dark blue eyes of her husband. Passion shimmered in them, a passion she had not seen in a very long time. But there was something else…control. Control of himself, of the situation—of her. A gateway opened inside her and she showed him the animal that hid inside of her as well.

"Let me feel its sting."

Drawing his hand back, he slapped the leather thongs against her skin. She cried out and arched her back as the sting across her breasts sent small daggers of pain to her brain. Before she could recover, he landed a second blow, and a third. Each time she cried out and writhed on the bed, tugging on her bindings and reveling in her helplessness.

Jack paused to survey his wife. Her breasts were turning a nice shade of pink, but he had not hit her hard enough to raise welts. Nor had the flogger yet landed on one of those beautiful nipples. He set the flogger to the side for a moment, running a hand over her supersensitive breasts.

"Oh, yes, Jack. Please."

"Please, what?" Today he would force her to ask for what she wanted.

"More," she whispered.

"Your wish is my command." But he did not comply right away. First he needed to get rid of these constricting clothes. Not making a show of it, he simply divested himself of his shirt and pants, underwear and socks, then picked up the flogger once more.

Jessica saw his cock swelling to his full eight inches now that it was free to do so. His size had alarmed her when they first married; now she squirmed in anticipation. She wanted that big, thickened cock to take her and take her hard.

But it was not her choice. Nothing at the moment was her choice and the thought made the juices gush again between her legs. The bedroom air brushed her pussy and made her even more aware of her readiness. Jack's arm rose again and she just had time to turn her head before the blow landed.

This time the lashes struck hard and right across her nipples. Jessica's scream was one of true pain, but Jack did not let up. Again he landed the lashes hard across her breasts, a different spot this time, but still getting her nipples with the ends of the thongs. Those hard, dark buds got the full effect of the sting.

Was there anything better than watching a woman squirm under the blows of a flogger? As his wife's cries filled the air, Jack's cock grew harder still, the purple veins marbling the stretched skin. Several welts sprang up under his blows and after one more well-aimed strike, he threw the flogger to the side.

Jessica had never felt such pain, nor such arousal. She could not explain it, and didn't want to. Each blow drove her closer to a climax...a climax she could not achieve on her own. She knew she cried out, but the cries were not of protest. And when Jack shoved a pillow under her hips, she raised them of her own volition, wanting his cock inside her.

With a single thrust, he plunged his cock deep, her cries music to him. Her hands grabbed onto the ties that bound her; she pumped herself onto his thickness as best as she could manage. But it was her very helplessness that fed his need...and hers. Savagely, he attacked her striped breasts with his mouth, sucking her nipple, pulling it up in his teeth.

She couldn't stand it anymore. Assaulted in so many ways, her body shouted for the release she needed. Mindless, she felt the tension in her pussy coil tightly as Jack slammed into her over and over, taking her body, possessing it with his own. Her back arched, hung for a moment, then convulsed as she screamed wordless cries into the room. Over and over the pleasure/pain washed through her; she could not escape the onslaught. Jack's teeth on her nipple bit down and she screamed again as fresh waves mounted and washed over her.

Her muscles contracted around his cock and Jack knew he could not hold back much longer. His control was rapidly slipping away. Slamming into her again with his cock while biting her nipple at the same time, her pulses around his cock as she came again tore his control to shreds.

And now it was his turn to pause, moans building in his throat. For a moment, he, too, hung motionless, prolonging the tension. Then, with a wordless oath of his own, he fell off the cliff and added his voice to hers. His come shot out in waves to match his thrusts as his wife's pussy contracted to squeeze him dry. The intensity of the thrusts increased then slowed as he emptied his seed into her.

Later, neither of them could say how long they lay there, his body collapsed beside hers. But both agreed they had never been so fulfilled. Hunting down the last of the buttons that had gone flying when he'd ripped open his wife's shirt, Jack grinned. Okay, maybe ripping a woman's blouse off was an activity that best remained in the books. By his count, he was still shy one button...and it could remain lost as far as he was concerned. Putting them in a neat pile on the table, he stretched, contented with all his life had to offer. Whistling, he went off to reexamine just what else he had hidden away in that locked drawer.

Upstairs, Jessica neatly hung the ties Jack had not used. Setting aside the ones he had bound her with to iron out later, she smiled. The reality of the flogging was so much more enjoyable than her imagination had ever been. Gently she rubbed her hand over her breasts, now hidden once again behind a blouse. Jack had informed her that the sensitivity would last for quite some time; her smile blossomed into a grin. Bending to retrieve the flogger from where he'd thrown it in his passion, she hung that in his closet as well, right beside his ties.

About the author:

For many years, Diana Hunter confined herself to mainstream writings. Her interest in the world of dominance and submission, dormant for years, bloomed when she met a man who was willing to let her explore the submissive side of her personality. In her academic approach to learning about the lifestyle, she discovered hundreds of short stories that existed on the topic, but none of them seemed to express her view of a D/s relationship. Challenged by a friend to write a better one, she wrote her first BDSM novel, *Secret Submission,* published by Ellora's Cave Publishing.

Diana welcomes mail from readers. You can write to her c/o Ellora's Cave Publishing at 1337 Commerce Drive, Suite 13, Stow OH 44224.

Also by Diana Hunter:

Irish Enchantment

Learning Curve

Secret Submission

Table for Four

LOOKING FORWARD

Mary Wine

Chapter One

"Leah, we must go."

Brother Paul tried to sound elderly but his lack of years didn't help. He reminded Leah of an adolescent boy wearing his father's suit to Sunday Meeting. But he'd been elected into the role of elder and she truly ought to respect him.

Leah pressed her lips together to hide her lack of enthusiasm for the task. It didn't matter anyway. She turned and joined the rest of the women as Paul ordered their caravan forward before they lost any more precious sunlight.

It shouldn't be so simple to bury a husband. Leah turned her head to look back over her shoulder at the rough grave her husband's body was resting in. They were three thousand feet up on the top of a pass, so no one bothered to mark the spot with a cross. The steady wind would have made quick work of knocking over anything standing in the recently turned soil.

"Look ahead, sister."

"Yes, I will." Leah snapped her eyes forward and never looked back. She didn't have the strength to worry about it anymore. Howard had been a sturdy man but the truth was, Leah couldn't think of another word to describe her departed husband.

And she had been his faithful, sturdy wife.

Now she was stuck on Tailarmar with a group of homesteaders and she was a widow. Well, maybe it would be better. Leah almost winced at her harshness. She hadn't wished Howard dead. But the truth was, she wasn't going to miss him very much.

Howard had yearned for the biblical version of life that he'd heard was available on the outer planets. His views on marriage were rather plain. So the result was she'd buried a man she only barely knew.

Leah truly couldn't grieve over his loss.

Instead she raised her head and enjoyed the slap of the wind against her cheeks. Tailarmar was a planet very similar to Earth but with one important difference.

Land. There was land here for those willing to brave the pioneering conditions to own it. Not a single inch of planet Earth had been sold in the last two hundred years. If you were not fortunate enough to inherit land from your family, you would never know the joy of owning a home.

So Howard had secured them a spot with the Sacred Heart Fellowship. The church held the precious permission from the Tailarmarian officials to homestead a parcel of land. But the pilgrims had to cultivate that land or it would never become their property.

Who could have guessed that Earth's past might also become her future. The farms these pilgrims would cultivate would feed the ever-growing population of the planet.

Life wouldn't be so different here. Leah smelled the air and felt her shoulders lift. Earth was overpopulated and stank of pollution. At least the areas of it that someone like her could afford to live in did. She would get

Howard's portion of land and somehow make it meet production standards.

The other members of the Sacred Heart Fellowship were strict and sober. That too could be endured. There was nothing better back on Earth, so she would look forward.

* * * * *

Elder Samuel puffed his chest out as Elder Paul stuck his finger into his chest. The younger Elder couldn't stand up to the years of age that glared out of Samuel's black eyes.

"Then what do *you* propose we do?"

"Patience. God will provide for his faithful children." The remaining eight Elders all muttered agreements to Samuel's words and Paul shank back as he was clearly put into his place by the senior man.

"The Tailarmarians will demand payment for the land as soon as we set foot on it. We have nothing to pay them with!"

"Your lack of faith is disturbing, Paul."

Paul felt his stomach drop in response. He had almost everything he'd ever wanted. Now that he was an Elder, his position in the community was a high one. His pride could cost him that if he wasn't wise enough to temper his words. Elder Samuel couldn't live forever.

"Forgive me, I am only thinking of our flock and their futures. The Tailarmarians will leave us in peace once they receive their land price. They are a violent race that will give poor example to our community if they linger in our midst."

Another round of mutters went through the tent, restoring Paul's pride. The remaining Elders agreed with him. Samuel began stroking his beard as his eyes considered their dilemma.

"We will have to trade some of the horses to the Tailarmarians."

This time the mutters that went around the tent were horrified. They needed the horses in the primitive environment. There wasn't even a power source. Their larger animals were worth far more than the money they'd bought them for.

"Unless they will trade for cloth. I have heard they sometimes trade for cloth."

That was valuable too. Everything they had became more valuable as civilization dropped further and further behind them. There was only one single season in front of them and whatever they produced would have to sustain the community until the next year.

Without the horses, the soil couldn't be turned for seed. Without their seed, they could not plant. The cloth would keep them warm in the coming winter. Every last thing they gave up could make their chance of surviving the winter slimmer.

Paying for the land could cost them lives when the snow began to fall.

* * * * *

"I like it not."

"Nor do I, Lucian." Aaron surveyed the group of pilgrims with sharp eyes. Their wagons were pulled together to shield them from the wind but not positioned correctly to defend against attack. Such lack of forethought made Aaron shake his head.

Ignorance was often paid for with death.

Leah stared at their visitors and didn't try to hide her response. No one else was. The men were huge. The horses they sat on even bigger. Twenty of the large brutes had ridden straight into camp at first light and they sat there inspecting the pilgrims like sheep. There was a deep arrogance reflected from their faces as their dark eyes moved over each and every one of the Fellowship members.

Solid muscle-bound legs gripped the sides of those horses as the animals pawed and snorted in the morning air. The men moved in almost perfect harmony with their mounts. They clearly spent a great deal of time riding the animals.

They wore their hair long. The dark strands were being caught by the morning wind. A few of them had it tied back away from their rough faces. Leah felt a moment of jealousy. Her own hair was braided and pinned to her head with a linen cap over it. It must be nice to feel the breeze against your scalp.

The Tailarmarian warriors all wore pants that clung to their legs and let her see the sharply defined muscles. A good many also wore only vests that left their arms bare. Leah let her eyes slip over the darker one in the center. His arms fascinated her. She'd never seen such sculpting of the male flesh except in pictures. A blush crept up into her face as she considered how it must feel to run your fingers over such strength.

His hands were at least twice the size of hers and Leah felt that blush turn hotter as she considered the confident way he handled his horse. Strength radiated from him in thick waves that caused heat to travel along her body and into her stomach.

Leah dropped her eyes and hid her smile behind her hand. Now that she was a widow such open admiration wasn't sinful, but it was certainly bound to get her into more trouble than she needed. Her body was actually warm and flushed. She felt bold enough to look him in the eye, but kept her face lowered instead.

Anger always interfered with empathy. Aaron didn't notice the female's interest in him until she dropped her face towards the ground. That angered him further but he strove to empty his mind so that he could feel her again. One slim hand was covering her face as she tried to dismiss him from her thoughts.

The dress she wore was ugly and shapeless. But her fingers were smooth and slim and delicate. He couldn't even tell what color her hair was because still more cloth was sitting on her head. A woman's hair was her crown. Aaron didn't understand why all of these females were swaddled up like infants.

She had been looking his body over with appreciation. Aaron had felt the path of her eyes and he wanted to see her face. Reaching out, he gently stroked her mind. She jumped and her face flew up so her eyes stared directly into his own. Aaron didn't touch her mind again because humans often reacted poorly to empathy. Instead he considered her large blue eyes and the tiny hints of light-colored hair.

Leah went from warm to hot in an instant as his bold eyes moved over her body. Sensation erupted in places that she'd never really thought sensation should be. Her breasts felt heavy and her nipples tightened into little buds. She was grateful her dress hid the strange reaction as that heat seeped into her middle and down toward her sex.

The sheer intensity of the heat made her shift in her tracks. The warrior's eyes seemed to know far too much and she walked toward the back of the women's group. A black eyebrow rose in response and Leah stopped her retreat. She wasn't a coward and she didn't like him thinking she was afraid of him.

Leah bent to pick up a bolt of cloth as if that had been her reason for moving in the first place. She straightened her back and moved forward to place it along with the other goods that were being presented to the Tailarmarians. She raised her chin and took another look at the man's muscular arms. As long as it made her feel so strange, she might as well enjoy it.

There was little doubt that she'd never see him again. Once the land was paid for, the Tailarmarians wouldn't disturb them. That was part of the agreement.

"You have the luck of a God, Aaron." Lucian felt the wave of interest coming from the female and lamented the fact that she was looking at his best friend. Boldness in a female meant she would be a good mate. Human women were always too afraid of their own bodies to become good mates. Looking at her blue eyes, he cursed silently. He would claim her in a second if her interest were for him.

Aaron wasn't sure if it was luck or a curse. His body was keenly aware of her. His staff had hardened in response to her arousal and he wanted to rip that cap off her head to find out what her hair smelled like. "It is most likely she has a mate." Aaron said the words and felt his staff throb with protest. If she were Tailarmarian, he would speak to her father before the sun set.

The men of her group began speaking and Aaron reluctantly looked at them. Their trade goods left a great deal to be desired. They had nothing as valuable as the land they wanted.

Worse yet, the pilgrims didn't seem to have brought unmated women with them. There was a lack of females among the rougher terrains of Tailarmar. Men like Aaron's father offered small amounts of land in order to bring in families that might then provide mates. His father had hoped that Aaron and his men might find females among the pilgrims. Now, it looked like there wouldn't even be payment for the land. Sending them back towards the spaceport would be a death sentence. They were not strong enough to make the three-month journey again.

Swinging off his mount's back, Aaron let the men show him their offerings.

"Enough." The men fell back as a group. Aaron held his temper in check. They were so foolish. Showing such weakness was an invitation to be conquered. "You cannot survive without your horses. The cloth will barely be sufficient to keep your women alive when the snow begins to fall. Do not offer what you cannot part with. There is no honor is taking the things that would leave you at the mercy of death."

His stiff arousal was making him harsh but Aaron didn't care. He didn't want to leave such a rare female in the midst of men who would not provide for her. He had never considered capturing a mate before. This morning the idea sounded appealing.

If he took her, she would be warm and fed and he would fill her belly with his seed until she swelled with his child. Instead she stood there trying to hide her desire while he felt it touch his mind. All of her companions were shaking with fear as they faced his men. But she displayed the type of courage that impressed him.

"We have gold."

That captured Aaron's attention. He aimed doubting eyes at the gray-haired man. These humans had promised gold in payment. It would seem they practiced deception.

"Come, sisters."

The women of the group came forward as they pulled on the small gold bands on their left hands. They left their offerings in the elderly man's hand. Aaron considered the meager pile of gold rings, but looked back at the woman who had not come forward. Her.

"Why do you not have gold to offer?"

His voice was as strong as his body. Leah felt her body tremble as the folds of her sex throbbed. She couldn't rip her eyes away from him. Her thoughts were full of him, almost like he was inside her mind.

"Sister Leah is widowed. Her ring was buried with her husband. That is our custom."

Aaron felt his staff grow painfully hard. He grinned as he looked the woman over.

"A female would be considered fair payment for the land."

Chapter Two

The humans reacted with frantic whispers. Aaron didn't care. He was only interested in *her* reaction. What he saw pleased him immensely. She lifted her chin and refused him with her eyes. The silent challenge fired his blood because she would pass that strength on to their sons.

"We do not sell our women."

"And we do not buy them," Aaron snapped his response out. "But we do barter for mates. If this woman is without a provider, I would bargain for her."

"That's barbaric." One of the older women pointed her long bony finger at him as she labeled him. Lucian stepped up beside him and Aaron considered the defiant form of Sister Leah again.

"Few women brave the harsh conditions of the Dritimti valley. Any woman that can make the journey is to be commended." At that, the older woman's face lifted with pride.

"You have little to provide for your people. Trade Sister Leah for the land. She will have her choice of mate from our warriors. That will leave you with one less mouth to feed this winter as well as settle your debt. Unless there is one of your own that has offered for her?"

"We have no unmarried members."

Aaron kept his eyes on the gray-bearded man. Victory was within his grasp and he would not leave without his prize. "Then I offer for her, unless she would choose another of my men."

"She would have a choice?"

Aaron gave the older woman a sharp nod in response and left it at that. Their customs were different but he wasn't leaving without Sister Leah.

Leah felt her temper rise. All around her there were sympathetic mutters but the hands that patted her shoulders began to push her forward. That big brute stood grinning as her own people offered her up to him in trade for their future! A future that was to have been her own. Instead, she was being fed to the local predators by her own herd so they could be safe.

The hands on her back became more forceful. Elder Samuel was giving her a smile while motioning her forward from behind the warrior's back. Her temper became boiling hot and she stepped forward with her chin held high. She would not be tossed out like some bleating lamb.

Elder Samuel caught her hand and pulled her closer. He leaned down as if to embrace her and whispered in her ear. "Bless your sacrifice, child. The kingdom of heaven shall reward you."

The Elder laid her hand into the warrior's huge one. Leah watched his fingers close around her own. It was a capture. Complete, secure, unbreakable. The warrior's dark eyes looked at her with an arrogance that Leah had never seen before. Over his shoulder his companion preened at her as well.

"It is done." His voice cracked open the morning air as his men gave a loud cheer from their mounts. The mutters of relief from her fellow pilgrims hardened her heart. Leah raised her chin higher. She refused to look back at the people she'd once called family.

The warrior turned and took her with him by their joined hands, then broke that contact as he swung up onto his giant mount's back. He held his hand out to her and Leah looked at the palm in indecision. The harsh round of gasps from the Fellowship made her thrust her hand into his with fury. No one cared what might become of her. Instead they were worried that she might keep them from their goals. At least this bunch of warriors look like they might eat better then she had in the last few weeks.

Her body left the ground as he pulled her up. Two solid hands grasped her waist to lift her so that her shoulder wouldn't take too much pressure. Leah turned her head to see the warrior's companion lifting her up to his friend.

She landed in front of the man and he immediately bound her to his body with a solid arm. His foreign smell wrapped around her senses as her body exploded with heat again. But Leah found herself battling the sharp sting of tears as she watched her people wave goodbye to her.

Some of them even had the nerve to look sorry. Leah fought off her tears as the animal beneath her turned and moved off in a powerful motion that made the wind slap her cheeks.

She must face forward.

* * * * *

"Welcome to Dritimti house." His lips grazed her ear as he leaned down to speak with her. Leah suddenly became hot as she tried to look at the immense but beautiful stone fortress carved into the canyon wall. The walls rose forty feet with the canyon.

She was pressed along his entire length and his strength surrounded her. His arm was draped across her and her breasts seemed to be swelling up to touch him. Leah suddenly hated her dress. She absolutely wanted to rip the thing off. She was too hot!

That arm moved across her nipples, making her gasp. The movement brought a moment of pleasure before the ache began to pulse from her nipples again. The motion of the horse between her legs made her ache far more.

But it was the feel of his engorged staff that held her thoughts the most. His arm secured her to his length and his staff was a solid rod pressed into her bottom. The folds of her sex became moist as she considered cradling that rod in the most primitive of fashions.

Leah struggled to clear her mind. She couldn't think such things! They were strangers, not only in name but also in species. What sort of man traded for a woman? He must have a harem full of consorts.

Aaron's lips lifted with pride as he rode into the inner yard of his home. Her strength raised his pride another notch. So did her desire. He knew her head was filled with his body filling hers. Riding her until she cried with pleasure.

"I am Aaron Dritimtar."

His lips nipped her ear again and then pressed a gentle kiss onto her neck. She wanted to lean her head back and let him kiss her neck even more, but scolded herself for wanton behavior. She must be in shock. There was no other reason for her to be so brazen with a man she'd met an hour past.

The strangest sensation came over her again and Leah recognized it from the moment she'd first stared into his eyes. It was like he was inside her head. Touching and examining her emotions. His presence communicated its amazing strength to her.

"Do not push your feelings aside. It is a natural thing to desire a man. To want his touch."

A vivid picture of him thrusting his staff into her body erupted in her brain and she did let her head fall back onto his chest. A tiny moan escaped her lips because the picture continued to move through her head with perfect clarity.

"I promise you, I will make that happen, Leah."

"Are you some kind of psychic?" Leah panted her question as she grasped for any tiny amount of self-control. The picture suddenly vanished and all she felt was the throb of denied hunger.

"We are empathic."

"Even with other species?"

"With humans, most definitely."

Leah felt her cheeks explode with color. He knew every last idea that had crossed her mind. His hand moved to cup her breast. Pleasure rippled down her body from the touch.

"Hum… I will remember that you like that."

Leah knew her eyes had to be as wide as saucers but that didn't keep her from arching her back and offering her breast to his touch.

They reached the stables and he pulled the animal to a stop. His friend appeared and lifted her from the saddle as

Aaron dropped to the ground beside her. He tipped her chin up to meet his eyes as he probed her face for information.

The strength Aaron found on her face pleased him. Strain stared out of her eyes but she returned his look without cowering.

"We will make fine sons together, Leah. Strong sons just like their mother."

His mouth caught hers and he parted her lips in a swift movement that demanded obedience. His tongue thrust forward to discover her tastes as she moved her lips in unison with his. There was nothing else to do. His smell was overpowering. Her body jumped forward and Leah used her own tongue to find his taste. He pulled back and his breath was rough as he smiled into her face.

The surrounding men laughed in low rumbles as many nodded their heads with approval.

"Best we finish this inside."

* * * * *

She had to be in shock. Leah stood in the middle of a bedchamber and twisted a part of her skirt. What was she doing?

Howard had never kissed her like that! Well, for that matter she'd never really dreamed about Howard thrusting into her.

There was something wrong with her. There had to be. It must be wicked to think about a man's…penis so vividly. It was sinful at the very least.

But it was making her wet as she stood there trying to figure out her new tendencies to daydream so vividly.

"Accept it, Leah. We are destined to be mated. The intensity is our calling to each other." Aaron came back into the room and aimed his dark eyes at her again. His stance was arrogant as he folded his arms across his chest.

"That makes no sense to me."

Her honestly pleased him. Aaron considered her a moment. "What I do not understand is that fabric covering your hair. Take it off."

Leah reached for her cap but stopped as she realized she was jumping to his commands. His face tightened as her action displeased him. Leah smiled back at him. She would not be his doormat.

"Aaron, stop bellowing at her like your warriors. You must learn to ask."

A woman came around the corner and aimed a wide smile at Leah. She was the most exotic thing Leah had ever seen. Her hair flowed down her back and her dress was the sheerest of fabrics that was hooked together under her breasts and draped behind her as she walked. Her large distended belly poked out and the pants she wore rode low on her hips. The outfit seemed to praise and frame her pregnant state perfectly. Leah looked again at the bare rounded belly that her child rested in. She couldn't imagine a more beautiful woman.

"Myra, if you bend me to your will, Leah will reject me for being too weak. Have mercy on me today and go find your mate."

Leah stared at Aaron in disbelief. His eyes had softened as he became the model of charming maleness.

He rubbed the mound of Myra's belly with a large hand while she gently stroked his cheek.

"A woman wants more than iron strength in her mate. Now be gone with you until Leah sends for you again." Myra waved her hand and smiled at Leah as Aaron frowned.

"Myra..."

"What? You would have your mating night without giving your mate the chance to bathe? Crude. What is wrong? Do you doubt that Leah will send for you?"

Aaron did doubt it. Humans were not as accepting as Tailarmarians about mating. The intensity of their mutual desire was all the confirmation he needed, but Leah might reject him out of fear. Staying with her now would prove the issue once and for all.

"What happens if I do not send for you?"

"You would have your choice of which warrior to ask into your bed."

So that was what he had meant by choice. Leah looked into his dark eyes and straightened her spine. It was him. Could only be him. She couldn't recall a single other warrior's face because she had been drawn to Aaron. There was no reason to debate the issue with her conscience. Lying to herself would be just as grave a sin as wantonness.

"Go. I will send for you."

Chapter Three

A completely different bliss captured Leah just five little minutes later. Myra pulled her across the room and through a doorway that led to a bathing chamber. A large steaming pool of water tempted her with its sparkling depths.

Leah hadn't had a hot bath in months. Her skin suddenly felt the weeks of grime and dirt that the trip had left on her. Myra began pulling pieces of her clothing off and Leah was most happy to help.

"What have you done to your hair?" Myra was trying to pull the entire bun off her head and Leah felt like giggling.

"There are pins in it."

"Well, it is a crime to hide your hair. Why do humans do this?"

"I don't know." Leah pulled the pins free and began to pull the braid out. She really didn't know why clothing had anything at all to do with faith. But today she was happy to pull her dress off and feel the air slip over her skin. She was still warm but not unbearably hot.

Myra waved her to the water and Leah stepped into it with pleasure. The pool was big enough for both woman but Myra simply kicked her long pants off and playfully dangled her feet in the water. The woman had a tiny pair of panties on and near-nudity didn't seem to bother her in the slightest.

"Do not do that."

"Do what?" Leah watched Myra with guarded eyes. The woman raised a single finger and waved it back and forth.

"Trust yourself and do not begin worrying about tonight. Aaron is a fine match. If he offered for you, he is quite taken with you."

"How would you know that?" Leah might be willing to admit they both seemed to want each other physically but emotions had never even entered her thinking. "We just met two hours ago."

"Ah... But warriors are very quick when they find their mates. It is a man's way, as my father told me." Myra reached for a small cake of soap and rubbed it over her feet. "Besides, if he doesn't please you tonight, you can choose another warrior tomorrow."

Leah raised her startled eyes towards Myra. "What do you mean?"

"Um... I forget you humans are different. You do things backwards. How can you swear pledge to a man before you have mated with him?"

Leah didn't know what to say. She still wasn't sure what Myra was talking about.

"Myra, do you mean you have relations with a man before you marry him?"

"No, goose. You have sex. How else do you know if he is the man who can drive your body to pleasure's edge?"

Well, that was clear enough. Leah watched Myra as the woman began to idly stroke her belly. She was exotic and sensuous. She just looked free. Leah envied her. The other woman wasn't awkward with her body. There was a grace there that Leah suddenly realized she'd been longing for her entire life. Myra had the ability to simply enjoy being a woman, without apologizing for the feelings that went along with her gender.

"Come out now, so your hair can dry. Don't make Aaron wait too long, there are only so many hours in a night."

Myra said it gleefully as she held a large piece of thick fabric up for Leah to dry herself with. There was an excitement about the coming night reflected on the girl's face and she simply didn't have any problem discussing sex. Leah's sisters back with the Fellowship would have passed out from sheer shock just because of their nudity.

Myra led her out into the main bedchamber again. Leah let her eyes rest on the bed this time. It was large and wickedly inviting. Thick covers were spread over it with pillows in the center. Myra giggled before pulling Leah along toward the fireplace.

"You see? Aaron has made a good choice. He knows what you are thinking about."

A deep carpet of some type was there and Myra pushed Leah down onto it. More giggles floated into the room as two women appeared in the doorway.

"Here are Faye and Syria." The two women immediately crossed the room and sat down. They both wore similar dresses with pants that left their bellies open to view. Myra began pulling a brush through Leah's hair as the two new arrivals took her hands and began shaping her fingernails. No one seemed to care that Leah was still as bare as the day she'd been born.

"Lucian is so envious that you chose Aaron over him." Faye sent Leah a naughty smile before the girl reached for a small jar and started to apply a colored paint to Leah's fingernails.

All three women continued to groom her as if it were the most natural of things. Leah simply let them. They painted her fingernails a deep gold color and then did the same to her toenails. Myra pulled the brush through her hair with endless strokes until it dried in silky wisps that hung down her back.

Myra began applying color to Leah's lips, but no one offered her any clothing. But then again, her skin was rosy and warm from the fire. Her breasts still tingled and Leah found her mind wandering to Aaron's body again. Howard had never let her touch him during sex; she wondered if Aaron would demand submission as well.

Leah didn't want to lie under Aaron without moving. Besides, she'd always thought Howard's rules very selfish. Why was she not allowed to touch? Howard often touched her breasts but she was forbidden to let her fingers wander over his chest.

A secret smile lifted her lips as Leah remembered the sculpted perfection of Aaron's arms. The way he'd moved that arm across her breasts sprang to mind and she watched her nipples draw into tight little buttons with just the memory.

Her companions giggled in response as they sat back to survey their work. They pulled Leah to her feet before they each embraced her.

"Welcome, sister."

"Be happy."

"And swear you will tell us everything tomorrow morning!"

Myra shepherded Faye and Syria out the doorway before she sent Leah a smile and departed the chamber. Leah was instantly aware of the slight crack and pop of the wood in the fireplace as it burned. She took small steps and noticed the chill of the stone floor as she left the carpet behind.

Her body was so very alive with each and every sensation. Suddenly she felt a surge of her own power and walked into the bathing chamber again. Large polished mirrors were mounted onto the walls. Stepping forward, Leah looked at her body with open curiosity.

She had never seen her entire body nude before. Curiosity made her turn to consider herself. She really didn't look so very different from Myra. Well, except for the pregnant tummy of course.

But that could change. Leah actually felt her face turn red as she considered just how she might go about getting into the same condition as Myra. She looked at her flat stomach and remembered the rather vivid picture of Aaron thrusting himself into her body.

The color on her face actually bled down her neck and onto her chest. Leah watched her breasts swell with just the idea of the man. She didn't know him but there was a deep awareness of the man inside her head.

Of course he'd said he was empathic. Which made her imagine some very naughty possibilities. Leah giggled because she didn't think she'd been considered "naughty" since she was five years old. But, well, the idea of sharing…intimate ideas through just her thoughts was…naughty.

It was such a tempting idea. Leah wandered away from the mirrors and back into the bedchamber as she battled her better judgment. Her entire life had been correct. Proper. Her few acts of boldness had always been kept tightly leashed inside her mind.

Now she'd met a man whom she couldn't hide those thoughts from. Leah moved closer to the bed and ran a hand lightly over the covers. All she had to do was summon the man.

"Your thoughts have already done that, Sister Leah."

Chapter Four

Leah almost shrieked, but tightened her lips to contain the sound. Her fingers ripped the top cover off the bed and pulled it in front of her body. Finding enough courage to be nude with the other women was one thing. With Aaron it was far more exposing.

He didn't like her decision to cover her body. Leah felt his disapproval as a small wave that brushed through her mind and had to fight the urge to laugh. Howard had *never* wanted to see her…bare! In fact he just might be turning in his grave at the mere idea that Leah was considering dropping her shield because Aaron didn't like it.

Her amusement confused him and Leah considered the way he held his jaw. He'd changed and bathed as well. His dark hair was pulled back from his face but still hung around his shoulders. He was the very image of strength. Leah considered his sculpted arms again as she found herself impatient to discover what his chest would look like.

His huge hands moved and her eyes followed them. The ties on the front of his vest took exactly three seconds to undo before he tossed the garment aside. Leah couldn't keep her gasp to herself. Instead she raised her eyes towards his face and caught his grin. She couldn't look at his bare chest. Really…she just didn't dare. Being bold was one thing. Foolishly flinging herself into utter madness was another.

Leah suddenly felt very stupid standing with a blanket gripped under her chin. The problem was, she had no idea what to do about it. She could wrap it around her body but that just seemed rather cowardly. She recalled the way Aaron had raised that dark eyebrow as she'd retreated from him and Leah decided she didn't like him thinking her spineless.

So she would just drop the thing and be done with it. Gravity made the action mercilessly quick. The second her fingers released the fabric, it dropped soundlessly to the floor.

Time became still and Leah listened to her own breaths. Each tiny movement made her skin tingle as Aaron took his time looking her over.

He stepped around her in a decreasing circle that made her heart rate triple. It reminded her of a lion as the animal hunted.

"You must be the boldest human I've ever met, Sister Leah." He was behind her and Leah turned to face him as she felt that same twist of betrayal from the Fellowship members.

"Don't call me sister. I'm not their sister any longer. My name is Leah." She watched his huge hand touch her hair and slip along the strands before his dark eyes rose to hers to demand submission.

"Don't resent their decision. It saved me from having to take you. I much preferred your acceptance."

"Take me?" There was far too much strength in the man. Leah felt her heart frantically pound as he twisted her hair around his fist and closed the gap between their bodies. She had been insane to think she could deal with a man like him. He was too big, too commanding. Too arrogant. But the trap was closed now as Aaron pulled her against his body and captured her mouth with his.

His hand controlled her head as his lips demanded complete surrender. He pushed past the remains of her restraint to explore her mouth as he caught her taste. His hand in her hair kept her submitting to the kiss as his other arm bound her to the hard length of his body.

Her fingers landed on his bare chest as Leah simply absorbed the power of the man. His kiss devoured her mouth and his mind seemed to be connected with her own as he groaned with approval.

"Touch me, Leah." His eyes aimed hot liquid command at her. "Touch me the way you wanted to out there when you saw me."

Leah spread her hands over his chest and felt the heat spike straight through her center. Her breasts ached as she rubbed the tightened nipples against his hard chest. The contact soothed her yearnings and she did it again as she felt the folds of her sex become swollen and moist.

Aaron lifted her off her feet and simply tossed her onto the huge surface of the bed. A large smile covered his face as he watched her bounce in a tangle of legs. Leah ended propped on her elbows with her legs askew and Aaron's eyes locked onto her breasts with their tightly puckered nipples. She shifted under his scrutiny as uncertainty crossed her thoughts again.

His hands undid his pants and he stepped out of them. Leah felt her uncertainty melt clean away as heat consumed her. He was completely magnificent. His legs were sculpted and molded like his arms. And his chest was wide and covered with dark hair.

But her eyes stared at his staff and the blunt proof of his arousal. Leah should have realized by how huge his hands were that this part of him would also be extremely large. His rod stood away from his body, stiffly declaring his intentions. Leah pressed her thighs together as she considered just where he wanted to put that weapon.

"Why do you show me a virgin's fear?" The bed moved as he dropped down beside her. It almost felt like he was pouncing on her but there was more control to the action. Still, Aaron had her drawn along his body's length and her thighs had opened before Leah found the strength to move away.

"We do not hurt our mates here, Leah." His voice was rough and low as he pressed a single row of tiny bites along her neck. Leah arched to give him move skin to nip. Sensation erupted from the tiny touches and traveled straight down to her sex, making it throb in rhythm with her heart rate.

"You're just very large…umm…everywhere." His huge hand landed on her belly as he moved it across her lower abdomen from hip to hip. His eyes lifted back to hers as he brought his hand up to cup her breast.

"You are not tiny. Your hips are broad and wide. There is no reason for fear but I will summon a midwife if you would like her opinion."

"What?" Leah felt her brows draw together because she had never heard of such a thing before in her life! "Did you say a midwife?"

Aaron almost laughed because she was so adorable. "Who else would know about such matters? But Myra has seen you. If she felt we were mismatched she would have come to me with her concern and brought a midwife to inspect you. Why are human females allowed to be so ignorant about common matters?"

"The marriage bed is considered extremely private."

"Allowing a woman to be mated with a male who will produce too large a child for her to carry is cruel. If you were too small I would have seen you presented to my men instead of in my bed. A Tailarmarian warrior does not willingly let a woman suffer." He smoothed his hand over her belly again. "I would put my own desire aside if you were a tiny female."

Hearing it put in such plain terms made Leah feel rather cherished. The emotion was odd but it settled into her brain and refused to leave. It would seem that Aaron considered her health more important than her modesty. But his staff was still twice the size of Howard's. Leah honestly hadn't known they grew so large, at least on humans.

Aaron tipped her head up and locked her eyes with his. "I brought you to my bed for pleasure, not pain." Cupping her breast again, he rolled the nipple between his fingers and listened to her tiny gasp. "The time for talking is done."

That same coil of fear snaked along her skin again but Leah resisted its pull. Her eyes wandered over his chest and simply accepted his superior strength. It was a fact that could not be changed but he wasn't dominating her. Instead, he was bringing her his strength as a symbol of his worthiness to become her mate.

His mouth captured a nipple and Leah fell back under the assault. She'd never dreamed that a man's mouth might be so hot or that her own skin could survive such a level of heat. His tongue flicked over her nipple, making it pulse and quiver with sensation.

One hand traveled back down her belly but it didn't stay there. Instead he covered her sex with it and used one finger to part her folds.

"What are you doing?" Leah jerked up from the bed in shock but he pressed her back down immediately as his face drew into a frown.

"Leah, did you have a mate or not?" Aaron couldn't keep the frustration from his voice. The woman dreamed vividly about his possessing her but she seemed to have less knowledge than his virgin sister. He deliberately stroked her folds with his finger and watched her face register surprise. He stroked her again and gently circled her center as she fell back into his embrace.

"I've never…felt this….before." Leah felt her eyes slide shut as pure sensation centered under his finger. Her hips began to press up as she sought something but she didn't know exactly what it was.

That finger didn't stop. Instead it settled over her sex and rubbed until Leah felt her body draw into a single tight ache that exploded, sending a wave of pleasure coursing through her.

Aaron waited for her to recover as he watched her face. The sweet smell of her release caused his organ to pulse with renewed hunger. Her sex was wet and ready for him but there was more to pleasing a mate than just her physical response. He wouldn't ride her until she demanded he do it. "Your mate was a selfish man, Leah."

Her blue eyes snapped open to consider his face. "Any man who simply mounts his female is less than an animal. Even a stallion takes the time to entice his mare. Now come and touch me. Exactly the way you have been thinking about doing."

It was another command but it was the most liberating thing Leah had ever heard. Suddenly she felt like the chains that had bound her were unlocked and she was simply free to be herself. She was impatient to begin.

Spreading her hand over his chest was amazing. Leah felt the pulse of life that radiated through his thick muscles. She found his nipples and felt them bead under her fingers. His dark eyes watched her intently, and that made her bolder. Leaning forward, she covered one nipple with her mouth and gently sucked on it. His sharp intake of breath fired her and she trailed tiny kisses across his chest until she found his opposite nipple. His huge hand lifted her onto his body as he rolled onto his back, granting her the liberty to explore his body to her contentment.

Their legs were tangled and Leah felt the pulse of his hard staff. The organ was pressed between their thighs and she moved away slightly as her hand went searching for it. He'd touched her sex. Maybe she should return the favor.

Closing her hand around his weapon, Leah delighted in his stiff gasp. Aaron had curled his fingers into the bedding beneath him as his hips thrust up into her grasp. She gently stroked his length and considered the harsh sounds she drew from Aaron's chest. Her own sex became increasingly hot as she touched his staff.

Suddenly the picture she'd had of him trusting his penis into her absorbed her thoughts. The organ in her hand jumped and pulsed with the vision as Leah felt her breath become small pants.

Aaron surged up from the bed and caught her head in his hand while his mouth captured her mouth. There weren't any boundaries between them and Aaron thrust his tongue into her mouth with the same rhythm as her vision. His body covered her as he moved her thighs apart to cradle his hips.

Her flesh opened as the tip of his ridged length bluntly probed for entry, making her gasp. "Shhh." His lips gently moved over her neck as his hips thrust forward again. This time Leah felt a stab of pain as her passage stretched for his length. Her body ached but she tipped her hips up for his next thrust. His hips flexed as he sent his rod into the hilt and she moaned as her flesh screamed.

In an instance, her body became a demanding inferno. Leah met the dark eyes of her companion, his face reflected fierce possession. He dropped a hard kiss onto her mouth as his hips began to thrust with a steady rhythm that made her moan with sheer pleasure.

Her body became taut again as sensation seemed to grip her in claws that began to crush her 'til everything shattered into pure bliss. Aaron groaned with her but he pulled out of her body before he gasped with release. He collapsed onto her and caught just enough of his weight with his arms to keep her from being crushed.

He hadn't let her have his seed and that confused her. The only purpose of the marriage bed was for children.

His hand began stroking her face as his eyes probed her. "Why do you worry?" His voice was harsh and rough but his eyes were as sharp as a blade.

"This will not give me a child."

Aaron rolled onto his back and pulled her with him. His hands stroked her body in long, powerful touches that made her skin warm.

"You must give me permission for that."

Shifting against his body, Leah tried to find some small distance from the man. She really needed to understand him but she couldn't concentrate with his body so close.

"Be still, Leah." His warm hands continued to stroke her back and even the curve of her bottom as he refused to let her move away. Leah simply surrendered. She liked lying there on his bare skin. He smelled so powerful.

She was definitely a sinful creature, but when she made it to the heavenly gates, Leah was certainly going to have a confession worth listening to.

Chapter Five

Her slumber was deep and relaxed, but Leah willingly left it behind as her nose caught the aroma of food. Her stomach suddenly growled low and deep as she rubbed her eyes and tried to think.

Another one of those long strokes from Aaron's hands traveled along her hip as the bed shifted. A tray of steaming food was sitting between them on the bed as he lounged on his side watching her. It was still dark and the fire had died into a bed of glowing embers.

He selected a piece of meat and offered it to her. Leah raised a hand but he immediately pulled the food out of her reach. He laughed as she sat up.

The hand with the food came back to her face and the aroma gained another low grumble from her stomach. "Eat." Leah raised her hand and the food left again.

"From my hand, Leah."

"Are you playing some game?" Her hunger made her grouchy.

Aaron smiled widely. "Yes. Why not?"

Why not, indeed. Leah considered the amusement twinkling in his eyes and smiled. "And if I don't play nicely?"

"You will pay a forfeit."

He offered the food again and Leah nipped it out of his hand. There was something rather arrogant about him demanding to feed her but it was also slightly erotic. As

Aaron fed her, she let her eyes roam over his chest. As the last of the food disappeared between them, Leah boldly licked his fingers and smiled. "So, now what?"

"Dessert." He said it in a husky tone that she remembered instantly. Aaron pushed her back as his hands spread her thighs apart but he didn't mount her. Instead his head hovered over her sex as his tongue gently lapped her flesh.

Leah frantically tried to escape. The sensation was too sharp. Too absolutely unthinkable! He simply pressed her back onto the bed and raised an eyebrow.

Coward or not, this was too much. "You can't do this."

In response his head lowered and his mouth caught her folds as he sucked the sensitive flesh into his mouth. Leah fell back as her hips thrust up helplessly, the waves of sensation becoming too powerful to resist.

"But you like it, don't you Leah?" His tongue flicked over her sex as she moaned in despair. "Just tell me to stop."

Her hips jerked up in search of his lips and she ground her teeth together as he simply smiled and flicked her sex again. "You are arrogant."

"Yes, but I know how to please my mate." His mouth took her sex again and this time he applied more pressure to the task. Leah felt her body draw tight but he released her sex and tongued it with quick licks until the tension ebbed. Then he sucked her flesh back into his mouth and took her to the edge of sensation again.

Aaron held her in the cycle for an endless time. Leah clawed at the bedding as she twisted under his mouth. She couldn't decide where one sensation began and another ended. Her body became a single pulse of feeling that consumed every conscience thought.

His mouth hovered over her as his eyes took in her surrender. Aaron smiled with wolfish arrogance. Being able to bring a mate to such pleasure was an accomplishment and he enjoyed the emotions that were bleeding out of her mind into his. It was a perfect blending of their genders, proving his decision right to claim her into his bed.

Her eyes snapped open and locked with his as he aimed his gaze at her. Aaron rubbed her belly as she watched him. "I want to put my seed inside you, Leah."

Everything was spinning out of control and Leah didn't care! Aaron floated around inside her head and all she felt was cherished. Tears stung her eyes because Leah couldn't ever remember feeling so wanted before. Aaron wanted a child but he wanted her as well. What the man wanted was a family.

He played her body like a master, yet he sat with a hard face that waited for her permission. He wanted her to want him just the way he wanted her.

"Come to me Aaron." Her voice was deep and husky, Leah almost didn't recognize it. Suddenly she decided she didn't need to understand anything. She was drunk on her own power. Aaron covered her body and she watched him smile in triumph.

His hips thrust forward with solid purpose. Her body immediately stretched to accommodate him again. Leah didn't need to remember her vision of him riding her, the reality was far more intoxicating. She lifted her hips for his thrusts and clasped him between her thighs.

He gave her his seed a split second after her body began to shudder with the pleasure. There were endless waves of sensation that carried both of them in their wake. Even when it ebbed Aaron pulled her along his body and secured her to his side.

Looking ahead had never served her so well.

"Someone is still sleeping." Three voices erupted into giggles as Leah snapped her eyes open. The warm covers of the bed were pulled off her as Myra appeared by her head.

"Come on, lazy! These two are driving me to near death with their excitement. Up! Up! Do you really want Aaron's ego to become too large?" Myra pulled Leah off the bed and shepherded her toward the bathing room again. "Let him think you will sleep the day away and there will be no living with the man!"

Faye and Syria collapsed into another round of giggles and Leah joined them, even if her face was turning red. The morning after her marriage to Howard no one would look her in the eye, as if it were some great shame. Leah decided she far preferred the Tailarmarian view on the subject of marriage relations.

"We must hurry. The warriors are all waiting for their chance to impress you."

Faye dumped a pitcher of water over Leah's head. Wiping the water from her face, Leah aimed confused eyes at Myra.

"Why would they be waiting for me?"

Faye dropped soap into Leah's hair and began to wash it for her. Being bathed by someone would take a little getting used to.

Myra smiled with glee as she held up a dress similar to her own. It was pale blue with gold shot through it. "You have until sundown to choose another warrior for your bed or accept Aaron as your mate."

"Only one day?" Somehow, Leah had thought she might have a little longer to make such a permanent decision.

"Warriors must not be given time to fight over a woman. It would cause trouble in the community. It is best this way. Besides, if Aaron has not captured your passion, you should choose another."

The two girls pulled her out of the water as Leah considered Myra's words. There were so many differences here, her head was spinning as she tried to keep them straight.

"How long do you have to choose a mate in your world?" Faye asked the question as she used a towel to dry Leah's hair.

"Well, my late husband spoke to my father. Howard did sit at Sunday dinner with us a few times."

Faye looked at her with pity. "You were life-promised to a man who had never touched you?"

"Well, yes." All three girls muttered with sympathy as they guided Leah into the strange clothing. They brushed her lips with color and traced her eyes with darker color.

Leah had been surrounded with sympathy on her wedding day too, but it had been so very different. These women helped her to display her sexuality instead of suppress it. Turning toward the mirror, Leah marveled at her transformation. She was exotic and sensual. Her hair was tumbling down her back as the dress moved with her to grant teasing peeks at her belly.

"Well, I hope there is food involved." Her companions laughed and pulled her along with them.

The front courtyard was filled with people. Laughter drifted up as they talked. Music filtered to her ears as well and Leah noticed musicians gathered in one area of the yard where a shade canopy was set up.

But the warriors captured her complete attention. There had to be at least two hundred of the huge men present. They were all together and their deep voices rose and fell as they jostled one another.

The entire group fell silent as Leah stepped out into the sunshine. She felt their eyes move over her body with blatant appreciation. But then her mind simply filled with Aaron's emotions. Leah searched for him as she considered the unease she felt projecting from his mind.

His face was completely emotionless when Leah found him. Aaron nodded his head in greeting but kept his face smooth and free from expression.

Oh, the man was arrogant. Leah let a tiny smile cover her face as she considered the way he kept his nervousness to himself. The rest of the men sent up a collective groan and several slapped Aaron on the back. His stiff composure cracked as his lips lifted into a wolfish smile.

"There will be no living with him now." Myra tried to scold her but Leah was simply ridiculously happy.

The entire group of men began to engage in games of strength and skill. Women mingled with them, but all the ones who walked among the men wore black. All the woman talking around Leah wore bright colors that sparkled with metallic accents. Pointing towards the women, Leah looked at Myra.

"Why do they wear black?"

"Those are maidens. The dull color reminds the men to treat them appropriately."

Leah understood. The games these warriors played gave the women the chance to see prospective mates. The girls in black floated among the men, watching them. The entire thing was done in full view of the community. One or two men even pressed light kisses onto the girls, but it never went beyond the carefree touch of flirting.

Leah suddenly felt very envious of the girls in black. She had almost chewed her fingernails clean off when she'd met Howard the first time. Unmarried members of the fellowship were never permitted to socialize before an engagement was arranged. Being allowed to interact often with these huge men would certainly make a Tailarmarian woman more at ease when it came to matters of intimacy.

Celebration permeated the air, and Leah felt herself join the emotion. She turned to Myra and grinned. "Just where is that food you promised me?"

The day turned into an endless festival of games and entertainment. Happiness surrounded her as the community gave her their welcome. She wasn't simply a possession to these people, instead she was an addition to their lives. Joy was openly expressed, as was affection. It was a freedom that Leah had never witnessed before.

It was barely afternoon when Leah stopped enjoying the games. Aaron was doing his best to defeat his friend in a wrestling match and all she could think about was how she'd rather have him wrapping his muscular arms around her instead. The past night had turned her into a wanton for certain.

Aaron dug his legs into the ground and tried to push his opponent over. Leah watched his muscles tense and her mouth went dry. Her nipples actually drew into tight little buds as she looked at his hands.

The things he could do with those hands made her tremble.

Aaron landed on his backside a second later and sent a furious look at her. His eyes aimed pure fire at her as he suddenly filled her mind. Leah felt a naughty little smile lift her mouth. She'd forgotten the man could read her emotions. Aaron rose to his full height with a menacing frown on his face. Leah let her smile grow larger. He wasn't really mad. She could feel his hunger.

In fact, Leah let her eyes slip down his body 'til she found the rather large bulge of his staff. She looked back up to find his black eyes attempting to reprimand her.

"I do not like losing."

Leah looked back at the growing bulge in his pants before she shrugged her shoulders. "I noticed."

"Aaron, I protest! You have clearly not fed your woman's appetite." Lucian stepped forward and tried to capture Leah's waist.

Aaron sent her a wink before he cut off his friend's movements. "She would be starving had you tried to feed her."

The two huge men charged each other like bulls and immediately began wrestling again. Leah stumbled back as she giggled with the rest of the women. Aaron made short work of the competition this time. He tossed the other man over and stood while the surrounding warriors cheered him.

Lucian grinned as he sat up. "Put some of that strength to work on your mate. She is making the rest of us pity her."

The blatant sexual joking made her face turn scarlet but Leah smiled as well. Her clothing was suddenly too hot again and she wanted it off her skin. Aaron stood among his men and waited. Myra's words floated through her memory.

It was her choice. Leah couldn't even look at the other warriors because her body only noticed one. She let her eyes slip over his arms again and she smiled as she saw his strength.

Lifting her hand, she held it out to her warrior.

Leah found herself wrapped in his arms a second later. Her feet left the ground and the rest of the warriors cheered Aaron on as he boldly walked away with her in his arms. The wide hallways of the house passed in a blur as Aaron set a determined pace towards their bedchamber.

Once again he dropped her onto the bed and stood watching her. This time Leah rose to her knees and slowly undid the top part of her dress. She let it hang on her breasts as she watched his black eyes focus on her chest.

A surge of power made her roll her shoulder until the garment fell free. Leah wanted this man and by bringing her into his world, he'd granted her the ability to take him. It was so completely freeing.

"Do you still think that you lost?" That wolfish smile covered Aaron's face at Leah's question, his hands worked quickly to unfasten his pants. Leah watched his erect staff thrust out at her.

Reaching forward she curled her fingers around his staff. The organ throbbed in her grasp as Aaron stiffly pulled his breath in. Leaning forward she let her lips catch the tip of it as she used her tongue to flick over the flesh.

"Nay, I won. For certain I have won." Whatever else he might have said died as she took him into her mouth. Aaron grasped her head and groaned. She was truly a fit mate. Stroking his hands through her hair he pulled her head back before he spilled his seed.

Pushing her onto his bed Aaron tugged her pants down before he let his fingers roam over her belly and toward the little nub at the top of her sex. She shuddered against him and he dropped his mouth onto hers in demand.

Sensation spun her out of control and Leah rejoiced in it. Aaron joined their bodies together as he filled her head. It became more than the quest for a son. Instead there blossomed the foundation for a family that would grow from their joined souls.

Beyond the boundaries of society there always lurked the permeate hand of fate. Destiny bound souls together with a force that couldn't be denied.

And Leah looked forward to it.

About the author:

I writes to reassure myself that reality really is survivable. Between traffic jams and children's sporting schedules, there is romance lurking for anyone with the imagination to find it.

I spend my days making corsets and petticoats as a historical costumer. If you send me an invitation marked formal dress, you'd better give a date or I just might show up wearing my bustle.

I love to read a good romance and with the completion of my first novel, I've discovered I am addicted to writing these stories as well.

Dream big or you might never get beyond your front yard.

I love to hear what you think of my writing: Talk2MaryWine@hotmail.com.

Mary welcomes mail from readers. You can write to her c/o Ellora's Cave Publishing at 1337 Commerce Drive, Suite 13, Stow OH 44224.

Also by Mary Wine:

Dream Shadow

RAPTOR'S PREY

Delilah Devlin

Chapter One

I dreamt of him. My dark warrior.

He pulled me from a deep REM cycle with the force of his summons. Standing with my toes sinking into heat, I found myself on a ridge of shifting sand—red as Mars and hot as the fury of his gaze. And I was naked. Again.

Rays from an orange sun beat down on my skin. Wind lifted my hair and brushed it against my nipples. Even knowing he was angry, my stomach tightened and my breasts grew heavy with desire. His hard, golden-eyed gaze raked my body, pinning me like a rabbit between his namesake's talons. And yet, I longed to thread my fingers through his long, dark hair and drag his mouth toward mine. He had taught me to crave the taste of his lips.

"I shouldn't be dreaming," I said, breathless with anticipation of what new sensual wonder we would explore.

"Are you?" His deep voice rumbled, and yet his lips didn't move. He stood still as a pillar, naked as I was. Aroused.

"I must be. How else am I here with you?" Emboldened by the thought that within my dream I was free to explore my fantasy, I reached to touch his face. He didn't move as I brushed his sun-warmed skin and feathered a light touch over his high cheekbones and sharply defined nose. My fingers paused at his mouth, and then I swept my thumb over his lower lip and pressed inside. The tip of his tongue stroked my finger and I gasped, imagining its moist heat teasing the hardening points of my breasts.

His expression didn't change, and his gaze didn't leave my face as though gauging my responses. The calculating gleam in his brown eyes gave me a moment's pause.

"If this is a dream, then why don't you give me what I seek?" he asked. "What harm would there be?"

My hands fell to his shoulders and I kneaded the muscles there, fascinated by his strength. "If I tell you, you won't call me back to you."

"Do you think your password is all I desire from you?" His gaze swept over me, scorching me everywhere it paused—my mouth, my breasts, my belly, the juncture of my thighs.

Heat licked at my loins and my glance fell to his erection. "No, but surrendering to you would give you power."

"I would not abuse that power any more than I would abuse the gift of your body." A strong hand lifted my chin. His steady, hypnotic gaze seemed to pull me closer and made me flush with warmth. "Have I caused you pain? Haven't I fulfilled your fantasies?"

I ignored his questions, knowing my blush colored my face and breasts. He had taught me to find pleasure centers in my body I'd never known existed. "I've watched you, while you sleep in your suspension chamber." The admission was difficult even knowing this wasn't real—he wasn't real. Unable to meet his stare while I confessed my intrusive behavior, my gaze dropped to his broad, bronzed shoulders.

"I wondered if your body is as powerful as it appears." Hesitantly, I smoothed my palms over his warm, lightly furred chest and felt the muscles beneath my hands spasm. "Am I only dreaming your body is this incredibly hard?"

He wasn't unaffected. His chest rose and fell more quickly now. I was pleased my touch inflamed him as well.

With my hands, I measured the breadth of his shoulders and followed the thickly corded muscles of his arms downward. "You've led me, invoking my responses each time we've met, but this is my dream. I would know if everything is as hard as it appears." I noted his hands clenched at his sides, and I smiled up at him. "Will my touch break your control? You've teased me, lured me to the edge, and left me wanting. Can you resist me?"

I spread my hands on the defined ridges spanning his taut, narrow waist. Then I glided downward, curving my fingers to rake the silky arrow of hair that broadened to frame his immense manhood.

As I encircled his cock, his head fell back and his jaw clenched. Feeling powerful, I stepped closer to press my aching breasts to his chest and slide my tongue along the crest of his shoulder. He smelled of exotic incense and warm, musky man. My hands glided up and down on his smooth, hard cock.

Suddenly, with a movement that left me gasping, his hands closed around my waist and he lifted me high. I was exultant. Now, he would come inside me. Now, I would learn the promises his body had hinted at—if only in my dreams. I clutched his shoulders and wrapped my legs around his waist, and he lowered me, impaling my moist flesh.

I moaned and his mouth curved into a grim smile. His hands shifted to my buttocks—but he held me still, while my vagina wept in anticipation of a vigorous coupling.

"Why won't you move?" My body ached for fulfillment and I tightened my inner muscles around him.

"Your password." He clenched his teeth. "Give me what I want and I will finish this."

The request jarred. But I was so lost in my flaming need, I ignored the warnings clamoring in my mind. "This is my dream, my mind. I command you to take me."

His eyes narrowed and his hands were hard steel bands anchoring me to his hips. "Do you?" His expression challenged me to prove myself.

I faltered and a prickle of unease crept up my spine to lift the hairs on the back of my neck. Khalim Padja of the Raptor clan, a Tirrekh warrior and the man embedded in my body, was a murderer and a traitor to the Dominion. But what else might he be? Was he somehow making this dream happen?

He'd been brought aboard my small transport ship, a cargo so precious and dangerous the governor of the outlying fortress had refused to hold him long enough for a military transport to arrive. I'd been promised a fortune to deliver him to the Dominion courts and assured his suspension chamber would hold him safely.

Before I slept in my own chamber for the duration of the month-long journey, I'd inspected his, and checked to be certain the sleep inducements would last. But I'd been unable to resist a thorough inspection of his body as he lay inside.

I was a woman who spent too many months alone aboard my ship in deep space, my imagination my only company. And his body was beautiful. What harm would there be to look and stroke my hands over his still flesh?

And I had, much to my shame.

But this dream was too vivid. Even for the elaborate fantasies I often built to while away the days and weeks of my travels. His scent, his warm skin, his hard hands. His cock that stretched me—achingly.

"I'm not dreaming, am I?" I asked, afraid of the answer and his knowing smile, and ashamed of my body's creamy response. My lips trembled and his gaze fell to my mouth. I closed my eyes.

"No. You're not dreaming." His mouth descended on mine and I was lost to his mastery. His firm lips pressed mine and his tongue stabbed between my lips, sweeping over the roof of my mouth, gliding along my tongue, inciting me to suck.

I moaned and my traitorous body released a fresh wash of liquid arousal.

He growled deep in his throat, and his hands squeezed my ass and lifted me, and then pushed me down—moving me, finally, up and down his thick shaft.

Mindless now, I threw my head back and clutched his shoulders, my nails digging into his skin as I climbed the precipice. "Don't stop," I begged. "Please, harder."

His body shuddered between my legs, and his hips joined our dance, working in contradiction to the hands that directed my hips, pulling out as he lifted me, thrusting deeper as he ground my cunt down his length. Deeper, harder, faster—until I shattered. My long, keening cry ripped through the stillness around us.

When I opened my eyes, my head lay upon his shoulder, rising and falling with his ragged breaths.

Drowsy, sated, I was less afraid and less believing because I'd never experienced such depth of passion in my life. I smoothed my cheek on his warm skin. "If this isn't a dream, then what is it?"

"A possession. You are mine."

Irritation cooled my body. I unwrapped my legs from his waist, and he lowered me until my feet sank into the sand. Although my knees trembled, I fisted my hands and stepped away from him. "I'm no man's possession. This hallucination ends now."

"The choice isn't yours." His words, not spoken, echoed around me, inside me.

I pointed my finger at him. "You're my prisoner."

His arms folded over his chest. "Am I?" Again, a small, mocking smile curved the corners of his lips.

"Damn you and your questions! I won't let you change the course of this ship. I'll never give you my password," I cried out, angry and frightened. Surely this was only a nightmare. "Leave me."

The sun glinted behind him, a corona so bright I raised my arm to shield my eyes. When I opened them again, he was gone and a hawk perched upon my arm. The bird sat so calmly, I wasn't alarmed. "Is this a trick?" I shouted over the endless red peaks.

The bird stirred, drawing my attention. His golden, unblinking gaze held mine for a long moment.

"Are you his, as well?" I dared to lift my hand and stroke the brown and black feathers on his head. "Such a proud creature. You know you're beautiful." I stroked his chest and the action calmed my heart. "I shouldn't be dreaming. This is his doing, isn't it?"

His talons pricked me and I raised my arm, hoping he'd take flight into the aqua sky. His wings unfurled from his body and a gust of wind arose. He flapped, his talons now digging painfully into my skin to keep his perch, then he flapped again, and his tawny wingtips fluttered across my nipples. The sensation was ephemeral, but erotic, tightening the tips into buds, and I gasped—

Andromeda O'Keefe choked. The aspirating tube had retracted and she was drowning.

"You're coming out of suspension too quickly," a deep voice, disembodied, came from beyond her gel-filled capsule.

She opened hers eyes, blinking against the light shining down through the clear hatch of her chamber and met a golden-eyed gaze. She recognized him instantly. Her prisoner was free!

She fought the urge to inhale more of the suspension gel and searched with her hands for the hood latch inside her chamber.

Before her hand connected with the latch, the panel popped and the dark-haired man tossed the hatch back and reached inside. A large, rough-skinned hand slid beneath her shoulders, another beneath her thighs, and he lifted her easily from her warm cocoon to the cooler air on the bridge of her ship.

Andromeda sucked in air and gagged. He knelt to lay her on the floor. Once her chest quieted, she realized her predicament. She was naked and wet, lying on her back with her prisoner Khalim Padja, also naked, standing over her. He held out his hand, palm up. Not an offer of aid. His implacable expression demanded she accept.

As she didn't have a choice, she laid her hand in his and he drew her up. Her legs threatened to buckle beneath her from disuse after her slumber. He'd obviously been free longer for he seemed to suffer no such weakness, and he slid an arm around her waist, pulling her close.

Still coated with a thin film of suspension gel, her body aligned with his from breast to hip. Disturbingly, her mind recognized they fit together well—just as they had in her dreams. Her body seemed just as accustomed to his embrace, and she found herself instantly, embarrassingly, aroused. Would he notice how tightly her nipples puckered against his chest? She tilted her head back to gauge his reaction.

A muscle in his jaw flexed and his nostrils flared. The heat in his dark gaze seared her. He'd worn the same expression in her dreams each time he'd seduced her. Oh God! How could she have known what he looked like when aroused, unless they really had shared those experiences? She shuddered, fear and desire warring inside her body and mind.

His hand reached toward her face and she flinched.

"First, we bathe." He smoothed back the strands of hair sticking to her cheek. "Then we'll talk."

Even his deep, rumbling voice was the same. With her heart pounding from the realization she was at the mercy of a murderer, Andromeda's mind raced. "The shower stall is in my quarters." She backed away from his hold. "I'll show you." Turning, she led the way down a narrow passage to her small, spartan room.

If she could get him inside the shower first and the door automatically entrapped him, she might have time to reach the weapons in the drawer beneath her bed. She couldn't hope to overpower a warrior without armament.

Conscious of the tall, muscular body following a step behind her, she sighed with relief when she reached her room. She'd forgotten how small it was, until she realized he would have to pass between her narrow bed and the storage cabinets to reach the shower—and she blocked the way.

She stopped in front of the shower, pressed the button to open the stall, and then looked over her shoulder. "If you'll step inside..."

"After you," he said, his gaze boring into hers.

Andromeda pressed her lips together in frustration and nodded, then stepped inside, silently cursing. She hoped he wouldn't poke around her things and find her cache of weapons while she bathed.

She needn't have worried. Her breath caught on a gasp, when he joined her inside the stall and the door slid shut.

Chapter Two

Khalim enjoyed his woman's discomfort. Her back stiffened, almost as quickly as her nipples had when they'd grazed his chest. More intriguing, her shapely bottom quivered where his erection pressed against her. He'd conditioned her body well to accept the forced intimacy.

He reached over her shoulder and pressed the button to start the shower, having already acquainted himself with the functions of most of the conveniences and machinery aboard her ship. The nozzles erupted with a soft misting of warm water all around them.

"Is this really necessary?" she asked, her voice sounding strained.

"I can't have you getting into mischief. For the time being, we'll do everything together." His lips curved when her body stiffened further and her shoulders rose and fell with angry breaths.

"The password. You've been after that all along," she snapped.

He detected an underlying hurt. Perhaps a previous betrayal. He filed that knowledge away. "And you," he replied, infusing silk and steel into his voice. "I've been after you, as well." He tapped the soap dispenser, and lather joined the water jetting from all nozzles, except those aimed at their heads.

She snorted. "You planned to seduce me into changing the course of this ship, then what? Kill me?"

She was adorably, irritatingly, intense. "I've much more interesting things planned for you." He braced apart his legs and grasped her hips, pulling her tightly to his groin.

Her body shivered—but not from fear. Her nipples rose to meet his palm, fitting into the hollow of his hand. "I won't give my password to you."

"You're wrong. You'll give me everything I want." He dipped a hand into the shampoo well and foam squirted onto his palm.

When he smoothed it over her head, she jerked away—or as far as she could in the cramped stall. "I can do that myself. And keep your hands—and other parts—to yourself!"

He pulled her against his body again and continued to wash her hair. He counted it a victory when she remained rigid—but pressed intimately to his belly. "You enjoy it more when I wash you. Remember?" He closed his eyes and summoned the vision of his underground keep on Qihar-Jadiid. Although aware of his hands massaging her scalp in her cramped shower, he brought Andromeda to the large, oval bathing pool in his quarters.

Instantly her body relaxed, becoming liquidly pliable, as she leaned back against his chest. In this dream-share state she always eagerly accepted his lead. He understood her subconscious refused to believe their travels were real—therefore, she could indulge in fantasy.

They reclined on the edge of the shallow pool. She was seated on his lap, her head lay upon his shoulder. Light from phosphor-pots illuminated the gold flecks swimming in the ruby-glass walls of his abode. Her body shimmered in the golden light.

He dipped a hand into the pool and scooped up water to rinse her hair, enjoying the lazy labor and admiring the sheen from the red-gold hidden among the dark strands.

"I remember this place. We were here before," she whispered.

He fit his palm to her small breast, cupping it, and then kneading it gently. He slid an arm around her taut belly to pull her deeper into the cradle of his thighs, until his cock rested in the crevice of her buttocks. "Yes, I made love to you in the center of the pool, and afterwards—"

"You brought me to completion with your hands, although I begged you to give me your cock." Her voice held a sulky note.

He nuzzled her cheek. When her head fell to the side exposing her creamy neck, he was satisfied she didn't bear him a grudge. "Will you give me your password?" He tongued her earlobe, and then bit it.

"Bastard." Her words lacked true outrage. Her body was aroused by the memory from their previous dream-share; her trembling abdomen told him so.

"Tell me what you want." His fingers dipped between her legs to flutter the folds guarding her feminine portal. "I will give it to you."

"Come inside me," she begged, her voice thin and needy.

He sank a long, probing finger into the hot, quivering flesh of her pussy.

She sighed and spread her legs farther apart. Then her head rolled on his shoulder. "No…not again. " She ground her buttocks against his cock. "I want this."

He plucked her nipple and her knees rose, encouraging him to delve deeper. "Which is it to be?"

Her body writhed against his, caressing his belly and lap. "Your cock...*please.*"

He shifted her off his lap and rolled, until her back rested against the edge of the pool and her arms stretched along the rim. With his hands beneath her buttocks, he lifted her hips above the water and lowered his face between her legs. He lapped at her cunt, alternating between stabbing as deeply as he could reach and rubbing the flat of his tongue over the hard knot at the top of her opening. He tasted her warm, fragrant arousal and thought he'd explode from the pleasure. His own body answered her call—his balls drawing up in their sac and his cock hardening further into steel.

"No..." she moaned, but her hips rose, pressing her pussy closer to his face.

His lips closed over her clitoris and sucked hard, and then released it to flutter his tongue over the engorged pearl. Again he sucked on her clit, and she keened loudly, her thighs trembling against his cheeks. When he released it, he soothed her pussy with long, slow laps. More of her salty essence met his tongue, the hot musky scent filling his nostrils. A surge of raw need swept over him and his body shook with anticipation. He groaned and lifted his head to watch her.

Andromeda's head lolled, her eyes squeezed shut. Her lush mouth was open, her breaths coming fast and with a ragged hitch. Ripening nipples, flushed red and pointing toward the ceiling, beckoned him, issuing a siren's call he could no longer resist.

He slid up her body, braced his arms on either side of her and looked into her face. Her green eyes opened, blinking dreamily. He leaned down and his mouth latched onto a nipple. He rolled it with his tongue while his hips aligned with hers.

Her legs rose, clasping him low around his waist so that his cock nudged the swollen outer lips of her pussy.

With a flex of his hips, he slipped inside. He groaned against her breast and his teeth closed on the nipple, biting her gently.

Her back arched, plunging her hips upward, forcing him deeper inside her vagina.

So hot! So tight! He gritted his teeth against the need to pound away and seek his own quick release. Her inner muscles caressed him, rippling along his cock, urging him deeper.

He rocked within the cradle of her thighs, delivering shallow thrusts, waiting for her to grow impatient and demand her satisfaction. This seduction was proving to be a battle of wills, although he was confident of the outcome. She hadn't the experience to hold back her body or her emotions.

Most importantly, she was a woman—her heart would follow her passion.

Eventually she would give herself completely and deliver her trust. Then he would have her password. He only hoped she'd surrender in time to avoid Dominion sentries detecting their change in course.

Andromeda's nails dug into his shoulders, and her legs constricted. "Please," she cried, her voice raspy. "Faster...deeper..."

Khalim resisted his body's desire to comply with her command. Instead, he teased her with one deep thrust and followed with more shallow ones…then deep…shallow.

Her nails raked his back as she tried to wrest control of his pace, slamming her hips up and down to force him to move faster.

He tightened his grip on her buttocks and ground his pelvis into her as far as he could reach and held himself perfectly still.

Her eyes fluttered open. He read stark, desperate need in her gaze and trembling mouth.

"You must trust me," he said, knowing his rising passion made his voice harsh.

"Damn you! Trust can't be commanded." Her eyes filled with tears.

He fought the need to soothe her, just as he resisted the urge to pump his hips at her hot pussy. She had to surrender—for both their sakes. He brought one hand to her dark thatch and combed his fingers through the hairs that floated in the water, until he found the hard, distended button between her legs. His thumb flicked it once.

Her breath hitched and she shuddered deep inside.

He rubbed it harder and her vagina clutched his cock, squeezing exquisitely tighter.

"How can you expect me to trust you…when you use my body against me?" A tear rolled from her eye.

He followed the moisture as it trailed down her cheek. His chest expanded with a deep sigh, and he leaned forward to lick the tear from her face. "Andromeda, you were mine from the moment you first touched me. Soon, you will know this as truth." Then he sealed his mouth over hers and kissed her, soothing her, caressing her mouth.

She sobbed against him and brought her hands to his head, gripping his hair to deepen the kiss.

Khalim slowly withdrew his cock until only the head remained in her warm well. He swirled his hips, teasing her—torturing himself.

She broke the kiss and stared at him. Khalim knew she didn't believe his words—would she read the promise in his eyes?

He let the rush of pleasure sweep over him and slammed inside her, all the way to her womb, before withdrawing and plunging inside her again. He'd give her this pleasure…then shape her desire all over again.

Urgency built inside him as he thrust into her vagina. He concentrated on the feel of her warm, tight channel as it constricted tightly around his cock, pulling him inexorably deeper.

Her hands glided down his back, squeezing and kneading, urging him to move faster.

His hips pistoned, causing the water lapping at their bodies to froth. Friction heated his cock until release tightened his body, rising from his thighs and hardening his balls. Knowing he was ready to come, he sought to bring her with him and ground his hips into her pussy at the end of each long stroke, rubbing the hair of his groin against her clit.

Andromeda mewled like a kitten, her nails biting into the flesh of his ass as she slammed her hips into his.

Khalim, spurred by her frantic movements beneath him, let the first wave of his release wash over him, carrying him toward the peak. He pumped once, twice, and then groaned. Cum jetted, lubricating his long, hard strokes. His arms trembled, but he continued to thrust until Andromeda gasped and tightened her cunt, arms, and legs around him.

And still he pounded into her, drawing out her orgasm until she keened long and loudly. When finally she lay spent beneath him, he gathered her close, pressing her face into the crook of his neck. Her arms wrapped loosely around his shoulders.

"Forgive me. I pushed you too far." He nuzzled her cheek with his nose, while his hands glided up and down her back. This aftermath was sweeter than any he had known. He had never wanted to linger inside a pleasure-giver's body after reaching his satisfaction. But Andromeda's sweet warmth and spicy scent bound him.

"Khalim," she said, her voice raspy, "I can't give you what you ask."

The sound of his name on her lips filled his soul with warmth. "Why do you believe that?" he asked softly.

She hugged him. "You're wanted for high crimes against the Dominion. I've already promised to deliver you. And I'd be a fool to believe you are anything other than what the governor told me."

Khalim kissed the top of her head and rubbed his chin there. "If I tell you that I committed no crimes and my only sin is my race, would you believe me?"

"But why would the Dominion do that?" Her hands lazily kneaded the muscles along his spine. "They're tolerant of many races and species."

"My planet and my people hold secrets deep within themselves. Some inside the Dominion would punish us for not sharing those secrets."

Her mouth skimmed his collarbone. "Are they so valuable?"

With his heart pounding from her tender kisses, he whispered, "Priceless."

She leaned away from him and looked into his face. Her somber expression was softened by her kiss-swollen lips and rosy cheeks. "Is this dream-making part of your treasure?"

"Do you now believe I brought you here?" he asked, squeezing her ass as he ground his reawakening cock into her.

Her lips opened around a soundless gasp, but she nodded. "I should be furious. You manipulated me when I thought I was safe inside a dream."

With a small rueful smile, he replied, "I only meant to bring you to Qihar-Jadiid to speak with you."

"Then why did you seduce me?" Her moss-colored eyes looked troubled.

"You appeared lonely." His smile stretched. "And you were naked. I didn't envision that—*you* wanted us without clothing."

Her blush deepened. "I don't have the power to shape the outcome of our shared dreams. You created the fantasy."

"You're wrong. And this isn't really a dream." He flexed his hips and withdrew partway, before sliding back inside her.

Her fingers clutched his back as tightly as her inner muscles gloved his cock. "While we're here, our bodies are still aboard the ship, right?" she asked breathlessly.

He wondered how she held the trail of their conversation. Her hot channel squeezed and caressed his rigid flesh, stealing his thoughts. He could only manage a nod and circled his hips.

"Then it's a dream—this isn't real." She sounded relieved and her hips answered with a delicate thrust.

Frustration over her stubborn denial of what they shared cleared his brain. "It's more than a dream," he ground out. "Has any dream of yours ever been this vivid?" He held her hips still and stared into her eyes. "What we experience here *together* is mutually remembered—and therefore real. If I were merely forming a vision for you to experience, you would have no choice."

Her eyes widened. "You could do that?"

"Yes! But I prefer to meld our vision to form events we both want to pass."

"Therefore we're naked?" Red suffused her cheeks. "It's what my mind wants?"

He nodded, satisfied she finally understood.

Her teeth nibbled the bottom lip of her lush mouth for a moment, and then her gaze narrowed. "But you didn't have to encourage me."

He arched one eyebrow.

"Once you realized I thought you were part of a dream, you didn't have to seduce me. You weren't being gentlemanly when you took advantage of the fact that—"

"That you were lonely? That your body ached for loving?" He pumped his hips to emphasize his point. "I couldn't resist becoming your fantasy. What man could?"

Her hands moved to the tops of his shoulders and she lifted herself up, and then ground her body down on his cock. Her eyes closed for a moment and her head fell back. "Don't flatter me. I won't believe you—I know what I am."

His hands assisted her movement, and they quickly established a rhythm. "Tell me." His lips skimmed her jaw. "What are you?"

"Only average-looking." She gasped as his teeth closed on her earlobe. Her back arched, pressing her pointed breasts into his chest. "Under other circumstances, you wouldn't give me a second glance."

He tongued the tender lobe his teeth had worried. "It's true. Of late, I haven't had time to pursue my pleasure. I've only known the purchased favors of professional pleasure-givers. But you are beautiful." He thrust faster, pushing her hips down to increase the friction between their opposing fleshes. "Would you believe me if I said that your *in*expertise is enchanting?"

Her breaths panted. "Still, you should…have told me…before you took me the first time."

"Would you have refused me?" he asked, his voice roughening with passion.

"Probably not… I wouldn't have…believed you." She moaned—a low sweet sound that amused him. Her body was already quickening.

Although their conversation was killing him, he continued to drive his point as his cock drove them both to distraction. "When I brought you to my chambers—only intending to talk to you—I read the hunger in your eyes."

"So…you decided to use my need…to soften me up…and get the password?" The first shudder of her orgasm racked them both.

Khalim slowed and sharpened his thrusts, angling his hips to glide his cock along the nerve-rich spot inside her vagina. He would deliver her maximum satisfaction. "No," he said, even as he felt her body convulse. "I wasn't thinking." His hips slammed against hers. "When your hands…went straight for my cock…and you knelt on the floor to take me into your sweet mouth…any thoughts of negotiation flew."

She groaned. "Don't remind me…this is…embarrassing enough."

"There should be no embarrassment…when we both are pleased with…where our imaginations lead us." He shouted then and his body exploded, his cock pummeling her sweet cunt as his ejaculate bathed her womb.

Dragging air into his starved lungs, he released a short bark of laughter. Never had a conversation been so torturous!

Once again, Andromeda cuddled in his embrace. "If I surrender to you," she whispered, "I'll become hunted. I'll lose everything I've worked for—my ship, my reputation. And for what?"

"For us?"

Her head shook in denial against his shoulder. "I'm not so big a fool to believe there's any 'us' beyond this dream."

He threaded his fingers through her wet hair and pulled her head back to watch the emotions her face betrayed. Sadness trembled at the corners of her mouth; wariness lurked in her wide-eyed stare. "Where do you think we go after this?"

"You to prison, me to the next job." Her expression grew closed. "We should go back."

Andromeda had much to learn. His wounded prey would resist his gentling every step of the way. His head descended toward hers, and she didn't resist as he pressed a chaste kiss against her lips. Then with a nod, they were back inside the misty shower stall.

Chapter Three

Andromeda found herself pressed to the metal wall, Khalim blanketing her back. The weight of his cock rested between her legs, nudging her swollen slit. With the memory of her recent orgasms humming in her mind and body, she had to fight hard not to tilt her hips. Oh, how she wanted for him to slide right in…

Being pulled between a wet "dream" and reality was too damn confusing. She took a deep breath and pushed away from the wall.

Khalim kissed the top of her shoulder, but stepped away.

With his body calling all her sensually deprived hormones, she knew she needed space. And time to sort out her jumbled thoughts, free from the distraction of his aroused body.

The man needed clothes.

She pressed the button to stop the water, and the door to the stall slid open. "I'd like for us both to get dressed. I need to check my navigation system to see where we are, then I'll fix us something to eat."

She didn't wait for his response and stepped out. The silent vacuum tucked around the doorway of the stall sucked the excess water from her body. Stepping farther into her cabin, she opened the cabinet above her bed and pulled out a reclamation suit.

"We don't need clothing." Khalim's breath stirred the hair resting on her shoulder.

She hadn't realized he stood so close, and shivered. "I'm cold," she lied.

"Then we'll tell life support to increase the temperature. There will be no lies between us."

Her hands clenched around the black fabric of her R-suit. "How does clothing constitute a lie?"

His hands gripped her waist and turned her. She let the suit fall to her bunk. Her breasts brushed his chest and pebbled instantly.

His gaze dropped to where their flesh met for a moment, then rose again. "Your body doesn't lie about what pleases you."

She lifted her chin. "And how do you know I'm not simply chilled?"

His hand stroked between her legs, and then he lifted his fingers and glided them across her lips. Without a word, he proved his point.

She inhaled the fragrance of her arousal.

How she wished she could reach for her weapons in the cabinet behind her feet. A tap from her electro-stun would wipe the smirk from his lips!

"Besides," he said, his voice a low purr that only heightened her awareness of the bunk pressed behind her knees, "you wouldn't have anything large enough for me to wear."

"I have clothing for you." Desperate to erect barriers between them, she continued, "There's a suit my last…partner left aboard the ship."

"Partner?" His expression grew alert. "Did he share this bed with you?"

"No, it's too small." Too late she noticed the narrowing of his gaze. He'd noted her choice of words.

"Then you shared the bed at the end of the corridor?"

She ignored his question. "You've been snooping in my ship?"

"Of course. I also found the weapons in the drawer behind you."

She jerked.

"They aren't there anymore."

No clothes. No weapons. How the hell was she going to get out of this fix? "I need to head back to the bridge." She shoved at his chest and slid past him.

"What happened to your partner?"

"None of your damn business." Had she not been acutely aware of her nakedness, she would have stomped all the way back to the bridge. For now, she'd do nothing to incite his anger or lust. If he expected her to be as easy a conquest as she had been in her dreams, he'd be disappointed.

He stayed one step behind her. "But it is my business. If he expects you to contact him—"

"He won't."

Khalim's hand closed around her arm, bringing her to a halt.

She pulled from his grasp and he let her go. "He won't contact me."

"Tell me why." His expression was implacable, but his narrowed eyes hinted at deeper emotion.

Sighing, she hid her hurt and blurted, "We parted company six months ago."

"Was this by mutual agreement?"

Her cheeks burned. "No."

"He has no reason to return?"

"He took our entire client list with him. There's nothing of value left here."

Khalim stood still, his penetrating gaze holding hers for a long moment, and then he nodded. "He was a fool."

With a nonchalant shrug, she turned, intent on ending the conversation.

Again his hand stopped her—this time, his fingers spread over her belly and he pulled her flush with his body. "If you don't care, why do you sleep in this narrow bunk rather than the larger bed down the corridor?"

She swallowed past the lump in her throat. "I don't care about him. But I hate to think about how foolish I was to believe he wanted me."

"I would never leave you," he said softly. His hand rose to her breast and cupped it. "And I wouldn't use your love to steal from you. I would cherish you."

Her hand rose and she pried his fingers from her breast. "Well, I'll never know that for sure, will I? Because I'm not going to love you." She whirled away from his embrace. "And I won't let you steal my ship."

His hands fisted at his sides directing her gaze downward.

"I'm getting you some clothes as soon as I check our coordinates." She ignored the look of masculine pride that curved his lips and stomped from the room.

Unfortunately, she couldn't stalk far enough to vent her anger. The end of the corridor opened onto the bridge.

She stepped down metal rungs to the captain's deck below and slid into her chair, extending the right arm of her chair to expose the controls.

Khalim eased into the seat beside her.

With the press of a button, the large bioluminescent screen in front of them flickered into life. A living recreation of the stars in their path glimmered against the blue-black screen. "Add vector," Andromeda said.

Instantly, a glowing red line stretched before them, disappearing into the hazy, spiraling cloud of the distant Milky Way galaxy. "Compute arrival time," she said.

[04 days; 03 hours; 24 minutes] appeared at the edge of the screen.

Andromeda blew out a breath. She'd slept longer than she'd thought. Her gaze slanted toward Khalim.

He stared back at her, his expression impassive. Only days away from imprisonment, perhaps for life, yet he betrayed not a single emotion.

Except that his cock remained rigid, rising from his lap.

Andromeda licked her lips. If Khalim had been persistent before—in her dreams—he'd be relentless now. He had maybe a day to gain her password and make his escape.

Lord, how would she resist, when her body already softened and oozed with her own arousal?

"I should get us food…" Her voice trailed off.

The flair of his nostrils as he caught the scent of her arousal made her squirm in her seat. His gaze grew predatory and slipped from her eyes to her breasts, and lower to her thighs, which she pressed tightly together.

Khalim turned his chair from the screen, never taking his gaze from hers and spread his legs. His invitation was crudely made, but Andromeda had no trouble understanding. He was hers to do with as she pleased.

Liquid gushed from her vagina and wet the seat beneath her. Her nipples puckered, drawing into tightly engorged points. Her hands started to lift to cover them, but he already knew how strong was her desire and she let them fall back to her lap.

She turned her chair and rose. Then she took a step toward him, and another, until she stood between his outspread knees, uncertainty and a touch of fear tethering her. He sat so still, she wondered if he drew breath, while her chest rose and fell more quickly. Did she have the courage to take what she wanted? No, *needed*.

Her body answered for her, and flowering warmth seeped down her legs. With her hands on his knees, she knelt before him and leaned close to rub her cheek along his erection. His cock was hot and velvety smooth against her skin. She inhaled deeply, savoring the musky scent of his arousal, so familiar and yet so new, her body shivered with excitement.

Then she nuzzled him higher, gliding toward the swollen head with her chin and cheek, never taking her gaze from his. His hands clenched the armrests. His head fell back against the headrest and his chest expanded, but still he didn't move to take her.

Andromeda opened her mouth wide and closed her lips around the crown of his cock and sucked.

"Ha'abib!" His hips rose and his cock slid into her mouth, caressing her tongue and butting against the back of her throat.

Gratified she could hold him in thrall with her seduction, Andromeda slid her hands along his thighs until she reached the crisp hairs at his groin. One hand sought the sac below and she cupped him there, enjoying his shiver of delight. The other hand encircled the base of his cock, lifting it from his belly to give her better control of his penetration. She lifted her mouth from him and trailed her open lips along his length, lubricating the shaft. Her hand followed, gliding moistly up and down his cock before her lips returned to chew delicately on the turgid head.

His fingers threaded through her hair, and he pushed her down his length.

Opening her jaw wide she accepted his guidance and let him surge deep into her throat, again and again, until she needed air and raised her head.

His gaze was still upon her. Perspiration gleamed on his forehead and heaving chest. "Come to me."

Determined to prove her power, Andromeda kept her gaze locked with his and opened wide to once again take him deep inside the warm cavern of her mouth. She moaned and the sound vibrated along his cock.

His hands tightened in her hair and pushed her down.

She tightened his lips around him and sucked, gliding up and down, her hand shadowing her movements to increase the friction, gently squeezing his erection.

Khalim's thighs quivered, his stomach grew rigid, and his chest expanded as he sucked air through his open mouth. "Enough!" he said, his voice harsh and grinding.

Not nearly enough! Andromeda stood and pushed the armrests up. With his hands at her waist to assist her, she straddled his lap, her knees sliding alongside his hips, until her pussy poised above his straining cock. Her inner thighs quivered and she no longer cared who led, who followed. She needed him inside her.

He leaned toward her and captured a breast with his mouth, tugging at the distended tip, and then flicking it with the point of his tongue before returning to his desperate rooting, nudging, pulling…

Her back arched. She'd never known how painfully sensitive her breasts could be.

Unable to hold back a moment longer, Andromeda braced her hands against his broad shoulders and slowly lowered her body. Her wet, swollen labia pressed against the head of his cock until it slipped inside her. She sank, her thighs trembling, unable to control the depth of his piercing erection. Emitting a whimper, her breath caught.

His hands slipped down to her buttocks and gripped a cheek with each hand, and he lifted her.

Then down she pressed again, taking him deeper this time.

His mouth switched breasts and his teeth bit the nipple, causing her to cry out. Her hands moved from his shoulders to his head and she clutched him, begging him with her action to continue his tender torture.

He murmured deep within his throat, and his hands squeezed her ass tighter, lifting her, pushing her down—farther each time, until she was seated, her hips flush with his, his cock deeper than any other man had ever reached.

A coil of sensual desire wound inside her, curling, twisting. She needed more. She wanted his powerful thrusts.

Dragging his head away from her breast, she leaned down to kiss his lips. Her arms wrapped around his shoulders. Her hips undulated, a jerking spasmodic movement. She was beyond grace, beyond thought. His cock stretched her, melting her core until she was ready to burst like super-heated lava. She gasped and threw her head back. "Please, Khalim, pleeeease!"

In a single surging movement, Khalim lifted her from his lap and pushed her to the floor on her belly. Andromeda had only a moment to wonder at his purpose, before he pulled her hips up and slammed into her cunt.

"Yes!" she shouted, coming up on her hands, rearing back to meet his thrust.

With his fingers digging into the flesh of her buttocks in a bruising grip, he delivered a rapid burst of quick, deep lunges.

Andromeda's thighs and arms threatened to buckle beneath his sensual onslaught. Still he pumped his hips faster and faster…deeper…harder…

His hips pounded at her cunt, the sweat-slick skin of his belly smacking her ass, loud as her whimpers and moans. Her vagina adjusted to the girth and length of his cock, his movements eased by successive washes of her body's liquid excitement.

Suddenly her orgasm burst around her like a brilliant, burning supernova and she screamed. Khalim's hoarse cry soon followed and together they melted to the floor.

Chapter Four

Khalim watched Andromeda stomp around the small galley, mumbling beneath her breath and slamming cupboard doors. Her actions, coupled with the stiff set of her shoulders and her closed expression, hinted loudly at her displeasure.

Feeling very relaxed himself, he leaned his hip against a counter and waited for the tempest to break. Like a roiling sandstorm, her thunderous frown threatened an ill wind. He guessed her conscience bothered her.

Yes, Andromeda's defenses were crumbling. Each time her gaze strayed his way, she assiduously refrained from glancing downward. He didn't blame her. His blatant arousal, a surprisingly constant state, had to be upsetting her. Unfortunate for her peace of mind, but extremely gratifying to his, her body recognized the perpetual, sensual cycle in which they were trapped.

She had only to gaze upon his erection and her breasts flushed with heat, drawing into exquisite, reddened points. The sight of her small breasts ripening with desire filled his loins, making his cock and balls heavy and hard. But while he relished their mutual dilemma, she resisted.

Oh, she'd fallen under the spell of her arousal while they'd sat side by side on the captain's deck before surrendering, much to his delight. But she was far from won.

In the meantime, his body needed sustenance to continue the long, hard battle for her heart.

"Can I help you choose?" he asked, anticipating her reaction to his voice.

Her back grew rigid. "No."

He pushed away from the counter and approached her, treading quietly. "Dehydrated turkey is so...dry, isn't it?"

She jumped and whirled to face him. "I love it," she said, her chin lifting, daring him to complain.

Reaching around her, close enough the hairs on his arm dragged across her shoulder, he plucked another packet from the open cupboard.

A shiver racked her rigid frame and her lower lip trembled.

"Mmmm. Reconstituted strawberries—they're edible." He dropped it on the counter next to her choice. Steeling himself against the urge to lean down and kiss her sweet mouth, he murmured, "Shall we add potatoes?"

She slid past him, her belly rubbing against his cock, and they both held their breath. "If you like!" The words sounded like they strangled her throat.

He hid a smile and replied, "You have a preference for Earth cuisine?"

"Of course. It's where I was raised." She placed the sealed packets in the dispenser above the oven and shut the door. A moment later, she opened the oven and their meals were ready. Fragrant steam rose from the meat and vegetable.

His belly rumbled, and he smiled ruefully at her startled expression. A small smile tugged at the corners of her lips and she turned quickly to find utensils. Khalim removed the trays, setting them on the fold-down table at the end of the counter. After she gave him a fork and knife and he poured the wine he'd retrieved from her pantry, they seated themselves on stools opposite each other. He raised his glass. "My thanks for your hospitality."

Andromeda coughed and laid down her glass. Her gaze fell to the metal table. His lap—and cock—were entirely concealed. The relief that showed in her deep sigh and relaxing shoulders made him feel extremely smug. He'd let her enjoy a moment's respite from his pursuit. Maybe.

She stuck a forkful of dry turkey into her mouth and proceeded to chew.

"Where's the pepper?" he asked innocently, and rose quickly from his seat.

She coughed and reached for her glass. When he returned with the shaker, her glare should have scorched his skin, but he merely gave her a bland smile and peppered his potatoes.

He swallowed a bit of his turkey and grimaced. "This is as flavorless as a shoe. For me, there's nothing more succulent than desert fowl in a bed of sweetgrass."

Andromeda shrugged, "To each his own." She took another bite and chased it with more wine.

He knew better than to mention the fact she found the need to wash the colorless meat down. Besides, the wine would likely work in his favor. He put down his fork and picked up a strawberry. He popped the berry into his mouth and closed his eyes, savoring the sweetness. When he opened his eyes, he found Andromeda staring.

She glanced away, but the color staining her chest betrayed the direction of her thoughts.

His cock pulsed. He reached for the wine bag and squeezed more of the fruity beverage into her glass.

"Thank you," she murmured, not lifting her gaze from her plate. She cleared her throat. "I've wondered…"

"Yes, *Ha'abib*?"

She looked at him then. "You said that before, when…"

"When we made love?" How easily she blushed! He smiled. "Do you want to know what it means?"

"Never mind," she said quickly.

"No, it's all right. It's an ancient term—an endearment. Roughly translated, it means 'darling'."

"Oh." She shifted on her chair, and her fingers tightened around her fork.

"Now, what were you going to ask me before?"

"Before? Oh, yes." She blinked and took a deep breath. "Why haven't you tried to convince me of your innocence?"

He grew still, sensing his next words would determine his fate, he replied, "Would you have believed me?"

Her troubled gaze locked with his. "Try me now."

He took a deep breath and plunged. "I was sent to accompany the Qiharan ambassador as his aide, but I was really his bodyguard. My people have no love for the Dominion—or trust. Before our oil reserves were discovered, we were beneath their notice."

"I was told you attacked the emissary, that you sought to disrupt the trade negotiations."

Khalim pressed his lips tightly together to quell the curse he wished to utter. "The ambassador was my uncle. Did the governor mention that?"

Her eyebrows drew together in a frown. "No. It did seem odd they would hold negotiations on such a remote planet. But I can guess what really happened."

Khalim nodded. "He was assassinated. It was well planned. We sat down to dinner our first evening there, and a guest at one of the lower tables stood up and opened fire. Out of my uncle's entire entourage, only I was left alive."

"They needed someone to blame," she whispered.

"I was labeled a militant who was opposed to the strengthening of our ties with the Dominion. Now, they've made it truth." Tension born of frustration stiffened his neck and shoulders.

"You weren't responsible, Khalim. How could you know—"

He shot her a look laced with irritation. How could she understand what he felt? He had been the one there—responsible for his uncle's safety. Instead, he'd watched him die.

"And stop glaring at me. I'm not responsible either."

He realized his stare upset her. "The deceit of your governing council still enrages me."

"Thank you for telling me, just the same. It explains a lot. I wondered why the governor wanted you removed so quickly." Andromeda canted her head to the side. "Do they know about your special gift?"

"It was kept secret—insurance, in case it was needed."

"Did you use it to warn your people on Qihar? Can you reach such a distance with your mind?"

"I spoke with my father before I was brought aboard your ship. He shares my gift." Khalim reached across the table and covered her hand. "I am thinking that perhaps, I ask too much of you. This isn't your fight. There will likely be a war."

"Your world appears so primitive, at least the parts I've seen so far—in the dreams. Can you win?"

"We don't have the technology our enemies possess, but we have weapons beyond their imagination. We don't expect to win battles, but the Dominion will not want to wage a lengthy campaign. We hope to wear down their resolution." He cupped her cheek. "You would be better off handing me over to the authorities."

She leaned her face into his hand. "I'm must be crazy, but I'm not afraid." Her eyes filled. "I couldn't bear to see you imprisoned."

"Why? What has changed your mind about me?"

She straightened and stared at him, her gaze steady. "You've seduced me from the start of this voyage, trying to win my cooperation. Yet when I resisted, you never once attempted to force me to give up my password. And you could have—you're stronger than I am."

"I told you, I would never harm you."

"And I believe you," she said quietly. "You've been tender and gentle, even when I angered you. You're an honorable man."

He lifted an eyebrow.

A small smile curved her lips. "Despite our appearance, I believe that's true. You've a twisted sense of humor, and this has been the oddest courtship, but I know I can take you at your word."

"You believe this is a courtship?" He waited, willing her to have the courage to believe he was honest in his dealings with her.

She took a deep breath and said in a rush, "Yes. As *in*expert as I am, I know a man couldn't be that hard all the time without being powerfully attracted."

Something inside him softened and relaxed. "And do you know what the purpose of this courtship is?"

"You mean, beyond taking over my ship?"

His narrowed eyes warned her not to tread that ground again.

"You want me to accompany you to Qihar-Jadiid?" Her expression was hopeful and pierced his heart.

"I want you to *remain* there with me."

A smile lit her face for a brief moment, and then she looked away. "But what of my ship?"

"If you give me freedom, you'll be viewed as a pirate by the Dominion and become subject to intergalactic piracy laws. You could be executed if you are apprehended."

"Do I have to scuttle her?" she asked, her voice tight.

"No." He squeezed her hand. "Someday, we may have a need for her. Do you think you can bear to be planet-bound for a time?"

"I love to fly, and it's been my whole life since before I reached adulthood, but I find the thought of losing my ship doesn't hurt me. I know I can't bear to live without you."

Satisfaction filled his chest and loins. It had come to pass, as his uncle had foreseen months before his death. He had found his mate, and soon, the hawk would tether its master. He tugged on her hand. "Come here."

"Wait!" Her eyes narrowed. "Just how many wives is a man permitted in your society?"

He pursed his lips against the smile threatening to break. Now that she was assured of her place with him, his little prey wasn't afraid to show her own talons. "As many as his first wife will allow."

"And do you already have a wife or two?"

He feigned nonchalance and shrugged. "I've been a warrior for most of my adult life. I've had no time to seek a suitable mate."

Her eyebrows drew together in a fierce frown. "Am I just convenient, then?"

"*Ha'abib,* you've been extremely *in*convenient." He jerked her to her feet and pulled her around the table. When she stood in front of him, his hands closed over her hips.

She stiffened, resisting his pull. "Will I be your wife or your convenience?"

Annoyance burned for a moment until he noticed her white-knuckle grip on his hand. The answer was not apparent to her—she still doubted her own appeal. "My wife, of course."

She nodded once. "And if I tell you there will be no other wives in our life?"

"Then I will expect you to provide all that a Tirrekh warrior needs from his *wives*." He suppressed a smile as the light of battle appeared in her eyes.

"Maybe one Earth woman equals several of your wives."

Needing to hold her, he stood up and circled the table, backing her up against the edge. "Perhaps we should test your theory." He leaned down and captured her mouth in a hot, hard kiss.

Andromeda sighed against his lips and their mouths softened, sliding together. He circled the sharp edges of her teeth and then stroked her tongue with his.

Her body yielded, sweetly opening her thighs to cuddle his sex. He circled his hips, rubbing her slit, wetting the tip of his cock in her moisture.

She drew away and framed his face with her soft hands. "This…attraction burns. I couldn't feel this way, if I didn't love you."

He rested his forehead against hers. "As I love you."

Her eyes glittered with moisture, and she rose up on her toes to press her lips to his, again.

Promises were exchanged as their tongues mated. His body stirred, her hips curved to accept his cock. He growled deep in his throat and lifted her off the floor. Her legs wrapped around his waist and he plunged into her wet warmth.

They strained together—mouths and hips fusing, desperate to deepen their emotional and physical connection. Khalim's hips rolled, pumping into her drenched pussy.

At first he didn't recognize the noise, he was so lost inside the wonder of his woman's body.

Andromeda pressed against his shoulders. "Khalim, that's a hailing signal!"

The alarm in her voice pierced his sex-drugged mind. Her legs were already lowering from his waist, and he helped her gain her footing, regretting the loss of their connection.

"What shall we do?" she asked, already heading toward the corridor. "We've been discovered by sentinels. We must be very close to the perimeter. How will we escape them now?"

He followed closely on her heels to the bridge. "You must distract them."

"How?" She reached the ladder, but rather than climbing down the metal rungs, she straddled it and slid to the floor below.

He imitated her action and followed her. "Do they expect you to respond?"

"If I don't, they'll assume I'm still in suspension." She slipped into her chair and flipped open the control panel. The screen opened, a midnight blue expanse dotted with brilliant lights from a billion far away stars. "Display all spacecraft."

As Khalim seated himself next to her, brackets surrounded a dark spot on the screen, and then illuminated the hull of a small cruiser.

"There's only one ship," she said.

"You will tell them you're experiencing some sort of trouble with your ship. Anything that will convince them there is a reason for your ship to halt its progress. While they await your ship, I'll pull them into another reality while we escape."

Andromeda glanced at him. "When I open the communications line, they mustn't see you."

Belatedly, Khalim's gaze fell to her naked chest and he frowned. "You need clothing."

Andromeda grinned, displaying a dimple in her right cheek. "You did say to distract them."

With her kiss-swollen lips and distended nipples, she'd certainly do that. It rankled that she was right. He glanced at the space beneath the console and screen. There might be just enough room…

Before she could gasp a protest, he was on the floor and underneath the console, his hands pressing apart her thighs.

"What are you doing?"

Without preamble, his long fingers slid inside her vagina.

Andromeda's toes pointed to the floor, lifting her heels and giving him greater access to her cunt. "Stop," she said, and then moaned. "I have to return their call."

"Do it!" he said, then leaned closer and kissed the inside of her thighs.

"You're insane!" Her head pressed back into the headrest and her hands gripped the armrests as if she were afraid she'd fly off the seat. "I won't be able get out an intelligible sentence."

He spread the pretty pink folds guarding her entry with his fingers and stabbed his tongue inward.

Her hips lifted off the chair, and he had to hold her down to accept his loving. "Make the call." He circled her opening with a lap of his tongue.

"Bastard!" He heard a click and then a breathless, "This is the captain of the *Osprey*. Identify yourself."

Epilogue

"What must they have thought when I cried out in the middle of their greeting?" I asked, rubbing his bottom absently. I'd never grow tired of exploring those hard, rounded muscles.

"Andromeda, does it matter?" His head rested on my shoulder and his breaths still held a ragged edge. "They will not realize how long they hover at those coordinates…until I release them from their dream."

The tip of my finger traced the crease between his buttocks. "Where exactly did you take them?"

I felt his shiver all the way to my womb. "To a place they will not be eager to leave."

I heard the smile in his voice, and I answered with a grin. "You took them to a whorehouse, didn't you?" I smoothed my hands over the rise of his ass, and then grabbed both cheeks and squeezed.

His cock lengthened inside me. "They are in a pleasure-giver's palace," he corrected me.

"They rate a palace?"

"Let us change the subject, hmmm?" The roll of his hips wasn't needed to remind me where his pleasure lay.

I was filled to the brim with his pleasure, so wet and sore from overuse the ache pulsed. Still, I couldn't have him complaining. I pumped my hips and drew a long moan from him.

"Mercy, Ha'abib!"

I hoped I exhausted him. While in my arms, he'd never feel the lack of wives.

He'd also never lack for laughter. His heart was lighter than when we had first met. He smiled often and I relished his sly sense of humor, even when the laughter was at my expense.

Once again, he had brought me to Qihar-Jadiid. His flesh still embedded inside mine, his weight pressed me into silken blankets. They were spread upon a sandy shelf of rock overlooking a shallow pond. We arrived at sunset and watched the aqua sky fade to mauve and the stars appear like a billion phosphor-pots set to light our way.

"If my ship were near enough, would we see us in the sky?"

Khalim grunted and lifted his head. "We aren't going to sleep, are we?"

"This is a dream," I reminded him. "You don't need to sleep."

He shook his head, then rose on his arms and disengaged our bodies. "You have much to learn." Rolling to his back, he placed a hand behind his head and yawned.

I climbed on top of him, stretching over him like a blanket.

His hands closed over my ass.

I folded my hands on his chest and planted my chin on top. I loved staring at him—his golden gaze warmed me to my toes. "This dream-sex could be the answer to birth control."

"Do you think so?" His slow smile was a study in masculine arrogance.

Unable to resist the curve of his lips, I leaned down and slanted my mouth over his, lapping at the tip of his tongue.

His body hardened beneath mine, his cock once again pressing at my cunt.

I broke the kiss and gasped. "You give me so much, I'll hardly miss flying at all."

Khalim's hands glided up my back and then his fingers combed through my hair, pulling me down for another kiss. "Close your eyes, Ha'abib. I have something else to show you." His mouth moved on mine, sucking softly.

My legs parted over his waist, and I straddled his hips. I pushed my chest away from him and his hands settled over my breasts. Circling my hips, I searched until my movements placed the head of his cock at my entrance. With a flex of my hips, I took him inside me. "I like what you show me," I said, my voice raspy with want. I let my head roll back and closed my eyes. I ground my hips down, swirling, screwing his cock.

Khalim's soft laughter drifted over me. "This is not what I meant."

"No?" I teased him with another slow, spiraling plunge.

His face darkened, his jaw tightening as I built his arousal. "I will show you. Turn around on me, love."

Never breaking the connection, his hands guided me until I faced the opposite direction. I felt him shift behind me until he sat with his chest to my back. "Now close your eyes," he whispered into my ear.

From one moment to the next, we left the oasis and our hard, rock bed. Beneath my knees, I detected the movement of muscle clothed in rubbery skin. I opened my eyes and found that we were flying above the shadowed surface of Qihar-Jadiid. Our conveyance was a great beast with wide wings that canted to catch the wind. With Khalim's arms anchoring me to his lap, his cock buried deep inside me, I raised my face to the starry sky and laughed.

About the author:

Delilah Devlin dated a Samoan, a Venezuelan, a Turk, a Cuban, and was engaged to a Greek before marrying her Irishman. She's lived in Saudi Arabia, Germany, and Ireland, but calls Texas home for now. Ever a risk taker, she lived in the Saudi Peninsula during the Gulf War, thwarted an attempted abduction by white slave traders, and survived her children's juvenile delinquency.

Creating alter egos for herself in the pages of her books enables her to live new adventures. Since discovering the sinful pleasure of erotica, she writes to satisfy her need for variety—it keeps her from running away with the Indian working in the cubicle beside her!

In addition to writing erotica, she enjoys creating romantic comedies and suspense novels.

Delilah welcomes mail from readers. You can write to her c/o Ellora's Cave Publishing at 1337 Commerce Drive, Suite 13, Stow OH 44224.

Also by Delilah Devlin:

My Immortal Knight: All Hallows Heartbreaker

My Immortal Knight: Love Bites

My Immortal Knight: All Knight Long

My Immortal Knight: Relentless

Garden of Desire

Prisoner Of Desire

Slave Of Desire

The Pleasure Bot

VOYEURS: OVEREXPOSED

Sherri L. King

Thanks to Joyce Schopmeyer for her incredible fudge and infectious laughter. Keep the oil lamps burning and your home as warm as your heart.

For D.

Prologue

"Hi. I am a human." Agate scrunched and then reschooled her features, affecting what she hoped was a flirtatious look of nonchalance, and tried again. This time using a breathy voice instead of her normal one. "Hello. I am a human." She beat her chest and scowled fiercely. "Human, I be."

No, that wasn't it, either. She glared at her reflection in the mirror, took a deep breath, and tried it again in a much deeper voice. "Greetings. I am a human."

An amused burst of laughter sounded from behind her as Cady, wife to the great Shikar Warrior Obsidian, glided into the room.

Glided? Cady Swann never glided. She marched everywhere she went. Agate was being fanciful again. It was from all those romance novels she smuggled down from the human world. They called to something soft and dreamy in her soul…and The Elder would have a fit if he knew about the stash she kept hidden in her room.

"You sound like a science fiction alien," Cady snickered, handing her a bundle of clothing.

"I'm trying to perfect my human voice," Agate defended, and immediately turned back to the mirror, practicing what she believed were human gestures and expressions.

"And you look like you're constipated," Cady pointed out. "Or drunk off your gourd. Look," she turned Agate around to face her, "you don't need to affect any kind of persona. Just be yourself and no one will ever guess that you're not human."

"But I don't look like a human," Agate insisted, looking into her friend's Shikar-yellow eyes. Eyes that were the same vibrant color as her own.

Large, dark pupils surrounded by starburst irises in hues of gold, orange and yellow fire—this was the trademark characteristic of all Shikars. Except for those of the Traveler Caste. Travelers' eyes were black as the shadows they walked in...but that was neither here nor there.

Agate would be wearing brown contacts for her trip up to the surface world, the *human* world. Her eyes would not be the trait to give her away tonight, so long as the contact lenses stayed put.

"You look just like a human with those contact lenses covering your pretty eyes." Cady's words echoed Agate's thoughts. "And I should know. I was a human once," she winked reassuringly.

Agate sighed and rolled her shoulders, trying to relieve some of the tension that had gathered during her ablutions. "I'm just nervous about tonight," she said unnecessarily.

"If you don't want to go and meet this man, then Steffy is willing to go."

"No," she protested immediately. "Steffy needs to spend more time on her music album. You can't go either," she hurried when she saw Cady begin to form the words, "you need to spend more time with Obsidian. He's been downright surly this week since you've been spending so much time with the Watchers—I mean, the Voyeurs." She grinned. "I want to go. I really do. But I want to make a good impression all the same."

"Obsidian is always surly." Cady snorted, but it was clear by the softening in her eyes that she dearly loved the man and all his quirks. "I don't see why you care that much about this. You're just going to wipe this photographer's memory clean anyway. Who cares if he doesn't find you convincingly human? It's not like he can do or say anything about it. And I doubt he'll be that observant—he'll be too busy staring at your boobs."

Agate frowned. "Do you think so?" She reached up and palmed her full, round breasts. "Should I wear a minimizer?"

"Are you serious?" Cady laughed then, a full and throaty sound, throwing her head back. "Oh lordy, girl. You are too much. The human world doesn't know what it's in for with you," she teased.

Agate smiled, liking the sound of her friend's mirth. When Cady had first come to them, a human orphan with powers beyond her understanding or control, she had hardly ever laughed or even smiled. But now she was a Shikar, mated to one of the Warrior males and was even a Warrior in her own right. She was also mother to a son, Armand. Whom she'd lovingly named after her dead brother.

When Cady was only a child, her younger brother had been eaten by Daemons—monsters that fed on flesh and on life. Cady had seen it all and it had changed her, hardened her. It had made her a fighter and a hunter, as fierce and deadly as any Shikar Warrior. She'd been fighting the Daemon threat, protecting both humans and Shikars from their rage, ever since.

"What clothing did you bring for me?" Agate asked, already looking through the pile of garments to see for herself. Her eyes widened at the dark navy skirt and matching buttoned jacket. It was made out of a blend of cotton and silk, an airy material that Agate favored. The blouse was silk as well, finely spun, a creamy ivory color.

She often used similar materials to cotton or silk when she fashioned serviceable undergarments for the Warriors. For the women, especially the wives, she used even silkier, decadent fabrics—no human material could compare. It was a hobby of hers, making clothes, and one she enjoyed. She also made sexual toys in her spare time for any Shikar who wanted them, and was well loved for her unique, stimulating designs. These things she did for fun, for relaxation.

When the time came for seriousness, for business instead of pleasure, she was a Voyeur. It was her greatest pride and her deepest secret. No one in their world of Shikars knew about the Voyeurs—a tongue-in-cheek, but appropriate sobriquet provided by the impish Steffy, another human turned Shikar. No one, that is, except for the Council and the other Shikar women who comprised the team of a dozen or so members.

Watchers or Voyeurs, whatever their group was called, it didn't matter. They were information gatherers for the Shikar Council. Spies, to put it bluntly. They kept their eyes on the human world, looking for any sign of Daemon activity so that the Warriors could go into battle on the surface with plenty of warning about the terrain and native people they might encounter.

Where it was the Shikar males' duty to protect the human world from the Daemon threat, it was in turn the Shikar females' duty to protect their men from the human world and its pitfalls. If there was a dip in the terrain, a stone, or a building, the Voyeurs noted it and reported it to the Council. The Council saw to it that the men received all the pertinent information. It had been this way for many years, ever since the Daemon Horde had first begun to invade the human world.

Agate was fascinated with humans. She tried not to let it show, she really did, but it was an impossible task. She was enthusiastic to a fault about the things that interested her. Steffy called her "bubbly".

Agate thought that sounded too much like soap, and while she liked the scent of soap, she didn't like her personality to be compared to it.

Speaking of the devil…

"I found some dressy shoes that should go with that outfit," Steffy said, breezing into the room.

Her hair was purple today. "Where did you get these?" Agate asked, holding the smart suit aloft, knowing that they hadn't procured the garments from the surface world. There hadn't been time. The email had only arrived the day before.

"Believe it or not, I unearthed them from one of my trunks," Steffy said, handing over the cute, black half-boots with their dainty heels.

Agate loved all human shoes! She almost snatched them, so eager was she to try them on.

"Along with these," Steffy waved a beige, diaphanous swatch of material wadded in her hands.

Agate knew that Steffy had over twenty trunks full of clothing—the former human and German DJ was obsessed with clothes. Agate had seen them herself when Steffy first moved in with her mate, Cinder. No one needed that many clothes, but Steffy had been emphatic that she keep each and every scrap of cloth.

"You never know when you might need a pair of vinyl pants," she'd said with much asperity when Cinder had threatened to burn half her trunks just to avoid having to transport them from her apartment.

And Steffy was right. At least in this instance, it seemed.

"I didn't know you had normal clothes," Cady raised an eyebrow dubiously. "I thought everything you owned was either skintight or black and shiny."

"Ha, ha." Steffy stuck her tongue out at Cady and the three women laughed at her comical, childish expression. "Actually, these are really old. I hope the styles aren't outdated. I wore these when I applied for a job as a bank teller once. That was at least three years ago. Damn," she mused. "Maybe I should go through those trunks after all. It's been ages since I saw what I had stashed away in them." She shrugged, letting the subject drop as quickly as she'd brought it up. "So, what's the plan?"

Agate grinned and started to disrobe, uncaring that she had an audience. "I am to finish my toilette, dress in these clothes that you have brought me, and go to find Grimm."

"I still don't like to involve Grimm," Cady pursed her lips. "I like to keep the Voyeurs business between us girls."

"Well I cannot Travel both ways. I am just not powerful enough. I have only enough strength to go one way, and I think it would be better if I got there with Grimm's help, so that if I run late I can just come back on my own…"

"You won't run late," Cady said emphatically.

"What if she finds a cute guy up there?" Steffy quipped suggestively. "If she took a little longer than normal to strike up a conversation, maybe go back to his place for a drink..."

"She won't," Cady sent Steffy a stern glare, "run late."

"Spoilsport."

Agate ignored them, putting on her clothes, reveling in the thought of the adventure that loomed ahead of her, even as she slightly dreaded it. She wasn't used to talking to strangers, especially human male strangers, but tonight she'd have to, at great length. "I will get Grimm to help me. And I will come back," she eyed her two friends, "*on time*. After I record Mr. Aleksandr Fromin's story, I will ask to see all his photos and documentation. For authentication purposes, I will tell him. And then I shall take his memory of me and anything to do with the Shikars and Daemons so that he remembers nothing that might hold value to any tabloid or newspaper that might find his story of interest. Also, so that he has no bad memories or nightmares because he was unlucky enough to stumble into an aspect of our world."

"Good. If you run into any problems—" Cady started.

"I won't," Agate assured her. She wasn't a child, for all so many of her friends seemed to treat her like one most of the time. "I do what I must, for the good of Shikars and humans. For the good of Mr. Fromin, too."

She wondered what he'd be like. She'd never spoken to a human man before. Unless one counted the...what had Cady called him? Ah, yes. Wino. The *wino* Agate had spoken to a few months ago had been an interesting fellow, if a bit smelly. He had told her a fascinating story about racing horses and crooked loan sharks. He'd been most grateful when she'd handed him a wad of green paper—American money—but Cady had given her a stern lecture when Agate had told her of the encounter.

Agate hated being treated like a child.

She was older than Cady anyway. At least fifty years older, for all they looked to be of the same age. Well, Agate had to admit that she did look a little younger than Cady—Shikars had much longer life spans than humans after all—and she wasn't happy about it. She wanted to look older, more mature; she thought it was sexier and more respectable.

At least she looked older than Steffy, who was quite a lot younger than either her or Cady. That was something, wasn't it?

Her mind was wandering again. It did that a lot. Because she was what Steffy called a Gemini. Whatever that meant. Maybe it was a human illness? She hadn't thought to ask at the time Steffy had told her the word.

"Here, put these on," Steffy handed her the wad of beige material.

Agate smoothed it out, frowning. "This looks like nearly invisible leggings or something."

"Pantyhose," Cady winced. "I'm impressed, Steffy. Your wardrobe is extensive. But are you sure Agate deserves that torture?"

"Here, I'll show you how to put them on."

After much labor, Agate finally managed to squeeze into the horribly uncomfortable garment. She didn't really see the need for such trappings, they were almost undetectable to the eye as they stretched over and around the length of her legs.

"Gorgeous," Steffy said, then laughed at the uncomfortable expression on Agate's face. "You'll get used to them."

"Not bloody likely," Cady muttered. "I never could."

"Me neither," Steffy admitted. "But it goes well with the suit doesn't it?"

Agate didn't think so, but she wisely kept her mouth shut. She didn't want to protest too much, she was afraid that her friends might change their minds about letting her do this thing. Cady already teetered towards doing so, and Agate daren't chance pushing her further.

"Time to go," she said breathlessly. More than a little excited now that the time to leave was upon her.

"Are you sure?" This from Steffy.

Agate nodded, smiling in what she hoped was a confident sort of way. "I am."

"Let's go find Grimm, then," Cady said, and Agate was relieved to hear the acceptance in her voice.

She couldn't wait to meet Mr. Aleksandr Fromin. Maybe he could tell her about these strange crooked shark creatures she'd heard about from the wino—after she wiped his memory clean of Daemons and Shikar and damning photographs, of course.

Chapter One

Aleksandr—Alek—Fromin felt his stomach do a wild somersault when he first caught sight of the woman.

Her wild red hair was so bright it nearly glowed under the dim lamplight of the Paris street. Alek had never known he was a man partial to redheads—he'd certainly never been before—but he felt himself grow hard just from looking at her long, waving locks.

She was young, a college student she'd said in her emails—though how any college student could afford to fly out here and meet him on such short notice boggled his mind. He'd nearly starved during his own college years, and probably would have if not for his scholarships and grants. Her clothes were neat and smart, quite flattering on her tall, delicate frame. The navy blue messenger bag slung over her shoulder matched the clothes well. But the color, so chic and serious, did nothing to flatter her delicious golden skin.

He hardened further, his cock straining at the fastening of his jeans. Shifting to ease the pressure, he casually lowered the newspaper he'd been perusing into his lap. He didn't read French all that well anyway.

Her emailed description of herself hadn't done her justice. She'd mentioned the red hair, of course, and her height. And her weight, a tidbit of information that had surprised and amused him. In his experience, women did just about everything they could to avoid the mere mention of their weight.

She hadn't said anything about how her full and round her breasts were, or how her legs seemed to stretch for miles and miles in their sheen of silken stockings. He raised his hand in greeting, eager to capture the attention of her dark brown eyes, and wasn't at all surprised to note that even her hands were lovely, as she returned his gesture.

Agate Jones approached the small round café table where he sat and smiled brightly. "I am Agate," she said, unnecessarily. "You are Mr. Aleksandr Fromin."

She had a voice to make any grown man weep with lust.

"Please, call me Alek." He offered his hand and she looked at it without taking it, frowning slightly.

"Alek," she said, and his name sounded like thick molasses on her tongue.

A long, uncomfortable silence reigned between them. He was about to withdraw his hand when she seemed to start, shook her head almost imperceptibly, then quickly reached for his hand with her own. She shook it almost violently, smiling even wider.

"I forgot," she said, and laughed almost giddily.

Alek wondered if she might be a little drunk. He breathed deeply, fully expecting to catch a whiff of spirits on her breath. Instead it was he who now felt drunk—on her wonderful scent. It was like nothing he'd ever smelled before, floral and sweet and spicy all at once, and he liked it very much. He shifted in his seat again. Agate was still shaking his hand and he was forced to disengage from her before she pulled his arm out of its socket. After a brief struggle—she had quite a grip—he had control of his hand again.

"You forgot what?" He prodded her, looking at her strange, ethereal beauty. He wondered what she looked like naked.

She sat down in the seat opposite him. "Nothing."

"Would you like a coffee?" he offered, at a loss for the first time in recent memory. He had no idea how to start this conversation with her, how to speak of this strange and unbelievable event that had brought them together. Emailing the details of his encounter to her and her group of fellow students was one thing, mentioning them aloud was quite another.

He was crazy to have come here. And this gorgeous piece of jailbait was just as crazy to have flown all the way out here from the States simply to talk to him. He'd told her to wait, that he was only on assignment here in Paris for a few days, that he would return to New York and tell her everything then. But she had insisted on meeting him, here, tonight.

It was odd. But then these past several days had been odd. This past week or so of wondering and waiting and second-guessing had his usually neat and methodical mind racing in circles of wonder and doubt and denial. His world had gone completely insane all around him.

Alek wondered dispassionately if he had gone insane too.

"Is it good?" she asked, cocking her head to one side. He couldn't help but notice how intense her eyes were, so focused and alert. Her lashes were long as hell and dark, but tipped with reddish gold. His stiff dick noticed it too, and liked it very much. Damn. He must be feeling the effects of all this recent stress more than he'd guessed; his libido had never been this out of control.

"I guess, if you like that sort of thing. There's tea if you'd prefer," he added.

"Do you like coffee?" The word sounded exotic coming from her somehow, though her accent had no inflection to give him a clue as to where she might originally be from. And he was something of an expert on accents and the people who possessed them. "Or do you like tea?"

"I suppose if I had to choose, I'd choose the coffee. Black with no sugar."

"Then I shall have coffee-black-with-no-sugar," she said the words so fast they nearly hummed together.

He motioned for a passing waiter and ordered for her, eyeing her all the while. She was looking about the place with wonder and awe, drinking in every sight as if to save it for later recollection. And then he knew. Knew why she was acting so strange and so jittery. She seemed so young to him then, and he felt almost guilty for wanting her as much as he did. Well, no, he didn't feel guilty at all. She was too damn appealing.

"You've never been to Paris," he said knowingly.

Her eyes were wide on his. "Yes, I have. For a few minutes only, but I have been here."

"Ah. You changed flights at the airport then?"

The look on her face was a study of puzzlement, consternation, and excitement. He couldn't read her, not at all, and it unsettled him. He was very good at reading people, he had to be in his line of work as a photojournalist, but he had no idea what the hell was going on behind Agate's wide, dark eyes.

The arrival of her cup of coffee diverted her attention then. She grabbed the cup in her long, elegant fingers and brought it to her lips. Alek gritted his teeth as he saw her lick her lips in anticipation, before taking a healthy swallow of the brew.

She sprayed the table with it as she promptly spat it back out.

"*Ack, by Grimm*, what is this vile drink!" She gasped violently, waving her hand before her mouth as if she might faint.

Alek winced, though her voice was beautiful even when she shouted, and watched the waiter hurry back to their table with a feeling of helplessness. Agate was still causing a lot of noise as she sloshed the cup back onto the table and coughed dramatically. Heads turned at every table to look at them.

"What is wrong, Mademoiselle?" The concerned waiter asked in English.

Agate surprised both Alek and the waiter when she responded in flawless French. "This coffee drink is awful. I need some water, please. Do you have water?"

"*Oui*. Of course we do," the stiff-backed server scurried off to fetch a glass.

"I think you insulted him," Alek murmured, studying her. "Most people love French coffee, you know."

"Do they? I must remember that. And *people* may love it but I do not. I hate coffee," she said with a look of distaste.

"You didn't have to order it, then." What was wrong with this strange woman? Was she a simpleton or something? No, she couldn't be, she was a college student at a very demanding and academic school—perhaps she was just something of a flake.

But she was a damned sexy flake. He wondered how easy it would be to get her wet and ready in his bed. And he wondered if he could get her that way tonight.

"I wanted to try it," she sounded forlorn.

Her water arrived, and the waiter thumped it rudely onto the table so that it splashed over the rim of the glass. He was French, and he was miffed, and Alek found the stiff man's attitude quite amusing.

Agate, apparently, did not. As the waiter turned away, huffing, she caught at his hand.

"Please do not be insulted, sir," she pleaded in her perfect, almost textbook French. "I did not mean to offend. I did not know I would dislike the coffee so and I apologize."

The man softened at once, and Alek found himself jealous. He'd have given a lot to have Agate look at him that way, her eyes pleading, soft limpid pools of brown light.

The waiter patted Agate's hand. "Of course Mademoiselle does not like coffee. It is perhaps too strong a drink for one so delicate as you. I am not offended, please don't apologize on my account."

Alek rolled his eyes.

"Thank you," she sighed then pulled away from the waiter, and reached for her water. She took a huge gulp, sighed, then took another.

She was so animated…why couldn't he read her? It bothered him.

"Do you have your photos with you?" she asked suddenly.

"Yes," he reached into a black portfolio case at his feet, removed the pictures, and handed them across to her. "Tell me you've seen stuff like this before and I won't believe you."

Agate studied the pictures, sharp photos of strange monstrous creatures and men throwing fire from their fingertips, pursing her lips in concentration.

He wanted to lick those lips. To suck on them. He shifted again in his seat, but it was no use, his cock felt full to bursting in his pants. It was nearly painful.

Her gaze locked with his, jolting him. She had such a powerful stare, such deep eyes.

He realized suddenly that she was wearing colored contacts. He wondered what color her eyes really were and became quite obsessed with how he might go about finding that out for himself. He supposed it would be easier just to ask her, but it sure as hell wouldn't be half as fun.

"These are all the photographs you have?"

He blinked. And remembered again why they were here. Damn but this woman wreaked havoc on his strict self-possession. He tore his eyes away from her face, looking at the photos instead. "Yes. What do you think? Do you know what those things are? What they were doing in a New York City park?"

"Where are the..." she seemed to search for the word, "...the negatives?" She blatantly ignored his questions.

Alek felt a little shadow of doubt, a small frisson of caution, and frowned. His instincts never led him astray and something about this woman didn't sit right with him. Well, a lot of things about her didn't sit right, but now it seemed important that he pay more attention to that instead of her luscious breasts.

"They're at my apartment in New York," he lied easily. Actually, they were in his portfolio, but she didn't need to know that.

"We asked that you bring them," she frowned. "When we emailed you."

"I was already here in Paris when I received your email. You don't need the negatives anyway," he pointed out, "the photographs show everything. I developed them myself."

She blinked. "I need them for authentication purposes." The words were well practiced.

She sounded like an automaton when she said them.

His curiosity and his caution escalated at once. "I can assure you that they are authentic."

"But I need the negatives," she exclaimed. "You'll have to go home and get them."

He choked on an incredulous laugh. "I don't have to do anything. What are you so bent out of shape about anyway? Those photos aren't doctored, they're real. What I saw was real," he started to get angry. "I'm not lying about this."

"Bent out of shape?" Her eyes rolled as if she were swamped with confusion and rising panic. "Doctored? Cady didn't explain these phrases, I don't know what this means—" she groaned and tears filled her eyes.

Alek felt like a heel. Even though he had no cause to—this woman was a nutter and he'd probably be better off getting up right now and leaving—he felt like he'd just kicked a puppy.

"Look, I might have the negatives back at my hotel here," he offered smoothly.

She jumped on the possibility, her eyes dried instantly and her smile was brilliant. "Let's go look."

His mind reeled with her mercurial changes of mood. But she'd actually offered to go with him, back to his room. Alek had never felt so lucky. He felt certain he'd have her in bed in no time once he got her into his room. Maybe once he'd had a taste of her, his mind would clear long enough for him to study her. To find out what it was about her that had him wanting to look over his shoulder every few seconds, as if he feared an ambush. Once he'd had her a couple of times, he felt sure he could read her better. Actually, it might take more than a couple of times…

God, she was so damn sexy he almost lost it, almost creamed his jeans merely looking forward to the night's promise.

He ignored his misgivings about her, of course. She was that hot.

The photographs disappeared into the messenger bag. She slung it over her shoulder, jumped up from her seat, threw a large bill note on the table, paused, then added another to it.

And then he had it. Again he felt sure he knew what it was about her. This woman was rich. So rich she was eccentric, flighty, and careless about leaving exorbitant tips behind for mediocre service. It made perfect sense now.

At least she wasn't snobby, her effusive apologies to the waiter had proven that beyond a doubt. He couldn't stand snobby, self-centered women.

Alek picked up his portfolio, well aware that the negatives to his photographs were inside it. Well aware too, that he was luring this eccentric, animated young lady to his lair with the full intent of fucking her brains out. And he didn't feel at all guilty about it.

She grabbed at his hand, tangling her fingers with his. It was an almost innocent gesture. But she was an adult—for all she looked so close to being jailbait—and so was he. Holding hands wasn't all they'd do tonight. Not if he had anything to say about it.

Chapter Two

Alek Fromin was extremely appealing. His hair was brown with bright blond highlights, hanging down to his shoulders in negligent waves. His skin was dark from the sun—oh how she longed to one day see the sun!—and his intelligent eyes were so pale a blue they looked like ice.

But they were too hot for ice. They fairly burned into her. She knew he was attracted to her. Knew, too, that he wanted to "get in her pants", as Cady might have said. She wanted him in her pants—skirt—as well, but she knew it was an impossibility. He was a human and she was a Shikar. A Shikar sent to steal this human's memory.

She felt so guilty.

But not *that* guilty.

She liked holding hands with him as they walked back to his hotel. Of course she knew what a hotel was—she'd been studying the human culture for years—but she hadn't seen one up close before. More than anything, Agate hoped it had an elevator—and that she would get a chance to ride in it.

The streets of Paris were teeming with people, even though it was night. Lamps illuminated their way and beckoned from the dozens of shops they passed. Agate felt the energy and purpose in the people around her, felt their enthusiasm—their joy of life.

She knew that her people were needed here, to help protect these humans from the threat they were so innocently oblivious to. It made her feel both sad and proud. Sad that Shikars must always keep themselves secret from humans who were known for fearing things they did not understand. And proud because her people would not hold such prejudices against the humans, the Shikars would always keep the world safe from the monsters that roamed the night. It was a Shikar's duty and privilege to protect those weaker than themselves.

And humans were, generally, much weaker than Shikars. But Aleksandr Fromin... Agate wasn't so sure about him. She sensed a core of steel underneath his brooding, handsome exterior. There was something about his eyes that warned her he was not a man to be underestimated, nor taken lightly. He'd seen much in his life—Agate could clearly see the jaded cynicism in him—he'd suffered much.

At least she could take some of his suffering away from him. He would not be haunted or dogged by the nightmarish memory of the Daemons or the Shikar Warriors he'd witnessed battling with each other, not after tonight. She would make sure of it.

"Have you ever seen these monsters?" He was obviously thinking along similar lines as she.

Agate nodded. It would do no harm to be open and truthful with him now—he wouldn't remember it later anyway. "Many times. There are more than you might think, far more."

Alek paused under the yellow glow of a streetlight and looked at her pensively for a long moment. "I've been trying to convince myself that this has all been some hallucination brought on from stress. I might have believed it eventually if not for the photographs."

"I know." She would help him with that, at least.

He shook his head, his lips twisting in a self-depreciating smile. "How can you know? Monsters do not exist. Seven-foot men who throw fire from their fingertips do not exist. They can't. If they did, everyone would know about it."

"Oh, you would be very surprised about that. Humans prefer to look the other way when something supernatural is going on. Not very many people have seen these Daemons. And even fewer have seen the Shikar Warriors. They refuse to see the truth that is staring them in the face."

"And what is that?" he asked, looking bored, but Agate knew better. The wheels of his mind were spinning. He was both fascinated and skeptical about their topic of conversation.

Agate felt her heart soften for him. He was so stoic, so reserved. Even when facing what must be a terrifying ordeal such as this.

"The truth of it is that these monsters, we call them Daemons, roam the Earth with increasing frequency and violence. They care for nothing and no one. Their one drive is to feed on humans with strong spiritual and psychic gifts, to feast on their life force to fuel their own horrible existence. The men you saw—the ones in your photos—they are Shikars. A species not too dissimilar from humans—though they live in secret underneath the surface of the Earth's crust—who are sworn to protect humans from the Daemons' violent hunger."

Alek laughed darkly, clearly not believing her story. "You must be joking. You don't really believe any of this crap, do you?"

Crap? Cady used the word often, and though Agate had never asked what it meant, she knew it was a derogatory word all the same. "You have seen this for yourself. You were caught in one of their battles, your pictures are proof that what I say is true."

He was silent for a long while, lost in deep thought. His eyes were hard as flint rock when they swept her from head to toe, and Agate was sure they held no small amount of suspicion. "If all of this were true," he said at last, "then these Shikars would hate for these pictures to get out."

Agate was shocked at his cunning, but determined to give nothing away. He was watching her closely now. If she faltered, this human—whom she now understood was quite dangerous when cornered, as he must no doubt feel in his present situation—would not allow her further opportunity to recover the proof he possessed, nor would he bother hanging around long enough for her to rob him of his memory.

Now was the time when all her cunning would be needed and though some might underestimate this in her, she had plenty of it when the situation called for such a thing. Agate simply chose, in most cases, not to flaunt it.

"You are absolutely right," she said truthfully, knowing full well that this man would see it if she lied.

Unable to resist the urge that had been growing inside her since she'd first heard his sexy bedroom voice, she leaned into him, rising on her tiptoes. He was taller than she'd first thought, even with her borrowed heels. She lifted her face and pressed her lips to his. Her hands came up to his shoulders to steady herself as the world reeled about her. He seemed to allow her the upper hand in this intimacy for but a moment. Then he took total control, dominating the kiss, and Agate was lost.

His hands came about her waist, lifting her hard against him. She felt his erection pressed tight to her belly, so hot and hard, as if there were no clothes separating them. She gasped, parting her lips, and his tongue filled her mouth. He tasted like hot, hard, demanding male and a swirling flame of lust licked at her womb. Visions danced in her head, swamping her, coming faster and faster—

And she could see inside of him. Images of war and battle and tragedy, graphic pictures of human suffering, of violence and famine and death—they flowed like raging whitewater from his mind to hers. Her empathic traits—dull and weak until now—flared as hot and bright as their kiss, and she could *see* into him. See his every secret, every thought, every memory.

The Daemons were there, as were the Shikars. The memory of the battle he'd witnessed haunted him, but not as she'd imagined it might. He was not so devastated by the possibility that such things existed, but that he had somehow misinterpreted them. That he didn't understand them and that these beings had been in his world all along without his knowledge aggravated and angered him.

And the memory of war was there also, human war. Agate had only seen pictures of such violence before—but now she was reliving the horror through his memories. He had been in the middle of the gunfire and the explosions, taking his pictures, documenting the events with a cool and detached ruthlessness. More than anything, he believed in recording the events that shaped his world, in documenting reality with as much detail as possible.

He was no different than she in this respect. The both studied the world around them, at times separate and alienated from all they must witness and record, even as they were caught up in the middle of it.

He'd been hit by bullets, cut with blades, burned and bruised and torn. He'd known such pain, physical and mental, but through it all he'd taken his pictures. Alek had been born in the midst of war, in the Ukraine, and his family's flight to America had done nothing to help him forget it. He understood war, even as he hated it. He could not sit back and do nothing as parts of the world lived in chaos.

Alek and his camera held witness as the world rumbled its discontent.

Agate saw everything, shared in his pains and his triumphs, lost in the wonder of his kiss.

His mouth ate at hers. His tongue uncovered and conquered every secret, tasting her, discovering her. The strength of his arms encircled and imprisoned her. A strong hand anchored atop the rising curve of her buttocks. The other swept up her back and tangled into the hair at her nape. He held her so tight she could have wept, her heart full to bursting with need and love and empathic understanding.

She could not take his memory from him. Not now. Not after touching his mind like this. Not after knowing his heart so well and so dear.

Alek sucked her lower lip, using his teeth to nibble erotically. His hand came around to cup her breast, nearly burning her through her clothing. Agate moaned. Then, with a gasp, she pulled away, nearly stumbling on her shaking legs. Too much longer in his arms and she would have willingly made love to him there on the street, with the whole world passing by unnoticed. She wanted him that much.

Their eyes met. And Agate saw that he had felt much the same as she.

"We'll finish this," he said roughly, gaze burning into hers.

Weakly, she nodded. "Yes," she breathed unsteadily.

His jaw clenched. Agate heard his teeth grit with his resolve. He took her hand this time, holding her fast and strong, as if he'd drag her along should she prove unwilling. She wasn't—unwilling, that is. Not at all.

With breathless anticipation, she walked alongside him, nearly skipping to keep up with his long strides. She smiled to herself. Cady was going to be so pissed.

It seemed she would be late getting back after all.

Chapter Three

A small shop caught his attention, dragging him out of his erotic thoughts—each involving his escort's naked body, long legs, and sugar-sweet lips. Her mouth fascinated him beyond all reason.

He wanted to fuck that mouth.

Wanted her on her knees in front of him, eager and willing, as she wet her lips with that wicked tongue of hers and opened for him.

Get it together, man. If he weren't careful, he'd lose all control, take her to a darkened side street and be done with any romance or softness. She made him that crazy.

But first he needed to buy a box of condoms. He only had one or two in his overnight bag—they'd been there for weeks now, he'd just been too busy and preoccupied to use them—and he knew he'd need more than that tonight. Making a detour in this shop would only cost a few precious moments.

He ignored the devilish urge to just forget about the extra protection, that time was too precious, he shouldn't squander it, even the few seconds it would take to make a quick purchase. But he'd never neglected to use a condom before and he wasn't about to make an exception now, no matter how hot he was to have the mercurial minx at his side.

Agate nearly tripped as he made the swift detour into the storefront door. He was loath to release her hand—he wasn't sure if he feared she might bolt or if he just liked the feel of their tangled fingers—but he did, allowing her to enter the door before him, an ingrained gentlemanly gesture he hadn't even given second thought to.

It amused him, as well as puzzled him, when Agate bounced excitedly over to a display of chocolate bars and candies. She seemed so childlike in her enthusiasm, but there were moments when he saw a seriously adult mentality behind her eyes. She was more than she seemed on the surface, he was certain of that.

There had been a moment, when he'd kissed her, when he'd almost felt as if he knew her far more intimately than he should have. As if they'd already shared many secrets about their lives, their pasts, their hopes and dreams with each other. But it was fleeting, and just as he noticed the incredible feeling of discovery—of the elemental and soulful *knowledge* of her—she had pulled away from him.

It was a good thing she'd done that, too. Alek wasn't sure, even now, that he would have had the strength to pull away himself. The tight need in him was stronger than any he'd ever experienced. He'd held onto his self-control by a thread, and it was a wonder he hadn't taken her there on the street.

"I love chocolate," she exclaimed with a bright smile, grabbing a generous handful of assorted sweets. She plunked them down on the counter before the bemused-looking cashier, and added several more to it. "These too," she added one of each of the local newspapers and two glossy magazines.

Alek dragged his gaze away—she fascinated him more than anybody he'd ever met—and made his way down the aisle he felt sure would lead him to what he was looking for. He grabbed a small box of three condoms—a French brand he wasn't familiar with, but it was latex and that was what he wanted—then decided to add two more boxes. Just in case.

He didn't pay much attention to the bell ringing over the door as it opened to admit another person into the small shop. Didn't notice the nervous, agitated young man until it was too late.

"Get over here, put your hands up," the man commanded in French, pulling a handgun from the pocket of his jack and pointing it first at the shopkeeper, then at Agate, and finally leveling it upon Alek. "Get over here," he barked again.

Alek raised the hand that wasn't holding his portfolio case and slowly moved to the front of the aisle where the man stood with his weapon. He wasn't afraid, merely pissed off at the inconvenience, as he patiently waited for the opportunity to diffuse the situation.

The man turned to the cashier and demanded that she hand over the money in the till. Quickly, as if he knew Alek was the more dangerous of the store's inhabitants, the thief brought his attention back around. His eyes, darting around in such a way that Alek suspected he was pepped up on more than just adrenaline, settled on the portfolio and lingered.

"Hand it over, mister."

Alek shook his head, smiling a little. "No." He really didn't want to hurt this petty criminal if he didn't have to. He didn't want to scare Agate with any show of violence. But he wasn't going to give up his portfolio bag—it held several rolls of film he'd yet to develop, not to mention the negatives that seemed so important to his soon-to-be lover.

Besides, it was his. He held on to what belonged to him.

The man, growing ever more agitated and impatient, waved the gun threateningly. "I'll shoot you dead. Hand it over, your wallet and your watch too."

His watch wasn't worth more than a few bucks, and the crystal face was cracked from a brush with a car bomb explosion he'd gotten to close too only a few days ago. Placing his portfolio at his feet, he removed his watch and held it aloft for the thief to take.

After he'd snatched it away, the man growled over at Agate—who strangely enough looked calm and unconcerned. "Come on over here, pretty girl, and give me your purse." He turned back to Alek. "And I'll have that bag," he insisted.

"No you won't," Alek said dispassionately, watching Agate come forward out of the corner of his eye. She seemed so unconcerned, so calm and casual…it didn't agree with the excitable, overly animated persona she'd shown until this point. He would wonder at that later, after he'd found a way to keep possession of his portfolio without resorting to killing the damned punk in front of him.

The man was angry now and swung back his arm to hit Alek across the face.

Three things happened all at once.

The cashier ducked behind the counter with a groan. Alek gathered himself, ready to make his move. And Agate seemed to disappear into thin air.

The thief's arm swung down and Alek easily dogged the blow. Grabbing his assailant's arm he wrenched it brutally, threw his fist into the man's throat, and swept his foot against the man's ankles, tripping him to the ground. Agate instantly appeared at his side and removed the gun from the thief's hand, easily, even as he struggled to bring it around to fire it at one of them.

"You shouldn't do things like this," she murmured, as if she were admonishing a recalcitrant child instead of a violent criminal. "Someone could get hurt."

It was so fast, taking no more than a couple of seconds, and then it was over. Alek was just grateful that no one had been hurt.

The man was on the ground now, clutching at his throat and choking, and Alek put a foot on his chest to keep him there—just in case he recovered and tried something else.

He frowned at Agate. She had put the gun on the counter, where the cashier was only just rising again, and gone straight back to studying the magazine rack. As if nothing out of the ordinary had just happened.

Who the hell was this woman? And, if his eyes hadn't deceived him in what he'd just witnessed, how the hell had she managed the disappearing trick?

Suspicions gathered in his mind and he determined to get her back to his hotel room as soon as possible for more reasons than the obvious one of making love to her until she screamed her head off. Something was going on with her, something big, and he did *not* like being kept in the dark about it.

As the cashier made to call the authorities, Alek grabbed his portfolio case again and paid for his condoms, as well as Agate's mountain of sweets and reading material. He threw everything into the case, grabbed her hand in his once more and marched with her out into the street. And he didn't slow their pace until they'd safely reached his hotel.

* * * * *

Elevators were every bit as exciting as she'd dreamed they might be.

Agate was having a hell of a time resisting the urge to press every single button on the control console of the elevator. She knew Alek already had his suspicions about her—he'd seen her Travel, even if he didn't understand what it meant.

There'd been no help for it. She'd had to use her Traveling ability to reach the would-be thief's side quickly enough to disarm him. Or so she'd thought at the time. How could she have foreseen that Alek was a Warrior and that he would defuse the situation before she could get close enough to even try?

Agate found herself even more attracted to him after such a heroic display of strength and courage. She wanted him. Perhaps more than was wise, given their circumstances, but she couldn't have fought the attraction even if she'd a mind to. Which she didn't.

He hadn't spoken to her for the past few blocks, nor when they'd entered the hotel. It was a little disconcerting, his somber silence, but she persevered. How could she not, while in the wondrous glass elevator as it rose through the floors of the towering building?

Her fingers fairly itched with the need to press the sleek, shiny buttons.

The doors opened to their floor. Alek ushered her forth ahead of him, but she managed to reach out at the last second and press one of the buttons. She almost giggled; it glowed in response to her touch. The doors closed behind them and she let Alek take her elbow and guide her to the door of his room.

It was dim in the room when she entered. When Alek closed the door, sealing them off alone from any intruders, she couldn't resist looking at him in the shadows. All Shikars were sensitive to sunlight; evolution had forced them to live in darkness but in losing the light the Shikars had gained much to make up for it. They possessed exceptional night vision, for one thing. It was because of this gift that she could see him so well in the dark, as clearly as she could when they were outside under the warm glow of the street lamps.

But now the teasing hollows of his face were traced by the darkness, giving him an even more dangerous appearance. His hair looked darker and softer, his face looked rugged and strong.

Agate shuddered delicately.

Alek's strong, square jaw clenched. His gaze swept over her hungrily. And then he reached for her.

"Who are you?" he rasped before slamming his lips onto hers.

The kiss was wet and hot and hard. Agate clutched at him, swept up in the vortex of passion. She wanted to crawl up his body, wanted to wrap herself around him and swallow him inside.

His teeth scraped against her lower lip and she moaned. The wide breadth of his hands held the sides of her head, directing the angle and depth of their kiss. His tongue filled her mouth, thrusting deep inside. Agate opened her eyes and was stunned to see his gaze staring deeply into hers, as if he'd waited for her to look at him.

With a rough curse he broke the kiss. Her mouth felt swollen and bruised and she licked her lips to gather his taste that lingered there.

The pale blue fire of his eyes flared hot, watching her mouth intently.

"Who are you?" he asked again.

"I do not know what you mean…"

She already knew it was useless to lie to him. He could see so much, was remarkably astute. "You know what I mean. You're strange, too strange for words. Elevators, chocolate bars, magazines, and coffee—they're so commonplace but you act as if you've never seen any of them before."

Her spine stiffened, affronted. "But of course I have seen these things—"

"You speak English without using contractions, yet you command the language as if born to it. You speak French like a native, but use it with textbook accuracy and precision. I can't place your accent—and I've studied accent and speech patterns for years in my work—and your gestures give nothing away. Except that you are uncomfortable with everyday conveniences, such as the elevator. So what the hell is going on with you, Agate—if that is your real name?"

"It *is* my real name." She scowled, at a loss for any explanation she could give him besides the truthful one—and that she could not do without permission from the Council or The Elder himself. Her mouth tingled, her breasts ached…she could hardly think beyond her simmering passion for this man.

Therein lay an answer, or at least a temporary one.

"Do you really want to talk," she looked at him from beneath her lashes, almost daring him to make a move, "or do you want to make love?"

Alek's eyes burned hotter than ever.

He pushed her back against the wall, lifting her up with easy strength to rest against the hard rise of his cock. Agate sighed into his mouth, parting her lips for the invasion of his tongue.

The kiss shook both their worlds.

Chapter Four

Those images again, bombarding her, filling her up with every secret he possessed so that she knew him. Knew him like she knew herself. His life, his memories, fed straight to her mind and heart through their kiss.

And she was lost in the wonder of…of love. Pure and uncompromising, it was there in her heart. She wanted him, with her body and with her mind. But she also wanted him with her heart. It was foolish madness. It would eventually tear her apart. He was a human; she knew she could not have him because of that.

But she could have this.

Wrapping her legs around his waist, locking her ankles at his back, she held on to him for dear life.

His mouth was so hot. It scalded a path from her mouth to her chin to her neck and she leaned her head back to allow him his sinful exploration. His hands came up to cup and mold her breasts, pressing and squeezing them until they ached and the nipples swelling to tight points.

"I wanted to fuck you raw the first second I saw you," he growled into her ear, biting her earlobe delicately.

Agate moaned. He rocked his hips in erotic circles between her legs, bouncing her back softly against the wall with his efforts.

"I'm going to tear this shirt of yours off and suck your nipples until you scream," he promised.

Her jacket disappeared. He removed it with efficient, practiced skill. The buttons of her shirt were no impediment to his desire. The strength of his hands tore at the fragile material, sending buttons and threads flying. She wore no bra, a fact that—from his lusty growl—pleased him greatly.

The tips of his fingers plucked at her stabbing nipples and she gasped. His head dipped, his hair tickled over her face, and he slurped one nipple greedily into his lips. His tongue stabbed at her, licked over her, while his lips and teeth drew at the delicate flesh. Such a sweet and gentle torture was beyond anything Agate had ever experienced—she of the hundreds of sex toys, which she both designed and tested out regularly.

No mere sex toy could have prepared her for the reality of this man.

His mouth savored first one nipple, then the other, feeding on her with moist, audible sucking noises that enflamed her senses and made her rock against him with need. One of his hands came around her, plumping and squeezing her ass, moving her on him so that her cunt ground against his erection deliciously. The other held her breast captive for his hungry kisses.

Agate held him tight, her hands moving to rake through the cool silk of his bright hair. "Please," she moaned.

"Please what?" he asked darkly, knowing full well what she wanted. What she needed. "Please suck you harder?" He did, teeth scraping against her until she shuddered and cried out. "Please get you naked?"

He lowered her to the floor, unzipped the side of her skirt and jerked it down to her ankles. The wall was the only thing keeping her standing, her knees had gone weak and her head was spinning with desire. His gaze burned into hers as he hooked his fingers into the waistband of her pantyhose and jerked them down to her ankles as well. Kneeling at her feet now, his hands swept up to feel her naked legs, leaving goose pimples in their wake.

Then his gaze lingered, caught and held captive, on the bright white gauze of her panties. A lacy confection of her own design, it was sheer and completely scandalous, revealing the tightly trimmed fur of her cunt.

As if entranced, he stared at her, at the stain of her gathering dampness and the shadow of her red hair. With a small, lusty sigh of male appreciation he lowered to her. His mouth pressed into her through the veil of her panties, teeth and tongue stabbing her through the fabric, wetting her with his moist breath.

Agate cried out, shaking, her hands moving to his head to help steady herself.

His fingers sought her, slipping underneath the fragile material to tease and tickle her. The tips of those fingers fondled her slit, delving into her wet need, spreading the lips wide. Her clit was swollen and throbbing, and when he unerringly found it, pressed it like a secret button, she keened wildly and pulled at his hair as stars exploded behind her eyes.

Alek jerked back from her grasp, tearing her panties with his teeth. His hands made quick work of removing that last barrier and then he rose before her again. His hands roughly opened the fastening of his jeans and his erection sprang free. Heavy and thick, it bobbed and stabbed towards her, a work of such beauty she could have wept. And then he was taking her up in his arm.

She wrapped her legs around his waist, spreading herself eagerly for him.

"Hold on, baby," he warned, licking and nibbling at her gasping mouth.

One long, deep shove and he slid home. Stretching her so tight and so full that she shrieked with the surprise and pleasure. He only had to rock against her once, sending himself deeper, and she was undone. Her climax rocked her, so swift and so hard that it shook her entire being.

Alek's fingers sought her out, moving between their bodies to stroke and tease her clit, making her come even harder around him.

"Let it go, yes. God, you're so fucking ripe." He sucked her bottom lip into his mouth and made short, gentle thrusts with his hips. "Milk me, just like that, come on. So tight. So wet. *Shit,*" he gritted his teeth and abruptly stilled against her.

Agate's body pulsed and shook with the wet eruption of pleasure that spilled from deep within her. The climax eased, but her desire and need did not. If anything, the force her release had rejuvenated her passion. She wanted more.

Using the strength of her legs she bounced herself upon him, impaling herself on his thick cock over and over again. The width and breadth of his penetration stretched her, burned her, and the friction of skin against skin was so exquisite. She was gasping and keening her ecstasy in his mouth, kissing him feverishly, deeply, offering herself completely.

Alek's hands moved to her hips to steady her, and he slammed deeper, harder in her. Filling her over and over again. Reaching nearly to her womb.

"Shit," he said again and stopped, holding still.

"Please," she tried to move on him, but his hands held her firmly, preventing it.

"I forgot to protect you," he kissed the corner of her mouth.

She frowned and tried move against him again.

"I didn't use a condom," he laughed darkly, pressing his forehead against hers. His gaze met hers directly, searing her with the passion that simmered in their depths. "Don't move or I'll spill."

Agate smiled and bit at his bottom lip playfully. Her arms looped around his neck, holding him close. "Spill all you want, I want to be messy with your seed."

He shuddered violently against her. "No. I've never…" he gasped harshly and moved in her once, hard.

"*Please,*" she begged, arching up against him so that her breasts brushed his chest through the shirt he still wore.

"Oh shit," he gritted out and seemed to let go of his rigid self-control, slamming his hips fast and deep into her. "I can't help it." He seemed to be saying his thoughts aloud, unable to hold back. "You make me want to come all over you, inside your pussy, inside your mouth," he groaned.

"I want to taste your come," she goaded, knowing he danced along the razor edge of an explosive release.

His mouth slanted across hers in a bruising kiss.

Her back bumped over and over against the wall, her breasts bobbed heavily. Every gasp he wrung from her, every moan, he captured with his lips, drinking the sounds into his mouth like a man dying of thirst.

Her body tightened, bowing against him like a reed. Pleasure burst forth over her, like liquid starlight. It seemed her very fingertips sang with ecstasy. Agate screamed into his mouth and held on tight, her cunt squeezing him mercilessly like a swallowing mouth.

"*Fuck*," he exclaimed and slammed into her hard enough to rattle her very bones. His cock pulsed like a heartbeat. The hot scalding wash of his come filled her, wet her, and burned her.

The skin of her thighs would bear the faint marks of his fingertips for days. They dug into her soft flesh, kneading and squeezing as he lost himself in the power of his release.

Long moments passed as they caught their breath. He continued to rock softly against her, small thrusts that kept the embers of her spent pleasure glowing hot. Their bodies were wet with each other, their scents mingled into one delicious perfume of passion and sex.

Alek kissed her again as if he couldn't resist, his lips parting hers, his tongue sliding deep and wet. Like his cock, so deep and hard inside her pussy even now, so soon after their explosion.

He never let her feet touch the ground. One minute her back was pressed tight against the wall, the next he was carrying her to the bed and laying her down on the mattress.

She rose up on her elbows, eyeing him.

"Keep your legs spread wide, baby," he urged softly. "Let me see that pretty pussy of yours."

With a smile, she did, glorying in the bright flame of approval in his eyes. Feeling shameless, daring, she lowered her fingers to herself, spreading the lips of her sex open like the petals of a flower.

Alek's hands were impatient and rough as he divested himself of his clothing. His eyes never left her, watching her fingers play over her clit and thrust into her hole.

Agate raised one of her damp, glistening fingers to her mouth. Her tongue licked out, tasting the honey and cream of their mixed fluids. Their eyes were locked now, their souls and hearts laid bare and open.

"Who are you?" he asked, so softly she almost didn't hear him.

"Your lover," she murmured.

"Yes. Mine," he said as if to himself. "All mine..."

Nude now, glorious and golden, he palmed his cock and stroked himself slowly, letting her see him. Agate felt her breath catch. He was so thick, so long. Still wet from her body, still hard. Perfect in every way.

"Spread wider for me, baby. Let me see you," his husky voice was a caress all its own. "Yes. Just like that."

He came down on the bed, on her, grabbing an ankle with one hand and the base of his cock with another. Pushing her ankle up high, almost to her shoulder, he positioned the head of his thickness at her slit. Rubbed her with it, smearing himself in her wetness.

"So beautiful," he breathed.

Agate sighed, feeling his heat and his touch throughout.

Slowly and gently, he pressed into her. He released her ankle and reached up to smooth away an errant lock of her hair that had fallen across her face. "I don't know what it is about you," he mused. "You make me feel…so much. Too much."

Their lips met. His cock filled her completely, one sure stroke to the hilt. His hands swept over her body, petting her, soothing and easing her beneath his weight.

"Alek," she sighed his name, feeling the echo of it sing in her heart.

"Say it again," he pressed light kisses to her eyes, nose and chin.

"Alek, Alek, Alek," she breathed it over and over again like a mantra.

"Lovely lips," he praised, licking and sucking at them. And he began to move on her, to rock into her body with his. Where before their passion had been a firestorm, it was now a warm and gentle wave that flowed sweetly. It took them deeper into something soft and dreamy that was somehow far more explosive than anything they had ever experienced.

Their bodies rolled, mussing the bed. Their limbs entwined, their hair tangled and their sweat dampened each other's skin. The sounds of their sighs and moans and gasps had the mysterious rhythm of primal music.

Alek's big toe skimmed her instep and she giggled. He smiled and nuzzled the side of her throat, nipping her just beneath her ear so that she gasped. When his lips moved down and drew on her tight, hard nipple, she cried out and bucked beneath him.

Her hands stroked down his back, feeling his muscles gather and roll beneath her fingers. The delineated muscles of his buttock fascinated her as they tightened and loosened with his thrusts. She couldn't resist trailing a finger into the crease of his ass, rejoicing when he moaned his response.

The push and pull of his cock came faster now. Alek pulled her legs up around his waist, and moved harder into her wet body.

"Mine," he gritted out. "All mine. Say it."

Agate could only moan and thrash her head, lost in the pleasure of their joined bodies.

"Say it," he barked through gritted teeth.

A drop of his sweat fell from his face onto her mouth. She tasted its saltiness with her tongue.

"Say you're mine." He ground down against her and she saw stars.

"Yes," she moaned.

"Say it."

"I *am* yours," she gasped.

His thumb rubbed against her clit, his cock stretched her to bursting. "You're mine. *Only* mine."

"Yes. Only yours. All yours." Agate screamed as he slammed into her, hard and fast, rocking the bed beneath them. Unbelievably, another climax crashed through her, taking her by surprise so that she screamed again.

"You're so fucking wet, so tight, so hot," he moaned his sex words into her ear. "Come on, squeeze me with your sweet little pussy. This is only the beginning. I'm not letting you leave tonight. I'm going to come in your mouth, and in your ass. Even between your gorgeous tits." He palmed them, still thrusting, still impaling her. "I'm going to fill you up with my cum until you're dripping with it."

She already was dripping with it. He slid in and out of her creamy wetness, an easy glide, and her body sang with delirious pleasure.

He thrust one last time, throwing back his head with a shout, coming deep. The release that took him, shook him, flooded into her like sweet, hot lightning.

The weight of his body collapsed on hers. His breath was harsh and deep and unsteady, and the thunder of his heartbeat pounded against her chest. They both lay there, stunned, as their bodies cooled.

Long moments passed. Agate stroked his hair, his head pillowed on her breasts. His mouth still pressing tiny, soft kisses against her. She sighed, smiling. Content.

Alek stilled, his body hard and unforgiving, like stone. He shoved off her, stood by the bed and looked at her with a wild stare. Raking his hands through his already disheveled hair, he seemed to be gripped by a strong and volatile emotion.

Agate frowned and reached for him. He swore, stepped back, turned and went into the bathroom. The door shut hard behind him.

It was a harsh withdrawal. Agate's eyes stung. He'd turned from her, denied her, in every way. She could see it—in his eyes and in his face—that he had pulled completely away from her. After what she had believed was an emotional bonding, a spiritual release shared between them, he had left her. For him to retreat this way must mean that he had not felt the same as she. It wrenched her heart, cutting like a blade.

She put her face in her hands and wept.

Chapter Five

What the hell had just happened? Alek splashed his face with cold water, gulping at it with parched lips.

He didn't know this woman. Clearly, she was hiding something—a lot of somethings—from him. He had no reason to trust her. But never in his life, never in his wildest dreams, had he experienced anything like what had just happened between him and Agate.

He smelled her on his fingers, tasted her on his tongue, felt the imprint of her body wrapped around him still. She lingered in his mind and his heart as no woman ever had.

No. He couldn't let this happen. Wouldn't. It was crazy. He knew nothing about her but what she'd told him in email and what he'd observed for himself throughout the past few hours. What had just happened back there, in that bed, was sex.

Just sex.

Then why did he still think of her as his? In an elemental way, he wanted it to be true. Intellectually, he shied away from it with a panic.

There was no room in his life for a woman—any woman—especially not one who acted as if she'd never tasted coffee, never seen an elevator. He no longer believed she was simply some rich, eccentric young woman. There was so much more to it than that, so many more questions that couldn't be answered by so simple an explanation.

He couldn't want this mysterious woman as badly as he did. It was insane. Totally unlike him. And he sure as hell hadn't just made love to her. He'd never made love a woman—he'd only fucked them. Fucking was enough, sex was not meant to mingle with love or tenderness. Not for him.

It had been so sweet...he wanted her again. His cock was hard again. His balls were tight, as if he hadn't just shot himself dry twice already. Oh sweet shit, he'd actually had her without using protection. After all the trouble of seeing that he had enough, he'd neglected to use the damn condoms.

He'd never taken a woman naked like that before. Their skin slipping wet and raw against each other, no barriers between to keep them apart. So many things he'd never done before tonight, and they had seemed so easy—so *right*—with Agate.

The water was cold on his face, but it did nothing to cool his fever. He wanted her again. He had to have her again—a thousand times more—before he could think clearly, before he could sort through this. Now, he needed her now.

His hand hovered over the doorknob. His heart teetered with uncertainty...

* * * * *

Agate pulled her contacts out—before tonight she'd been fascinated with the very idea of wearing them—and threw them to the floor. It didn't matter if Alek saw her Shikar eyes glowing now. She wanted him to see, wanted him to know their true color. She wanted him to know everything.

With a sob, she wondered how she could face the rest of the night. Her duty to her people was to ensure that Alek remembered nothing of this. But her heart cried out that she let him remember, that she win his heart in return and keep him.

But she couldn't. So many times she'd already said this to herself, that she just couldn't keep him. They were so different from each other, indeed they were different species entirely. He still regarded her as a stranger, as an odd human woman at best. A life with him would be nearly impossible.

Thinking on the choices that faced her made her cry all the harder. Must she see her duty as a Voyeur done, or could she follow the dictates of her heart and soul?

The choice was taken from her. And no worse outcome could she have imagined.

"Where is he?" The Traveler—Grimm, a Shikar Traveler Caste of blackest eyes and most dangerous past—appeared at her side, his voice like midnight. "I'll kill the bastard and be done with it."

Unfortunately Alek chose that moment to return from his sojourn in the bathroom. He froze, catching sight of the ebony-cloaked man who towered over her.

"What the fuck…?"

Seeing an imminent showdown between the two men, Agate rose from the bed and grabbed at Grimm's arm. "Do not—"

His eyes swept down over her nude form, but she was not embarrassed nor was she intimidated. This was her lover's life on the line—she could see the truth of that in Grimm's eyes—and she would show no weakness.

"Do not what?" The words flowed like wine, smooth and rich. "Do not protect your honor? Do not see to it that this stupid human pays for making you weep?"

"He did not—" she protested, tugging at him when he would have flung her off.

"Do not lie to me, woman. I can see he has been with you, I can smell his touch all over you. He stole your purity, in every way, and must be punished."

Alek scowled. "Now wait just a minute. She wanted it just as much as me, and she was no spring flower, I can assure you. Now who the hell are you and what are you doing in my room?"

Agate felt his words cut her like a knife and gasped.

Grimm disentangled himself from her and approached Alek like the predator he was. "She was pure. No man's hand has touched her before yours. You take and you take, but you see nothing of the worth of what you have stolen."

"Grimm! There was no theft! I gave myself to him," Agate marched to his side, deliberately avoiding Alek's gaze. "Willingly. And I would do it again. He is my first and last lover."

Grimm's anger blazed with waves of heat. "You dare to claim him? A human male?"

"I do," she heard Alek's teeth grit and wondered if he understood any of the byplay between her and her Shikar protector. She glanced at him and remembered her eyes, how strange they must seem to him, but there was only a miniscule twitch at his lips to prove that he had even noticed them. "Let it go, Grimm. Please."

"Get away from him, Agate," Alek's command surprised her. "Come here."

She moved to his side immediately. His hand came up to her chin, tilting her face, his eyes studying hers. "I am sorry," she said.

"You have a lot to tell me," he murmured. "But not yet. Later."

"You'll be lucky if there is a later, pup," Grimm intoned. "Tryton can deal with you." He came forward, laid his hands on their shoulders, and the world disappeared.

Chapter Six

Four days passed. Long, lonely days in which Agate was confined to her home, ordered by Tryton—The Elder himself—to stay put and obey until further notice. She didn't see or hear from Alek, but she knew he was still here. Still in her world, so far beneath the surface of his own that no human could have ever found their way to it. She could feel him, close by. And her heart ached from the separation.

She wondered what he felt, if he was too consumed with the uncertainty of his surroundings and situation to think of her. Or if he thought of her with every waking moment, as she did him.

It was no surprise to her that Grimm had known of her innocence that night in the hotel. He seemed to know everything about everyone; it was just like him to know something so personal and secret.

It had, at first, surprised her that he'd made an issue of it. And she had tried to divert him with the bold claim that she meant to keep Alek, to mate with him. It had been a foolish claim and it had done nothing to save her lover. It may have, in fact, sealed his fate.

Unmated Shikar women took lovers if they wished, it was not taboo. But she had never done so, she'd always had her toys to keep her occupied. Sensuality and self-love were delicious pleasures to be enjoyed and explored by all. Every Shikar knew that, man or woman. She was no virgin, but neither had she taken a lover before Alek. She hadn't wanted to. Agate had always seen Shikar men as brooding, arrogant beasts, so she'd never felt lonely without one to call her own. Alek, a human, had been the most perfect man she'd ever encountered and she'd wanted him as she'd never wanted another.

But she feared now that she might have gone too far beyond the boundaries of what could be accepted when she had taken a human to be her first lover. She feared for Alek and what Tryton might do to him.

The hours stretched on and she waited…longing for her love.

* * * * *

"I am continually surprised by humans," Tryton told him, clapping him so soundly on the back that it nearly sent him tumbling.

Alek looked about his new home with a satisfied eye. All of his things had been fetched from his room in Paris and his apartment in New York City. His pictures, his camera equipment, his books, everything was here in its right place.

But Agate wasn't. She was still in her rooms, where Tryton had confined her while drilling him and testing him to see if he deserved her. A Shikar woman.

His mind still reeled from the whirlwind of events that had so drastically reshaped his life over the past few days. He could hardly believe all that had happened. And so quickly.

"You hardly know her. Yet you're willing to give up your life above just to be with her. Are you sure this is what you want?" Tryton gave him one last choice. "You could stay here, live here and fight with us, even if you didn't want her."

Alek had made his decision. And he knew it was the only decision that had been worth making. Four days without her had been hell, despite the hospitality Tryton and the other Shikars had shown him. He missed her. Knowing her one night had been enough to know that this was the right choice to make. "I need her." And it was as simple as that. "Staying here, becoming a photographer for the Shikar Voyeurs, that's just a perk. But it doesn't mean a damn thing without her."

He was incomplete without Agate. The time he'd spent with her, seeing her joy of life, holding her in his arms…had been the time of his life.

Tryton nodded, as if he'd expected that response. "You are a good man, Alek. Shaped by war and by human suffering; hardened. But still good. You will take proper care of her."

"I will."

"Grimm still wants to kill you. Or at least bloody you a little."

Alek fingered his jaw, wincing at the memory of The Traveler's fist hitting it like a battering ram. He had enough sense to know that the man had held back to keep from breaking the bone… He didn't want to find himself in another skirmish with the shadowy man in black. But for Agate, he'd risk any danger. "He can try."

Tryton chuckled. "You will do just fine here. Now to fetch the recalcitrant Watcher," he sighed. "I mean *Voyeur.*

Damn Steffy and her cute little puns anyway," the seven-foot, blond Adonis left the room while still muttering to himself.

Alek smiled and waited for his Shikar mate, hoping that she would be as happy to see him as he would be her.

Chapter Seven

She raced into his room, not even bothering to knock. "You bastard! How could you keep me waiting like that?"

Alek laughed. "It's good to see you too, baby."

With a sob and a laugh, she launched herself into his arms, raining his face with wet kisses. "I was so scared that I would never see you again."

"I wouldn't have let that happen."

"How could I know that?"

"You looked into me. You saw me. You know me." He kissed her long and deep.

"How did you know about that—?"

He grinned. "Tryton told me a lot of things. I admit, I wasn't sure at first what I wanted to do. But after learning about you and your people, I know this is right."

"You'll stay with us? Work with the Voyeurs?"

"Only if you'll be part of that." He searched her eyes, noting how much more lovely they were without the dark lenses covering them. "Do you still feel so strongly about me, after so short a time?"

"I feel like I've been waiting for you forever," she exclaimed. "Of course I still want you."

"You're mine—say it," he smiled.

"I'm yours. Now your turn," she prodded.

"You're right, it is." He had her naked before him in seconds, her head almost spun with his determined efficiency. "I'm going to use that great big new bed of mine to its full advantage tonight," he promised. "You're wet," his fingers cupped her scarlet curls, "and hot. And tight."

She sighed as he lifted her and carried her to his bed.

His hands spread her knees and his head came down between them. His breath scorched her, as did his gaze. Alek pressed a wet, open-mouthed kiss onto her sex, licking her slit up and down like he might an ice cream cone. He sucked on her clit and probed her with his finger, thrusting it deep into her pussy like a cock.

Minutes later and she was bent over him, taking his cock so deep into her mouth she almost choked. He was velvet over steel in her mouth, hot and hard and heavy. The twin weights of his testicles were tight in her hands, and his scent was drugging and delicious in her lungs as she sucked and licked him to a creamy, jettisoning orgasm.

"*Shit*, baby, swallow it. Yes, oh god, your mouth is so good," he moaned, caught and lost in the spell of pleasure she wove about him.

Certain she had never tasted anything sweeter, she swallowed every last creamy drop of him. And found herself wanting more.

Then she was on her knees before him, feeling him sink balls deep into her slick, drenched cunt.

"So tight," he panted, riding her like a stallion covering a mare.

He licked a finger and probed it into the moue of her anus and she screamed her release aloud, uncaring that someone might hear.

"I love it up my ass," she panted. She'd often used toys there before.

"Then I'll give it to you," he promised and moved to fulfill it immediately.

She'd never been stretched so full. His cock buried to the hilt in her rear made her see stars. Her fingers rubbed her clit and his hands came around her to cup her breasts, to tease and pull at her nipples.

When she came, Alek joined her, his release so intense it almost hurt. He filled her ass with his cream, smearing it between their bodies. It was the most amazing orgasm he'd ever known.

He pushed her back onto the bed, spread her legs, pushing his mouth hard against her juicy pussy. Licking her, he tasted himself there too and found that he liked it. Agate bumped against his face, grinding her clit against his lips and mewling like a cat in mating season.

"I could eat you out all night and half the day," he said the words against her, knowing she would feel the vibration of his voice. "You smell so damn sweet. You taste so damn good, baby."

He watched the tiny contractions in her pussy as soft orgasms racked her. He knew he'd never get enough of her. He was already hard again, aching and full of enough juice to drown them both in it.

There was a convenient carafe of water on his bedside table, put there just for this purpose. He splashed it all over them as he prepared himself for her again. It fairly sizzled and turned to steam as it fell on their hot flesh.

The hot, wet core of her welcomed him like a mouth. Better than a mouth, it swallowed every inch he had to give. And he was soaring.

Agate nearly swooned, and it was as if she could feel the head of his cock bumping her heart, he was so deeply joined with her. Alek was stretching and filling up all her empty places with his love and with his passion. The bed creaked and protested as they galloped towards oblivion.

"I nearly went crazy without you," he panted.

"Me too," she moaned. "Let us never part again, please."

"No. Never. I don't know what's happened. Fuck it, I don't care. I just know I can't be without you," he slammed his cock deep, his balls slapping against her skin loudly. "I need you, baby. Just like this. Always like this."

Her orgasm ripped through her, nearly knocking her unconscious it was so unexpectedly violent. The bright hot explosion of him, so deep in her, burned and scalded her most tender flesh and she cried out. Their mouths met, each tasting of the other's release, and their cries echoed out into the night.

Hours later, they were both so spent they could barely move. And still their bodies were joined together, tight and hot and deep.

"I want to try some tea," she murmured sleepily.

Alek groaned, and moved his cock inside her wet heat with as much strength as he could muster. It was enough to make her moan.

"Remind me to wear a raincoat when you do."

Agate swatted him playfully. They laughed together until the morning sun rose high over the lands of the world so far above their new home. And they loved again and again and again.

About the author:

Sherri L. King lives in the American Deep South with her husband, artist and illustrator Darrell King. Critically acclaimed author of *The Horde Wars* and *Moon Lust* series, her primary interests lie in the world of action packed paranormals, though she's been known to dabble in several other genres as time permits.

Sherri welcomes mail from readers. You can write to her c/o Ellora's Cave Publishing at 1337 Commerce Drive, Suite 13, Stow OH 44224.

Also by Sherri L. King:

Bachelorette

Chronicles of the Aware: Rayven's Awakening

Fetish

Manaconda

Midnight Desires

Moon Lust

Moon Lust: Bitten

Moon Lust: Feral Heat

Moon Lust: Mating Season

The Horde Wars: Ravenous

The Horde Wars: Wanton Fire

The Horde Wars: Razor's Edge

The Horde Wars: Lord of the Deep

The Jewel

Why an electronic book?

We live in the Information Age—an exciting time in the history of human civilization in which technology rules supreme and continues to progress in leaps and bounds every minute of every hour of every day. For a multitude of reasons, more and more avid literary fans are opting to purchase e-books instead of paperbacks. The question to those not yet initiated to the world of electronic reading is simply: *why?*

1. *Price.* An electronic title at Ellora's Cave Publishing runs anywhere from 40-75% less than the cover price of the exact same title in paperback format. Why? Cold mathematics. It is less expensive to publish an e-book than it is to publish a paperback, so the savings are passed along to the consumer.
2. *Space.* Running out of room to house your paperback books? That is one worry you will never have with electronic novels. For a low one-time cost, you can purchase a handheld computer designed specifically for e-reading purposes. Many e-readers are larger than the average handheld, giving you plenty of screen room. Better yet, hundreds of titles can be stored within your new library—a single microchip. (Please note that Ellora's Cave does not endorse any specific brands. You can check our website at www.ellorascave.com for customer recommendations we make available to new consumers.)
3. *Mobility.* Because your new library now consists of only a microchip, your entire cache of books can be taken with you wherever you go.

4. *Personal preferences are accounted for.* Are the words you are currently reading too small? Too large? Too...**ANNOYING**? Paperback books cannot be modified according to personal preferences, but e-books can.

5. *Innovation.* The way you read a book is not the only advancement the Information Age has gifted the literary community with. There is also the factor of what you can read. Ellora's Cave Publishing will be introducing a new line of interactive titles that are available in e-book format only.

6. *Instant gratification.* Is it the middle of the night and all the bookstores are closed? Are you tired of waiting days—sometimes weeks—for online and offline bookstores to ship the novels you bought? Ellora's Cave Publishing sells instantaneous downloads 24 hours a day, 7 days a week, 365 days a year. Our e-book delivery system is 100% automated, meaning your order is filled as soon as you pay for it.

Those are a few of the top reasons why electronic novels are displacing paperbacks for many an avid reader. As always, Ellora's Cave Publishing welcomes your questions and comments. We invite you to email us at service@ellorascave.com or write to us directly at: 1337 Commerce Drive, Suite 13, Stow OH 44224.